A Charlie Draper Thriller

Sonoran

Justice

By

Dave Folsom

Sonoran Justice by Dave Folsom

This one's for Sandy, my wife, best friend, editor, live-in critic, and our three daughters who made our life complete.

This book is a work of fiction. Names, places, or incidents are either products of the authors imagination or used fictionally. Any resemblance to actual events, localities, or persons, living or dead, is purely coincidental.

Scaling Tall Timber Press
Box 35
Roscoe, South Dakota 57471

All cover art and photography by the author.

Paperback Edition

ISBN-13: 978-0615614083
(Scaling Tall Timber Press)

ISBN-10: 0615614086

Chapter One

Southeastern Arizona

The killer stood behind granite boulders high above the surrounding landscape. His custom-built M98B Super Magnum sniper rifle, chambered for .338 Lapua, rested on a wool blanket cushion spread carefully over a flat-topped granite outcrop. A finely-crafted rifle costing just under five thousand dollars, it had a two and half pound trigger pull, a customize barrel with a muzzle brake, a 4x16 power high optic scope, a built-in biped in front and desert camouflage. Two important facts Damián Sanchez learned during his years of contract killing included: *use a precision weapon* and *be patient*. His specialty, killing at distance, ranked as his only employment. Demanding complete anonymity, and working only through a broker, he required fifty percent payment up front. The drug cartels kept him busy and made him rich.

Still early, the morning sun beat on his back through a desert camouflage-colored shirt and threatened to drive the afternoon temperature into the nineties by noon. Damián Sanchez ignored the heat since he anticipated the job would be done quickly. He watched his prey through the rifle's scope. The man sat tall on a slowly moving four-wheeler winding his way closer. The assassin waited for the moment his target would stop for even a second, a fatal moment when he would squeeze ever so gently on the rifle's hair trigger. The killing ground below his perch lay flat for a distance of several hundred yards, an ideal selection for his work. Populated by towering Saguaro cactus, the remaining vegetation sat low and widely scattered, surrounded by sand and an occasional rock outcrop. Not much in the way of cover for his victim to hide. The M98B was capable of kills in excess of two thousand yards, but Sanchez preferred a distance under a thousand. At any measure under that he could put five out of five shots through the center of a man's chest with ease. When the distance lengthened a rare chance of a sloppy kill or even a miss arose. Not likely, but not a sure thing either. Therefore, he waited, knowing from his study of the target, a closer opportunity would afford itself before the day became much older. Damián Sanchez earned a tidy five hundred thousand American dollars for each kill and in ten years he'd never failed. His employment took maybe one or two weeks, rarely more. Four or five times a year his phone would ring and he'd have to work a situation leaving him considerable time to cultivate a lavish lifestyle. The western beaches of Isla Mujeres, off the coast of Yucatan, Mexico suited him; and best of all, they were located near the tourist city of Cancun. The shooter owned and piloted a Cessna Citation Mustang hangared at the Aeropuerto De Isla Mujeres less than a mile from his estate. The plane's 391 mile-per-hour cruising speed could place him anywhere in the North American Hemisphere in a short time with the M98B and ammo concealed in a custom-built hidden compartment. His mostly wealthy neighbors thought him an inherited-money playboy and he cultivated the image. The cartels paid well for his services and this day he intended to add to his already bursting coffers.

***

John Quinn worked at chores two thousand yards distant, unaware of the watcher. Standing tall and heavy set, Quinn was a long-time rancher pushing sixty, still hard as nails. Ornerier than a grizzly bear with a toothache, Quinn owned two thousand acres of dry Arizona desert supporting no more than one cow per several acres in a good year. He'd buried two wives in that Sonoran sand and raised three daughters, now grown and gone. Two were married with families and lived across the country. The third taught school in Phoenix, lived alone and rarely visited. Inheriting her father's disparaging outlook on existence and the idiots who inhabited it, she rarely socialized.

John Quinn's Silver Buckle Ranch butted against Sonora, Mexico on the south and the Tohono O'Odam Indian Reservation on the west. The ranch buildings were sun-baked, tinder dry and paint naked from years of neglected maintenance. Quinn rose early every day to tend his dwindling stock because he always had, if not for any other reason. The land was windswept, drier than bleached bones and needed constant irrigation. A single deep well supplying his irrigation needs had, in recent years, pumped dry at the height of the growing season. Quinn was forced to reduce his herd each succeeding year to match the available feed. In today's market he knew he'd be lucky to find a buyer for either the cattle or the land at anything but giveaway prices. At ten minutes before eight in the morning, Quinn walked to his old Honda four-wheeler to start his daily hunt for strays. Quinn's cattle, like all bovine critters, habitually searched for food, a continuing quest occasionally finding trouble. This morning, his count came up two short.

His dog, a mixed breed Border collie stray that found Quinn's doorstep six years before and never left, followed behind at a safe distance. Quinn and the dog shared a love-hate relationship. Quinn liked the dog because it didn't talk back and was pretty good at rounding up stray cattle. The dog on the other hand didn't much like Quinn and growled if he got too close, but scarfed down the table scraps provided. After his master backed away the dog would eat. After a while the animal began to follow everywhere behind the old man at a discreet distance. Quinn started calling the Border collie *Dog* and the name stuck.

"Come on, Dog!" Quinn growled, mounting his four-wheeler. He started the engine and twisted the throttle, not looking to see if the dog followed. Quinn rode west toward the sloping hills that split his property into two distinct sections. The western side over the hills shared a common boundary with the Reservation. The eastern side served as the main ranch and went as far as the highway. His cattle usually hid from the afternoon heat in the steep valleys and deep gulches that divided the ranch. Quinn was a hundred yards short of the beginning of the elevation change when the .338 copper-jacketed bullet slammed into his chest slightly to the left of his breastbone.

The dog cowered in the shade of a mammoth Saguaro watching the inert body of his master for the rest of the day. For most of that time the Honda continued to idle. The next morning, hours after the Honda ran out of gas, the dog trotted over to the body, sniffed, and turned away. The dog looked back once from the top of a low hill a quarter-mile away, before continuing back toward the ranch home site.

***

Alice Quinn felt anger mixed with growing concern when she called to check on her father and he didn't answer. She bought him a cell phone two years earlier and struggled to teach him how to use it.

It took three months of nagging before he'd answer it and almost six before he called her the first time. Alice had been dialing for two days with no response. When school was out on Friday, she loaded up her five-year old Nissan Quest and headed south on Interstate 10, beginning a hundred-seventy-five mile drive to her father's ranch southwest of Tucson.

The nearly three hour drive would have pleased her had she not worried about her father. Her feelings ranged from concern to anger during the trip and settled on anxious during the last fifty miles. The sun began to set and the spring weather cooled the temperature into the seventies immediately. This time of year it would be in the low fifties by morning and she'd need a jacket. At Tucson, where she entered Interstate 19 toward Nogales, Alice shut down the air-conditioning and cracked the rear passenger windows to drag in cool air. She stood five-nine in flats, the oldest and tallest of her siblings by several inches, supported mousy-brown hair that defied all attempts to control it and pretty much always looked like she'd just risen from sleep. At thirty-one, she'd quit worrying about her lack of male suitors, despite attempts of her few friends to arrange things. Alice knew she wasn't movie-star material, but her slim figure and natural beauty were better than average. In those rare moments when she reflected on it, she knew her downfall included hating beer and sports compounded by few potential suitors wanting to discuss quantum physics.

Alice turned into the single lane driveway that meandered through stately Saguaros and green-barked Palo Verdes forming a sparse canopy over low-growing creosote. She saw the house in the distance and her father's old beater Ford pickup parked in front. As she drove closer, a second pickup alongside became visible. Parking, she recognized one of the local boys she'd known since high school.

"Hi, Alice," he said, grinning through white teeth and a sun-aged face that made him look older than she knew him to be.

"Hi, Buck," she answered.

"I came over to talk to your dad, but he doesn't seem to be around."

"I know," Alice said, "I've been trying to call him for several days with no answer. Have you checked the house?"

"Couldn't, the dog wouldn't let me on the porch."

Alice noticed the dog, lying on the front porch with its head resting on its front paws, watching. She approached him knowing, like always, she'd have to make friends again. The dog had never been friendly, only letting her pet him after an introductory period becoming longer depending on how extended the time was since she last visited. She moved slowly, talking to dog in a low soothing voice while she let him smell her hand. She sat on the step and gently touched his head letting her hand slide down to his back. The dog moaned and crept forward placing his head on her lap.

"Where's your master, Dog?" The dog moaned again, got to his feet, jumped off the porch, ran a short distance before stopping and looking back.

"I think he wants us to follow him," Buck said.

Alice climbed into Buck's pickup and they followed the dog for a mile into the desert following a meandering course to avoid washes, standing cacti and occasional boulders. Finally, the terrain became rougher and they were forced to walk. The dog led them through rolling sand hills and deep gullies to a plateau of soft sand where Buck spotted the Honda several hundred yards distant.

"Maybe you'd better stay here," he said. His suggestion met with a hard stare from Alice.

"He's my father," she said, "I need to take care of him".

10

Alice Quinn didn't cry until hours later, long after the Sheriff's Department personnel, the coroner and Buck left her alone with the dog, sitting on the front porch of her father's house.

"I don't suppose you'll tell me what happened out there, right?" she said to the dog, her rhetorical question hanging like a cloud in the hot desert air.

The dog cocked his head and looked at her, but didn't respond. Then the crying started. When her blubbering finally stopped, the dog moved over and placed his head on her lap. She knew the dog and her father never got along, but the animal seemed to be mourning also, a surprise to her as much as her own tears. Her father had been a difficult man; distant, silent, and unreachable. Alice couldn't remember her mother and her step-mother's short vision lasted only brief years before she died when Alice was nine. After that her father threw himself into running the ranch and expected Alice to run the house and raise her siblings. Alice called her sisters the next morning, neither one of whom expressed interest in making the trip to Arizona. She supposed the decision-making rested in her lap.

"Guard the place," she said to the dog and slipped into the Nissan. Her father might have been a disagreeable asshole, but he didn't deserve a bullet in the chest on his own place. As Alice thought about it the angrier she became. First thing on her agenda included making sure someone paid for his death. The Sheriff's Office in Ajo seemed a good place to start.

***

Molly Sorenson, the elected Sheriff of Ayo County was acutely acquainted with grieving relatives, angry crime victims, and an array of genuine criminal assholes. The mousy-haired woman sitting in her office didn't match the usual anguished next-of-kin. She sat in Molly's overstuffed faux leather guest chair straight-backed, knees tight together, with hands-in-lap demureness, yet Molly detected sand in her voice. Her eyes read angry. Molly's twenty-year career in law enforcement enabled her to recognize the look.

"Sheriff, someone killed my father. I want to know why and I want them punished," the young woman said.

"I understand, Miss Quinn, and we are doing everything we can. I have to tell you though, there are no witnesses, no bullet since it passed through him and chances of finding it in the desert are slim, but we are trying. We know it was a very large caliber. Now, is there anyone you know who would want to harm your father?"

"My father was a disagreeable man. His only friend I know of was his dog and they didn't get along. I don't know anyone who'd want to kill him, but it wouldn't surprise me if there were a few," Alice said.

Molly's phone rang and she said, "Excuse me just a second," to her guest and "Yes," to the dispatcher who she knew wouldn't interrupt unless it was important.

"Sheriff, Mr. Draper is here."

"Tell him I'll be right out," Molly said and hung up. She looked at Alice Quinn and made a decision. Something about this young woman made her want to help more than her department could afford to.

"Miss Quinn, would you mind excusing me a moment, I will be right back." Without waiting for an answer Molly left her office and closing the door behind her, walked down the short hallway to the dispatch room. Rachael, her dispatcher, a twenty something five-foot tall cutie, who flirted with anything male over the age of ten, ranked as the calmest and most efficient dispatcher since Molly's election. This day she had an embarrassed-looking Charlie Draper standing at her desk.

"Can I talk to you for a second in an interview room?" she said to Draper knowing his silence begged rescue.

"Sure," he said, "what's up?"

"I've got a favor to ask."

"For you, anything," Draper said.

"You better wait until you hear what I have to say before you agree."

Chapter Two

Southwest Arizona

Charlie Draper followed the Sheriff into an Interview Room casually admiring Molly's backside while wondering if he was in trouble. The Sheriff looked taller than she actually stood, a result of the law enforcement uniform, Draper decided, and the intimidating chrome plated S&W nine millimeter automatic she carried on her right hip. He also knew the weapon wasn't for show; she could use it effectively and had on more than one occasion. Their relationship stood on pretty solid ground, at least in Draper's mind, so he walked somewhat puzzled. He surmised from her formal attitude that something might ruin his day. He guessed only half right.

Molly closed the interview room door and walked over to him, put her arms around his neck and kissed him, holding it long enough for Draper to wish they were somewhere else. She stepped back and smiled.

"What was that for?" Draper asked, "Not that I didn't like it, you understand, but...?"

"I have a favor to ask and the last time I caused you a lot of trouble."

"True, but the payback has been very enjoyable."

"This is serious, Charlie. I have a young woman in my office whose father was murdered a couple days ago and there's almost no evidence. Would you listen to her story and maybe you can give me some insight as to what to do to help her? We're kind of at a dead end."

"The rancher killed over by Nogales? Quinn was his name I think the paper said."

"Yes, it was very much like an assassination. We couldn't find a trace of where the shooter stood. No vehicle tracks, no sign of foot travel, no indication of any one around. Nothing; it was almost as if he'd been shot by a ghost. We spent two days scouring a half mile around where the body was found and came up empty; *Nada.*"

"What would you like me to do?" Draper said.

"Listen to her story and maybe look around out there and see if we could have missed anything. Kind of a spook's eye view; I'll make it worth your while, promise."

"How could I refuse? You know there a number of sniper rifles made today that are capable of pretty long range accuracy. In my day I could take out a target at around a thousand yards consistently, but with modern barrels, muzzle suppressors, and sophisticated sighting optics, two thousand yards and up are not impossible," Draper suggested.

"We found a likely spot about a thousand yards away in the direction the ATV was headed, but there was no indication of anyone having been there. The question is why a high-paid assassin would, or anybody else for that matter, be interested in killing an old, worn-out rancher. It looks to us like he was barely able to keep his head above water."

"Don't know, but you have me intrigued. I'll listen to her story."

Back in Molly's office, Draper shook hands with a tall, rather pretty woman he guessed to be about thirty. Her eyes read tired, testifying to the burden she carried, while at the same time appearing determined, almost hard, as if she'd resolved to find answers. Draper couldn't see a big stick, but bet she owned one.

"Miss Quinn," Molly said, "I asked Mr. Draper to join us because he has some unusual talents that you may find useful. Please understand he does not represent the Sheriff's Department nor does he have any affiliation with us. I need you to understand that. Mr. Draper is a private citizen who occasionally helps people in need."

"Like a private detective?" Alice Quinn said, looking at Draper.

"No, he's a private citizen; period. Are you willing to let him ask you some questions that could be personal in nature?"

Draper studied the woman through Molly's making sure the department's 'denial of responsibility' was documented. Draper knew everything in Molly's office was recorded on a digital video camera located behind the one-way mirror on her office wall. Alice Quinn looked wound up tight, though not altogether because of her father's death.

"O-kay," she said, drawing the word out as if she had reservations.

"Do you have any siblings, Miss Quinn?" Draper asked.

"Yes, I have two younger sisters, why?"

"No real reason," Draper said, "I'm trying to understand your father and why anyone would want to kill him."

"Well, I suppose you should know they are only half-sisters. My step-mother died when I was nine, leaving my father with a nine-year old, me, and two baby step-sisters who were one and three. Neither of them remembers their mother and I raised them since my father wasn't interested in anything other than providing food, shelter and clothing. They both left the day they graduated from high school and I haven't seen them for a number of years."

"Do you know where they are?" Draper asked.

"Oh, yes. They call once in a while and at Christmas. They both think I'm going to be an old maid and one of them will have to take care of me." Alice Quinn smiled as if debating which one most deserved that chore. "Betsy lives in Maine and Jane in upstate New York."

"You don't think they could be involved?"

"Heavens, no; why do you ask?"

"No reason, just eliminating all the possibilities." Draper said. "Would you be willing to show me the ranch?"

Alice Quinn thought a moment before answering. "Today is Wednesday, the funeral is Friday and I have to be back in Phoenix on Monday, so it would have to be tomorrow. Otherwise, I'll have to get someone to show you."

"Tomorrow would be fine. How about I meet you at the ranch around ten in the morning?"

Draper debated over whether or not to fly down to Alice Quinn's place since he hadn't had the 182 out for a while, but he'd purchased a newer Dodge Ram four-wheel drive pickup and decided on it. The Arizona sky, with its usual azure cloudless hue, contrasted with the desert colors in a pleasing way that made the drive relaxing and the two-year old pickup held the winding highway like the tires were glued to the pavement. Pleased with his purchase, Draper mused over the mystery surrounding John Quinn's death wondering who would most benefit. No likely candidates appeared as the desert flew by alongside. Alice Quinn, would profit if she became the sole heir, but from the sounds of it, the ranch had only minimal value.

John Quinn's oldest daughter stood on the porch watching his pickup drive in. Draper parked next to an old Ford three-quarter-ton four-wheel drive converted to a flatbed. The flatbed was covered with rancher-type necessities including a couple spools of barbed wire, steel fence posts, a rusty post pounder, tools and an assortment of wooden corner posts. A mongrel Border collie cross stood next to his new mistress.

Draper stepped out of his pickup and said, "Morning, Miss Quinn."

"Call me Alice, Mr. Draper, only my students call me Miss Quinn."

"Fair enough, my first name's Charlie. That your dog?"

"No, he was my father's. He's not very friendly so you'd best keep a little distance."

"Sounds like my kind of dog. How about it, boy, are you going to bite me?" Draper talked to the dog in a low even voice and reached out his hand for the animal to smell if it wanted, but far enough away just in case. He looked the dog directly in the eyes and waited.

For a moment or two the dog didn't react, until finally it stepped forward and sniffed Draper's hand. "You can trust me, dog," Draper said in the same even voice continuing to talk while slowly moving his hand toward the dog's head and letting the animal move into it. Soon he was petting its head. "Somebody beat this dog when he was a puppy," Draper said.

"You are very good with animals, Charlie," Alice said.

"Animals are easy, all you have to do is treat them right and feed them. People are the hard ones."

"That's a very cynical viewpoint; though one I happen to agree with. What kind of work do you do when you're not rescuing fair maidens and taming wild dogs?"

Draper continued to pet the dog while assessing his new client. "Mostly I fly the Sheriff around when she needs it and occasionally help folks with troubles. Used to work for the government, but I'm now retired."

"What do you want to do first?" Alice asked.

"I'm thinking the dog and I should take a little walk and maybe explore the area around where your father was shot, but first maybe you could give us a short tour of the buildings."

Draper wanted to get a feel for the man his daughter described as uncaring and disagreeable. He followed her and the dog through the house, barn and numerous out buildings. All suffered from long years of neglect and deferred maintenance. The machinery, few in number, sat old, but showed faint signs of care. Most of the paint sun-baked off years ago, yet the moving parts were oiled and greased. The entire place confirmed a long-term struggle to make a living. At first blush, Draper couldn't imagine why anyone would want it.

"How many cattle are we talking about?" Draper asked.

"I'm not sure; it used to be in the thousands, now probably less than a few hundred."

"Is the land free and clear?

"It seems to be," Alice said. "I've been through all my father's papers and it looks as if the place was paid off years ago. I've looked everywhere but can't find a will, so I suppose probate will establish any outstanding debt."

"That's more than likely," Draper said, noncommittal. What he'd seen so far didn't associate with a contract killing. "Would you mind if I took the dog and just wandered around a bit? I'll probably take a look at where your father's body was found. No need for you to come as we'll probably be gone for several hours."

"That would be great; I've got a lot to do before Sunday when I've got to go back." Alice Quinn hesitated a moment before continuing. "There was something yesterday. I don't know if it means anything, but a lawyer from up in Phoenix called and said he had been working with my father on selling the place. He wanted to know if I was interested in continuing the process."

"What did you tell him?"

"I said not at this time, that I was still trying to get my head around what's happened. I did indicate maybe later when things settled down."

"Might be a good opportunity," Draper said. He knew little about real estate prices but he was certain the place wouldn't go much over three hundred thousand in good times and at the current market probably less than one-fifty. Split three ways, that would be less than fifty grand for each child; nice, but not exactly life-changing. Draper couldn't help feeling there was something he was missing.

An hour later, after wandering around to get a feel for the place, the dog led Draper to the spot where Quinn had been killed. The dog whined before parking himself next to a big Saguaro cactus. Draper could see the dark stain in the sand next to four-wheeler tracks. He stood studying the terrain around him and decided the killer had to have placed himself on higher ground. The best bet seemed a low gravely ridge to the east. He estimated the top at a little over a thousand yards; not a difficult shot by a competent marksman with the right equipment.

"Come on, Dog, let's see what we can find at the top of that ridge," Draper said. The morning had started out cool, but as typical in springtime Arizona, the temperature rose rapidly. Draper expected it to top out in the mid-nineties by mid-afternoon when he planned to be in his new air-conditioned pickup. At noon he and his new canine companion stood next to a large granite outcrop Draper felt would make an excellent rifle rest. Its location matched perfectly with the distance and gave a nearly one hundred degree view of the kill zone. He studied the exact spot where the four-wheeler sat without difficulty. In the far distance the Quinn ranch buildings made a tiny etch in the landscape over two miles away. As his Apache friend William Alan DeCollado had taught him, Draper began slow ever-widening circles around the boulder, stepping carefully and studying not only the ground but low vegetation for signs of disturbance. Around the boulder there were obvious Vibram-soled boot tracks which Draper dismissed as likely law enforcement. He concentrated on the eastern side of the small ridge. The killer, an obvious pro, made every effort to conceal evidence of his presence. It took the dog to find the first sign. The black and white colored Border collie mix barked a few yards to Draper's left and downhill. Draper walked carefully to the dog's location stopping short and studying the ground, moving forward only when he satisfied himself that he wouldn't disturb anything. Two feet in front of the standing dog Draper spotted a distinct heel indentation in the sand. DeCollado had taught him to walk on the balls of his feet, a practice fairly easy going uphill, requires some effort on level ground and much practice going downhill. Draper knew that a person's normal stride tends to land heel first. When walking downhill considerable weight is exerted on the heel and leaves a distinct mark in soft ground. Draper surmised the killer had become careless the further he'd traveled after the kill, not expecting anyone to follow.

"You're a damn good dog, Dog!" Draper rubbed behind the dog's ears, looked him square in the eye while he voiced praise. After an initial hesitation the dog leaned into Draper's leg and wagged his tail. "Are we going to be friends? Maybe we can catch this asshole together. What do you think, Dog?"

The dog didn't answer but when Draper started down the shooter's trail, he noticed the dog followed close behind. He figured that was progress. A half hour later they found tracks looking like a small Jeep-like vehicle at the end of a two-path road leading toward Puertocito. He called Molly to see if someone could come and take a cast of the tire impression and maybe track down the vehicle since Draper would bet it was a rental from somewhere. He doubted it would lead anywhere but worth a shot.

After talking to the Sheriff, he and dog started the long trek back. After they crossed the ridge, the dog started running ahead then stopping and waiting expectantly. "What's the matter, boy, you anxious to get home?" Draper said when the dog reacted again.

Draper and the dog approached with the ranch outbuildings shielding them from the house. Fifty yards from the barn, the dog stopped short and emitted a low growl. Draper became instantly alert. Long ago training took hold and he crouched while pulling his .40 Glock from its shoulder holster. He wore the legal concealed-carry weapon habitually since his run-in with the Mexican cartels a year earlier. He peeked around the corner of the barn and spotted a dark-colored Lincoln sitting next to his pickup. Draper touched the crouching dog and whispered "Stay, Dog, we have company."

The dog quivered under his hand telling Draper that something wasn't right. The house looked peaceful enough, but Draper waited, studying the area between him and the building. Noises from the barn reached his ears, a voice muttering in Spanish, loud sounds as if searching for something. Draper followed his outstretched Glock to the open door and peered in. A heavy set

Hispanic man, dressed in black clothing ripped at the tops of cardboard boxes and pawed thorough the contents, tossing each one aside when failing to find anything. Draper couldn't imagine what he was looking for but it became obvious Alice Quinn wouldn't approve.

Draper stepped through the door and said, "You're making a hell of a mess, asshole. Why is that?"

The man whirled, his hand reaching for a hidden weapon; Draper waited a millisecond until he saw the black-handled gun appear before he double-tapped the man's chest with two .40 caliber slugs, dropping him to the dirt floor. Draper grabbed the man's weapon, a nice Beretta 96 in his favorite caliber. He thumbed the safety on and shoved it into his waistband. Since Plan B was now in effect, he exited the barn and sprinted to the house expecting more shooters. The dog beat him there and when a second man ran onto the porch, pistol in hand, the dog leaped and hit him chest-high sending the gun flying. By the time the third man came through the door, gun in hand, Draper closed the gap and double-tapped him. His effort hurried, the first round splintered the doorjamb, but the second found its mark and the shooter dropped. On the low porch, Draper looked at the second man, his eyes wide and filled with terror. The dog's jaws clamped on the gunman's neck made it hard to see his weapon, so Draper stuck the Glock against his forehead and said, "Move and you're dead; how many?"

The shooters voice almost a whisper, he said, "Three."

"That better be right, or I'll come back and let the dog tear your throat out." Draper searched for the weapon and found it under the dog. Adding it to his arsenal, along with another Beretta near the third shooter, he stepped over the body and cleared the main room of the house. Fortunately, there weren't many places to hide as he worked the rest of the house, slow and careful. In a back bedroom, he found Alice Quinn unconscious on the floor, her clothing torn, her face covered with blood and swollen from a serious beating.

"Dammit!" Draper muttered and pulled out his cell and called 911.

Chapter Three

Southwestern Arizona

D raper picked up the unconscious woman easy, laid her on the bed and covered her with a blanket. He couldn't do much else until he secured the second shooter. How long the dog would hold him was a question and he needed to finalize that detail. Back on the porch, the dog still had a death grip on the man's throat. Amazed, Draper knelt down, patted the dog's head and said to the shooter. "You move a muscle and my dog will tear your throat out, so you behave yourself for a couple of minutes and I'll be back. Capish?" The man didn't move, but blinked his eyes rapidly which Draper interpreted to mean he understood.

Draper returned from the barn where he found baling twine to secure the dog's captive. Not anticipating a fight, he'd neglected to bring along zip-ties. He selected the baling twine knowing the material to be almost impossible to break under normal effort.

"Let him go, Dog," Draper said, standing over the disarmed shooter, still held down by the dog. Draper had his Glock out pointed at the shooter. The dog backed away a few inches, growling deep in its throat as if warning the captive that he was still close. Draper noticed multiple canine tooth marks in a ring mixing with gang tattoos circling the man's neck; he felt glad he wasn't the recipient of the dog's fury.

"Listen closely, friend; I want you to roll over and put your hands behind your back, slowly, remembering I have this big gun and you know I'll use it. And remember also, any sudden moves and I can't guarantee my dog won't tear you to pieces before I can stop him. Do it now."

When the man complied, Draper pressed his right knee into the man's back using all his weight and secured his hands with the baling twine. "Watch him, Dog, if he moves, eat him," Draper said. Clueless as to whether the dog understood, he felt damned sure the shooter did.

In the house, Draper unloaded all the guns except his own and laid the weapons, clips and chamber loads on the kitchen table. He couldn't tell which deputy was coming along with the paramedics, but since they knew there was a shooting involved, he didn't want to tempt a green deputy into shooting him. That completed, Draper turned his attention to Alice Quinn. She hadn't moved. Draper felt her neck for a pulse, at first not finding one. After a moment his inexperienced fingers found it, weak and thready. Draper checked his watch and noted the fifteen minutes since he put her on the bed meant that law enforcement and medical help was another forty-five out. He hoped the Sheriff's Department had a deputy close because help would be great. Draper located a blanket and covered the woman, slid a straight-back chair close and sat next to her holding her hand. A few minutes later she pulled her hand away and looked him with terror lighting her eyes followed by tears when she recognized him.

"The men...?" she mouthed and a rivulet of blood leaked out.

"They're gone. You're safe now. Just lie still, an ambulance is on the way. Don't try to talk."

"They were after some papers they said my father had. When I said I didn't know what they were talking about, they didn't believe me and started hitting me. After that, I don't remember much," Alice Quinn said, ignoring Draper's suggestion.

"Don't worry about it, we'll figure it out later," Draper said.

The first arrival, a vehicle with siren blaring slid to a stop outside moments later. Draper ran to the open front door, cautiously peeked out to see a Sheriff's Department marked pickup and a shotgun armed officer. He didn't recognize the man so he yelled out, "I'm Charlie Draper and I'm a friend of the Sheriff. I'm armed, but it's holstered." Draper stuck his hands out the door so the deputy could see them. "I've secured the scene."

"Step out on the porch, Mr. Draper and keep your hands where I can see them." the Deputy said, standing behind his county-issued pickup with the twelve-gauge across the hood.

Draper complied, but not without grumbling silently; just his luck to get a new guy following the rules. Draper stepped onto the porch with his hands outstretched while the officer called in using his shoulder mike. He heard Rachael answer, "Ask him how tall I am."

"You heard her, how tall is she?" the deputy said.

"She's not an inch over five feet, cuter than hell and her name's Rachael," Draper said.

"I guess you know her, but I'd appreciate it if you'd remove your weapon with two fingers and place it on the porch and step back away from it." Draper noticed the shotgun barrel never quivered off the center of his chest so he did as told. By this time Draper could hear a siren announcing backup since it was too soon for the ambulance. A second unmarked county pickup pulled in and Tom Pickett, Molly's Undersheriff, stepped out. Ignoring Draper, he said to the deputy, "Clear your weapon, Jim, I know this guy."

"Good to see you, Tom," Draper said.

"Any way we could get you to move to a different county, Draper, say in Maine, so we could go back to real police work, like giving out tickets and eating donuts?"

"Tom, I'm just trying to save you from gaining weight. You should appreciate that."

"Right," Pickett said. "What the hell we got here?"

"Three shooters, beat up the daughter of the rancher that was killed out here last week. Two dead and one tied up."

"Where's the third one, inside?" Pickett asked, noting the two bodies on the porch.

"He's dead out in the barn."

"Jim, say hello to Charlie Draper, local masked avenger and, as you can see, not unknown to leave dead bodies lying around."

Draper shook hands with the new deputy.

"Go check out the barn, Jim." Pickett said. The deputy headed for the barn still carrying the twelve-gauge. Pickett stepped onto the porch, gazed at the other two shooters and said, "This looks secure, let's go see what we can do for your young lady until the ambulance gets here. They are still fifteen to twenty minutes out."

The two men moved to the bedroom where Draper had left Alice Quinn. "Alice, this is Undersheriff Tom Picket. Do you feel up to answering a few questions?" Draper said.

Alice Quinn nodded. Pickett sat in the straight back chair leaving Draper standing. "Miss Quinn, have you ever seen any of the men who came here today before."

"No." The answer came out low and Draper could see it hurt to talk.

"Miss Quinn, if it's too uncomfortable to answer questions now, we could wait, but it will delay our efforts to find out who killed your father."

"It's okay."

"Do you have any idea what these men were after?"

Alice Quinn's eyes closed and she didn't answer for a moment.

"She told me they were looking for some papers they said her father had." Draper injected.

"Yes," Alice said, so quietly Draper could barely hear her words.

Draper watched Pickett slowly and carefully extract what little information Alice Quinn knew. Draper felt considerable respect for Pickett even though he knew Molly had hesitated in promoting him. Low-keyed, sometimes a bit reserved almost to the point of distant, Pickett had proved himself a competent administrator and a damn fine law enforcement officer. Draper liked the man, somewhat a rarity for him.

The ambulance came and went, transporting Alice Quinn to the hospital in Tucson, nearly sixty miles distant. A short time later, the coroner came and removed the two bodies followed by two deputies who took custody of the live prisoner. The crime scene folks had brushed, swept, dusted and vacuumed the entire place to the point that, Draper speculated, had there been any paint, it would be now gone. The first deputy left to continue his patrol duties leaving Pickett and Draper sitting on the porch stoop in the late afternoon sun. The Sonoran Desert, its quiet beauty spread far into the distance with Saguaro shadows lengthening rapidly, lay before them as far as they could see. The desert sands, accented by huge plateaus and gravelly hills were guarded by steep granite mountains and volcano chimneys on all sides. At a distance it read peaceful and serene in startling contrast to its rugged dangers close up. Winters could be bone-chilling at night and summers ran blood-boiling hot in the afternoon. The two men sat for several minutes in silence. The dog lay next to Draper with its head resting on its paws.

Finally, Pickett said, "Need to have your gun, Charlie."

"I know. I have a spare in the pickup."

"Somehow I knew that," Pickett said.

"I figured you did," Draper said, petting the dog who moaned low with satisfaction.

"What do you think of a man who spent a lifetime trying to make a go of ranching in this country?"

"He'd have to be one tough son-of-a-bitch," Draper suggested.

"Yeah, but tough doesn't necessary translate into asshole, which apparently describes Quinn as well. There surely doesn't seem to have been much affection between him and his daughters."

Silence ensued for several minutes before Draper said, "You know, my Apache friend, Bill DeCollado, likes to say 'don't judge a man unless you've walked a distance in his moccasins.' It's an old tired quote but it apparently applies here since Quinn surely was a cantankerous old bastard if I read his daughter right."

"You think there's more to this than appears?" Pickett asked.

"Yeah, I do. I just can't lay a finger on what it could be. The old man gets shot dead in a way that smacks of an assassination, followed by three clowns with guns who beat up his daughter. The two incidents are too close together not to be linked, yet neither one makes sense."

"Well, I have to go. This case is giving me a headache, so give me your gun before I shoot you myself out of frustration," Pickett, said, grinning.

"Wouldn't want that," Draper said, pulling his Glock out of its shoulder resting place. He dropped the clip, cleared the chamber, slid the clip back home, clicked on the safety and pocketed the chamber round before handing the Glock to Pickett, butt first. "I'll even donate the test rounds, since I know you guys are on a tight budget."

"No shit on that one." Pickett looked at him as if he wanted to say something, so Draper fell silent and waited. Finally, he continued, "Mind filling me in on your plans? I know you too well not to suspect you're involvement in this mess isn't complete."

"I guess you're right. I'm involved now since those three clowns beat up my client. I'd considered just leaving it lay, but now they've made it personal. I'd really have liked an hour or two alone with the asshole I didn't have to kill. I don't suppose you could arrange that?"

Pickett gave Draper a sardonic look saying, "I'm going to pretend I didn't hear that."

"Since that isn't possible, suspect I'll have to do as I always do, shake some trees and see what falls out," Draper said.

"Just be careful not to let anything hit you on the head. I'd hate having to comfort my boss at your funeral."

"I'd hate that as well," Draper agreed.

Draper continued to sit on the porch watching Pickett's pickup disappear into boiling dust. He wished he'd been able to work on the lone surviving gunman at least a few minutes, but tending to Alice Quinn eliminated that, not to mention the first deputy had arrived too quickly. The dog moved over and put its head in Draper's lap.

"I guess this mean we are friends, right dog? I suppose I'm going to have to take you home with me. Well, come on; let's take a little look-see around the place."

Draper spent the next hour until full dark threatened, searching the outbuildings, exploring every nook and cranny he could find with no success. The barn and its periphery buildings contained a dirt and dust-covered accumulation of the assorted treasures a lifetime in one place tends to generate. As a time-saving measure, Draper ignored piles of boxes, barrels, and various other containers that lacked signs of recent disturbance. The boxes the first shooter had disturbed were part of a dirt encrusted pile supporting water stains and considerable deterioration. Draper's hunt resulted in failure.

Draper moved to the house, followed by the dog, and it proved more difficult. The rooms were clean, but only in the way a long-time bachelor would clean, ignoring corners and cobwebs overhead, but clean enough to mask any obvious disturbance. He spent many minutes in each room, the front including the kitchen, dining area, living room as well as the back containing one large bedroom and two smaller ones. Draper stood in the middle of the larger bedroom last, which he assumed from the strictly male furniture and sparse accessories had been Quinn's private cave. The bed, carelessly made, had metal foot and head boards that had once been painted blue. The original color faded and its heavily chipped surface spoke volumes of long-term apathetic use.

He sat on the bed and studied the walls for several minutes trying to guess where a lonely old man would hide something if there were anything to hide. His eyes followed the six-inch rough pine baseboard molding surrounding the room. A length of quarter-round added to the bottom of the baseboard dressed the final finish. Pretty standard carpentry, Draper thought, until he caught the flaw. In one two-foot section across the room the seams of the baseboard and the quarter-round lined up exactly, something no carpenter would do unless it was intentional. He also remembered in the rest of the house the baseboard stood no higher than three inches. Draper knelt in front of the apparent mistake, and studied it. The seams were architecturally tight, indicating craftsmanship, yet out of place. He tried to pull on the section to no avail. There were no obvious indications of a lock or trigger. Draper's knees began to bark in protest, so he stood and sat again on the bed. After studying it for a few minutes, it occurred to him it could only work one way. He crossed room and knelt again. Using his hand, he pressed on the baseboard between the two seams. At first, nothing happened; then with a little more effort the piece slid into the wall about a quarter inch. When Draper relaxed, the piece popped out an inch or so revealing a carefully constructed hidden drawer. He pulled it fully open to expose the drawer contents. Watched closely by his new canine buddy, Draper systematically inventoried numerous trinkets, some jewelry, a single gold locket on a chain, and a red book with a simple latch that looked like a diary; the mementoes of a lonely man saved from better times. Included were letters, with female appearing handwriting, and few black and white pictures of a pretty young woman holding a baby. At the bottom, Draper found an old property deed and a newer bundle of papers that appeared to be an unsigned buy/sell agreement.

"It seems, Dog, we've found what the assholes were looking for. I'll bet Alice couldn't have told them where it was, because likely she didn't know." The dog barked a single woof and wagged its tail.

Draper boxed up the items he'd found in the hidden drawer in an empty cardboard box and took it to the pickup. His next effort included locking the barn and out buildings. In the house, he shut off everything he could find that needed securing for an extended time and locked the windows and doors. He wasn't concerned that he didn't have keys since he felt it likely Alice had a set and if not or if the need arose, he and half the criminals in the world could pick the ancient door locks blindfolded.

Securing the box behind the rear seat, Draper opened the front passenger door and looked at the dog. "Are you coming with, Dog?" The dog hesitated, then walked slow to the door, spent a moment sniffing the seat and leaped in, sitting upright on the passenger side.

"Guess I've got temporary custody of a new dog," Draper said.

Chapter Four

Southern Arizona

Draper woke the next morning with a cold canine nose prodding his back. He rolled over and opened one eye to see the dog standing next to the bed. "What the hell, Dog, can't you let a man sleep?" In response, the dog woofed a single demanding bark hinting at impatience.

"Okay, okay, I'm moving." Draper struggled out of bed and padded to the front door followed closely by the dog. "Don't go getting into any trouble, Dog. I'm a bit grumpy until I've had my morning coffee." The dog didn't seem to care and bolted through the open door.

Draper, dressed and scrubbed, made coffee, located a clean cup and prepped it with his favorite flavored cream and a healthy shot of cheap brandy. He found the dog lying on the front porch guarding the desert, waiting patiently for Draper's arrival. Coffee cup in hand, he moved his chair to the sunrise position where he could watch the sun begin to peak over the eastern mountains. Draper liked to watch the sunrise and set. He oriented his front porch to the north during construction, first because it lay shaded in the afternoon and second, he could watch both sunrise and sunsets by simply moving his chair.

George, a large gecko, who started arriving for breakfast shortly after Draper finished the house, waited while Draper went back in for a half slice of bread. The Dog cocked its head to one side

37

and studied the gecko; decided it belonged, and thereafter ignored it. Draper returned food in hand. George accepted the offered slice, ate a bit of it and scurried off with the remainder.

Draper watched the sunrise light the thin morning clouds with brilliant pink hues, a sparkling show that never lasted more than fifteen minutes or so. It relaxed him and convinced Draper that anything so beautifully designed had to have a purpose.

While he studied the sunrise Draper plotted his day. It included a trip to Tucson, an opportunity to blow the dust off his Cessna 182, a fixed gear, high-wing airplane that had a lifetime of gentle care and low flying hours. Draper bought it five years earlier anticipating his current early retirement. He used it and his commercial pilot ticket to make a few extra bucks here and there and satisfy his love of flying. This day it would be a convenient way to get to Tucson.

Draper took a swig of coffee and pulled out his cell phone. The cell, his single acceptance of new technology that didn't have Cessna attached to it, provided a convenient communication source and therefore acceptable. The result of an exhausting search, his single function model made only phone calls. His first call, directed to his favorite female County Sheriff Molly Sorenson, was answered instead by Rachael, the dispatcher, who explained Molly wasn't available.

"She's in a meeting with the County Commissioners," Rachael said. "Could I help you? I have a weakness for big strong guys who shoot people."

"I promise you, if Molly ever throws me out, you will be the first one I'll call," Draper said, continuing an on-going banter that Rachael played with anything male between the age of ten and the grave, told him his activities on the previous afternoon ranked high on the office rumor board.

Draper's second call found Detective-Lieutenant John Pérez of the Tucson Police Department up to his eyebrows in crime. Recent years populated by a significant uptick in gang violence, illegal immigration and the proliferation of hard drugs had law enforcement everywhere bombarded almost to the breaking point. Draper sympathized and he and Pérez had become friendly, though not exactly friends, since Draper's activities occasionally deviated from Pérez's strict definition of legal. He included Draper occasionally in a "band of brothers" coffee klatch that included other law enforcement agencies.

"What the hell do you want?" Pérez said.

"Now is that any way of greeting an old friend who helped you get that Lieutenant designation in front of your name? I'm hurt."

"I'll talk to you as long as there aren't any outstanding warrants in your name. There aren't are there, since I heard you were busy yesterday?"

"None that I know of," Draper said.

"Okay, talk."

"Need your help," Draper said.

"What else is new? You aren't planning to come anywhere near Tucson are you?" Apparently, an eight month long break wasn't long enough for the Tucson cop.

"Can I come if I promise not to shoot anybody and buy you lunch?" Draper said.

"Now that's altogether different. For lunch I can put up with you for an hour; you coming today?"

"Yeah, I have to check on my client in the hospital there and then I'll call you." Draper said. Draper hung up and patted the dog standing waiting for favors next to him. "I gotta fly up to Tucson today, Dog, so I'm going to leave you in charge. Okay?" The dog wagged its tail and Draper assumed that meant agreement. Draper had made arrangement with Rachael at the Sheriff's office to have a patrolling Deputy check his place whenever he had to leave. He'd added feeding and watering Dog to those duties.

The dog watched from the porch as Draper opened his Quonset building--converted to hanger--doors and using a nose-wheel hook, dragged the 182 out into the daylight. Silver with light blue trim colors, it seated four, had a tricycle gear, a constant-speed prop and a wing-high configuration that made it rock-solid stable and easy to fly. Draper had invested a princely sum in a state-of-the-art navigation system that included GPS and a sophisticated autopilot. Its turbo engine allowed a 167 mph cruise speed making fast, easy hops to either Tucson or Phoenix under most weather conditions possible.

Closing the big sliding doors on the hanger, Draper did his pre-flight and run-up on the concrete pad designed for that purpose. His runway, a two thousand foot packed-sand thoroughfare he'd built himself, lay nearby. He'd packed a small suitcase just in case there was time to detour up to Phoenix to see Gabriella, his unofficial adopted daughter that he'd rescued from the Mexican cartels and now a nursing student. The bag included his spare Glock .40 and several fifteen round clips alongside his Arizona concealed-carry permit.

Ready to go, Draper gave the plane full-throttle and pitch. At rotate speed Draper eased the 182 into the air and climbed to his cruising altitude, before settling back to enjoy the barely half hour flight to Tucson. A cloudless sky stretched clear to the horizon and light winds provided a smooth ride. Draper enjoyed the trip; happy to be flying again, but the problem with Alice Quinn nagged at him like a desert thorn. Why in hell, he asked himself, would anyone spend money on a pro shooter without a reason? An angry neighbor or enemy could simply walk up and shoot the son-of-a-bitch without spending the coin required to enlist a sniper capable of pulling off a thousand-yard kill. If old man Quinn was negotiating a sale, why send three goons to steal the paperwork? That by itself begged the question why would anyone want two thousand acres of Sonoran sand? Unless..., Draper pondered a moment; what if Quinn had changed his mind...? He considered several scenarios, none of which answered the questions. The amount shown on the buy/sell listed at three hundred-fifty thousand, not an exorbitant amount but certainly generous considering the location and the current market. Five years ago it might have meant a subdivision of ten or twenty acre "ranchettes," a term invented by the real estate industry, but that market stank today like last week's fish, so no answer there. No question the ranch stood directly in the path of the so-called *Devil's Highway,* a corridor in southern Arizona infamous for drug trafficking and human smuggling. The more he thought about it the likelier that scenario fit. The only hitch belonged to the fact those illicit activities weren't new and remained a part of the landscape despite the heroic efforts of a gaggle of federal and local law enforcement agencies.

Draper's 182 crossed the last remaining mountains corralling the Tucson valley and he could see the Tucson airport in the distance. After talking to the Tucson tower, he made a standard into-the-wind approach and let the heavy 182 settle gently onto the runway. Twenty minutes later, the plane refueled and tied-down, he located the rental car booths and selected a plain-Jane Chevy Malibu, much too small for his over six-foot stature, but good enough for the day. He'd learned from the Sheriff's office that Alice Quinn had been taken to St. Luke's, a hospital he was intimately familiar with due to his previous case earlier last year. He'd hope never to see it again.

Alice Quinn's room, located on the fifth floor, looked exactly like the one's he'd visited before, small, undecorated, sterile-smelling and depressive. The woman in the bed could have been anybody since he could see little of her face not covered by white gauze and steri-stripes. She appeared asleep, but his movements opened the single eye not covered. "Oh, hi," she said. Tears began to flow from the eye dripping on her pillow. Draper took her hand and she squeezed his hard. "God, I thought they were going to kill me. How bad is my face? They won't give me a mirror."

"Not any worse than a damned good bar fight; nothing that won't heal," Draper lied. He didn't really know, but considered it likely there would be some scarring, both physically and mentally. The depth of either one would depend on her inner strength, although Draper guessed her sand might run deep.

"What were they looking for?" she asked.

Draper debated on telling her what he'd found, deciding later would work better. Alice Quinn had more than enough to fret about already. "You need to worry about getting well. Let me be concerned about everything else," he said.

"I need to call the school. I've got to be back in school Monday and my father's funeral is today."

"What's the number of the school, I'll call them right now and that'll give them time to find a substitute." Draper ignored the last part as a rhetorical question. The funeral would go on without her.

Alice Quinn gave him the number just as a doctor and a nurse came in and asked him to step out. Draper walked down the hallway to an empty waiting room and phoned the school principal to let them know Miss Quinn had been seriously hurt in an accident and would likely require several weeks for recovery. The principal indicated their concern, thanked Draper for calling and asked that he tell Miss Quinn that they wished her the best and hoped she could return soon. On the way back to the room, Draper ran into the doctor, a short, obviously middle-eastern man with dark eyes covered with frameless glasses and coal black hair. Draper had little doubt he felt right at home around the sands of Arizona.

"Are you a family friend?" the man asked.

"Yes, how is she?" Draper said, a tiny exaggeration made easy by twenty-years of covert activities and a required course at Langley.

"The young lady is in very serious condition at the moment. She has numerous broken facial bones, a broken nose and likely a concussion from all the blows to her head. She also has two broken ribs. We expect full recovery, but she may need plastic surgery to reduce scaring."

"How long will she require hospitalization?" Draper asked, suddenly angry that he hadn't killed the second shooter, or at least let the dog gnaw on him for an hour or so.

"Possibly a week; maybe a little more depending on how she does."

Draper continued on to Alice's room and peeked in to see her eye open and waiting. "I talked to the school and they said not to worry, just get well and come back when you can."

"Thank you, Mr. Draper."

"Listen; as long as we're working together call me Charlie. I'm already old enough, don't make me any older."

"Okay, Charlie," she said, wincing because it hurt to smile.

"I know it hurts to talk so let me do the talking. I have a couple of questions and you squeeze my hand for yes and do nothing for no, how would that work?"

Draper didn't belabor the session since the woman seemed almost as clueless as he was about the whole situation. When he left she was sleeping. The only thing he'd discovered was that at thirty-one, her BA in Secondary Education allowed her to teach, an occupation that while personally satisfying, likely would never make her rich. Draper found it odd she couldn't name a single friend close enough to call to assist her in recovery. She reminded Draper of what little he knew about her father.

Out in the hallway, a young man approached Draper. He looked like he'd walked out of a John Wayne western, tall, but shorter than Draper by several inches, his face sun-darkened to a permanent leathery color, his hands gripping a dusty hoof-stomped Stetson, standing in rolled over cowboy boots that hadn't seen polish since new. He stood in the hospital hallway sans the .45 holster rig, but looking like knew how to use one. "Sir," he said to Draper, "Are you Charlie Draper?"

"Yeah," Draper said.

"Sir, my name is Ralph Bauer, though most people call me Buck. I'm a friend of Alice Quinn. If I could bother you for a moment of your time for a quick talk somewhere? The Sheriff's office in Ajo gave me your name."

"No problem," Draper said, "Let's go into the waiting room."

"I appreciate it," Bauer said, and turned toward the space. Draper followed wondering where this guy came from. He looked about Alice Quinn's age, but certainly not her type. He appeared as if bovine obstetrics would be a breeze. In the small waiting room, they grabbed chairs and Bauer seemed to be assessing him, so Draper waited.

"It's your dime, friend," Draper said finally to break the ice.

"Yes, I'm sorry I was trying to figure out where to begin."

"How about at the beginning," Draper suggested.

"I'm not very good and this, but here goes. Alice Quinn and I went to high school together. I took her out a couple of times, nothing real serious, but I kind of assumed that would come. Then all of a sudden she left without a word and I didn't see her again for five or six years until I happened to be at the Quinn Ranch helping John with a problem cow calving. He was far from an expert in veterinary practice so whenever he had a problem, he'd call me. He was a strange man; hardly spoke except when he needed help. Anyway, they argued and she stormed off and I didn't see her again until last weekend when she came down because she couldn't get her father on the phone. She and I found his body."

Draper waited when Bauer stopped as if he was plotting where he was going next, hoping he'd get to the point soon.

"I guess I'd like to know what your interest is here, because it looks to me like Alice needs help and if you are her boy friend or something, I'll back off. Otherwise I intend to look out for her. No offense meant," Bauer said.

"I only met Alice after her father was killed. The Sheriff in Ajo is a friend of mine and she asked me to talk with her and see if there was anything I could do to help her. I met her again at the ranch yesterday. I was out looking around with the dog and when I came back three goons had beat her up and were searching the place."

"You're the one who killed two of them and captured the other one." Bauer's inflection made it a statement, not a question.

"No, Dog gets credit for capturing one."

"Are you a cop?"

"Nope," Draper said.

"But you are going to help Alice?"

"That's the idea."

"And she's going to pay you?"

"I doubt she can afford me."

"But you're going to help anyway."

"I'm going to try."

"Why?"

"Because, like you said, she needs it." Draper began to tire of the man's third degree.

"I'll pay you. I have a little money saved," Bauer said.

"Good, I'll send you a bill and you can decide if you want to pay it. Now, are you done? If you are, I have a couple questions for you."

"Go ahead," Bauer said.

"You have any idea why anyone would spend a ton of money on shooting the old man?

"You mean other than he was a disagreeable son-of-a-bitch?"

"Other than that," Draper said.

"I can't imagine. John certainly was a strange dude, but I can't see anyone caring enough to kill him. He kept to himself and I was probably closest to him other than maybe the feed store owner in Ajo who put up with him."

"The shooter was a pro. Probably someone from out of the country and likely paid in the hundred grand range," Draper said.

"No shit? That does put a little different perspective on it. But who would do it?"

"There's only one possibility--one of the Mexican drug cartels. The question is why?"

"I don't have a clue. Certainly no one has offered to buy my place. The way things are I'd have probably jumped at it," Bauer said.

"The problem is Alice Quinn is now the owner along with her two sisters I suppose, which means it's likely there is some risk to their lives. I don't know how much, but there's no doubt the cartels are capable. Do you have a gun?"

"Yes."

"Know how to use it?"

"Two years, Army Rangers."

"How long ago, say ten years? I'd suggest some heavy practice. If you are going to be around Alice Quinn, be prepared to suspect everyone, be cautious whenever you go outside and if necessary shoot to kill. Dead men don't shoot back."

"I know the rules of engagement."

"No, you don't. It's similar but different. This is more up front and personal. Can you kill someone when you can see their eyes?"

"I think so."

"You have to know. What kind of gun do you have?"

"A Smith and Weston nine millimeter," Bauer said.

"Get a .40. That'll knock down a man and he'll stay down. Take it to a range and practice until you can put most of a fifteen round clip in a silhouette target body mass. You'll live longer. You have a week or so to prepare. After that, I know a place she can stay out of harm's way. Who's going to take care of your ranch?"

"I have a hired man taking care of it. We moved all John's cattle over to my place. I've got them inventoried and we'll tag the calves. What are you going to do?"

"Pester the cartel so they concentrate on me instead of Alice Quinn."

Chapter Five

Tucson, Arizona

D raper called Tucson Police headquarters a few minutes before noon on his way to the St Luke's parking lot and asked for Detective-Lieutenant John Pérez. He sat in the Malibu on hold for almost two minutes before Pérez answered.

"About time you called, I'm starving," Pérez growled.

"I've been busy making your life more difficult," Draper said.

"No doubt in my mind about that. Where you taking me for lunch?"

"You name it," Draper said.

"It's tough to think of a restaurant you haven't killed somebody in," Pérez said.

"Surely there is more than one restaurant in Tucson?"

"How about *Juanita's?* I called the boys and told them you'd be in town. They grumbled a little but agreed to join us when I told them you were buying," Pérez suggested.

"You are pretty free with my money."

"I know, ain't it great?"

Draper hung up and pointed the Malibu toward downtown Old Tucson where *Juanita's* sat squeezed in between two rundown warehouse buildings. The water-stained stucco and sun-bleached sign

49

greeted only those customers who knew the inside shone with fresh primary-colored paint scrubbed spotless every day. The earth-colored floor tile looked clean enough to eat off of and the healthy-sized proprietor mastered the art of Mexican-style cooking at an early age by practicing daily. Draper first joined the coffee group the previous year including meeting, in addition to John Pérez, DEA agent Wayne Jones, Larry Whitcomb from ATF and CBP officer Vicente Arteaga. Draper liked and respected them all.

"Hey, stranger," Whitcomb said when Draper entered the room.

"Hey, yourself," Draper responded, shaking hands, and moving around the room.

Food came immediately as they always ordered the same thing. Lunch included general conversation, some lies and considerable jesting. After an hour of light banter and the food cleared away, the mood turned more somber. Draper outlined the events of the last week while the others listened in silence.

When he finished, Whitcomb said, "Do you advertize for trouble or does it just follow you around?"

"No need to advertize, lots of assholes out there," Draper responded.

"What about the three who beat up the girl; find out anything about them?" Jones asked.

"According to the Sheriff's office all three have been in and out of the system since they were teenagers. Gang ties in Phoenix and Tucson. They're mostly just muscle if their records are any indication. The one I didn't shoot is a small time drug dealer slash gangbanger with a long record and two stints in the prison at Florence. I think these guys are just low-level punks. Whoever is behind this is bigger, ambitious and has financing." I'm guessing, but the shooter they hired to kill John Quinn stinks of a very expensive pro. The kill was made from over a thousand yards with a large caliber sniper round, probably a .338."

"That's a hell of a shot," Whitcomb said.

"For the average Joe, you're right. This wasn't any run-of-the-mill gang shooter. This guy's had sniper training and tons of practice. I suspect he could have done it at twice the distance with the right equipment and practice."

"And you know this how?" Jones asked, always a skeptic.

"I read a lot," Draper said, smiling.

"My ass," Jones snorted.

"Just believe me, Wayne, the weapon he used cost something near five thousand a pop, plus extra customization if you want it," Draper added. "I'd bet on it."

"So what do you think this is all about?" Pérez asked.

"I wish I knew. The only thing that makes sense is the cartels. The ranch butts up against Mexico for several miles. The only thing that comes to mind is based on the plans we found last year." Draper's comment met with silence. He scanned the table and could see doubt on every face. His statement referred to the tunnel plan he and DeCollado had lifted out of a cartel leader's estate in Mexico the previous year.

Vicente Arteaga from Customs and Border Protection spoke for the first time. "You think there might be or a plan for a tunnel in that area?"

"I honestly don't know, but what else make sense? I found an unsigned buy/sell agreement hidden in the house as if someone was interested in buying the ranch. I think that was what the goons were looking for that beat up Alice Quinn."

"I'm skeptical of any tunnel; yes we have found a few, but they are mostly crude, dangerous and short. Any place on a ranch would necessitate a miles long tunnel. The vibration alone from mechanical digging would trigger sensors. Upper management scoffed at the plans you shared with us last year as a pipe-dream. Besides, the cost would be enormous," Arteaga said.

"I guess I'd have to agree; it's likely the problems would overshadow the end result --if your estimates of total cartel income are close--but what if they aren't?" Draper wasn't convinced himself, but playing the devil's advocate seemed prudent. He knew the tunnel plan he and Bill DeCollado found in the late cartel *Jefe* Carlos Armenta's estate in Mexico rang grandiose in cost and engineering yet nothing else explained Quinn's death. Armenta died in his bed trying to shoot Draper with a .357 revolver hidden under his blankets causing Draper to double-tapped him with his Glock .40 in response.

"Management doesn't think a tunnel of that magnitude is feasible or cost-effective," Arteaga said.

"Think about this," Draper said, his mind constructing a scenario even he had trouble believing. He spit it out as he built it, not bothering with much mental editing. "The Quinn Ranch buildings are at the end of an existing road capable of supporting large trucks. They haul cattle over it all the time so trucking wouldn't raise suspicion. If the cartel was able to acquire the land and build a new large metal building in the same area, no one would raise an eyebrow. Now, could they construct a tunnel the ten odd miles from the border to under that building? The answer is yes; it is both engineering-wise and construction-wise a no-brainer. There are currently sixty-two tunnels in the world longer than ten miles in length, railroads, highways and enclosed aqueducts are some of the longest. The Delaware Aqueduct in New York is an enclosed tunnel 85 miles long.

Ten miles seems child's play in comparison. The Chunnel from England to France is 31 miles long and over 250 feet deep at its deepest point much of which is under water.

"There'd have to be a portal somewhere on the ranch that would stick out like rose in a thorn patch. How could they hide it?" Vicente Arteaga argued, unable to shake his Border Patrol mentality of chasing illegals and drug traffickers through the nighttime desert brush.

"Not necessary; think in terms of a tunnel that ends a hundred feet below the building and you lift people and product up to the inside of the building with a nice set of dual freight elevators."

Arteaga looked unconvinced. "A hundred feet underground, would that be possible?"

"Easy, that's a little more than a six story building. In any circumstance less than ten stories, either electric or hydraulic freight elevators can lift up to just under ten thousand pounds per load. A two elevator group could transfer nearly twenty-thousand pounds up. They've been doing it in mines for decades," Draper said.

"Okay, let's concede it's possible to build," Arteaga argued, "but what about cost; the Chunnel was government financed, I'm sure."

"Granted," Draper said, "I spent a little time researching cost and it depends on soil type, tunnel diameter and total length. A twenty-one foot diameter tunnel is about $200-500 million per mile, so for ten miles we have a total cost of 3-5 billion dollars. That's a lot, but if you consider it spread over a couple-three years, a billion a year out of a minimum gross exceeding, according to estimates I've read, reaching $20 billion or more, not so much."

Silence dropped onto the table like a stone.

"Since TBM's are built especially for each job, say reduce the tunnel height to fifteen feet, although I'm not sure you can because of engineering issues, but for the sake of argument, that's thirty percent less or $140 to $350 million per mile." Draper was on a roll and continued, "When you're done you have a concrete-lined perfectly safe, engineered tunnel capable of transporting people, drugs or money either way using some sort of high-speed shuttle."

"What's a TBM?" Pérez asked.

"Sorry, that's short for Tunnel Boring Machine," Draper said.

What sort of engineering issues?" Vicente Arteaga said.

"Primarily ventilation, room for an emergency walkway, maintenance equipment and so on." Draper freewheeled a bit here since his research didn't really cover the technical engineering issues.

"What about all the people involved. How could they keep it secret? Surely someone would blab; right?" Arteaga said.

"I agree," Draper said, "I've thought long and hard on that one and my only conclusion would be they, meaning the cartel, uses intimidation in ways we can't even imagine. A promise of a good job that includes a real threat of harm to them or their families could do the trick."

"Seems a little far-fetched, and I'm sure my upper level management would agree with the thinking of CBP," Wayne Jones said.

I'd don't doubt it," Draper said. The trouble is, I can't see any other answer. Give me a better one and I'll jump on it."

No one at the table said a word and Draper conceded that while as individuals they might agree, it was probable their bureaucratic superiors would balk. Not surprised, he conceded any forward progress would only come if he initiated it. "Listen," he said,

"I appreciate your patience and if you come up with anything I'd like a call."

Later, after everyone left, Draper stood in the parking lot with John Pérez. They watched the others drive away silently until Draper said. "I don't blame them. It sounded pretty incredulous even to me."

"You planted the seed. Give it time to grow," Pérez said. "Believe me when I say they all know you are trying to find the answer and they'll be thinking about it. If anything turns up you'll be the first to know."

"I know. I was hoping not to have to go back to shaking trees."

"Maybe so, but I happen to know from experience you are pretty good at it," Pérez said as he turned while walking to his car.

Draper watched him pull out onto the street before he slipped into the Malibu and headed for the airport. It was time to go to Phoenix.

Draper settled back to enjoy the roughly two hour drive to Phoenix thinking about Gabriella, his barely eighteen-year-old quasi-daughter whose schooling in nursing bill he paid without question. They'd become close in a father/daughter way totally foreign to Draper but considering the circumstances, a situation to which he slowly adjusted. His first twenty-years of adulthood spent mostly in Middle Eastern and Far Eastern countries didn't allow much in the way of long-term relationships with anyone. He first met Gabriella on the wrong side of the US/Mexican border when in desert-night blackness he'd grabbed her around the throat and stuck his Glock .40 in her ear followed by a serious threat to blow off her head. Only when she yelped did he realize his captive wasn't a Mexican bandito. Instead, he had a tight grip on an emaciated seventeen-year-old, foul-mouthed, escapee from a Mexican whorehouse, who a day later saved his life by shooting a bandito intent on cutting out his heart. He owed her and surprisingly he began to like her. He admired the internal strength that allowed her to shed her three-year captivity like an old set of clothes and start him on a path to cast off his own demons. She studied hard, called him often and would shortly end her first year with a better than average academic record that improved with each passing day. She had to pass the Arizona General Equivalency Diploma test in order to enroll, which she tackled like a tiger taking down a water buffalo. With fierce determination and long nights of study she hit the ninetieth percentile on the first try. Draper couldn't help but be proud of her. He pulled into a parking spot at her apartment complex in time for dinner. He called to take her somewhere but she'd surprised him by insisting on cooking, a newly acquired talent that Draper didn't know about.

"Hi, Dad," Gabriella said, answering the door after his knock. She grabbed him around the neck and kissed his cheek, "I've missed you."

"Missed you, too, girl."

"Come in, I've got everything ready," Gabriella said, holding the door.

The apartment was small, far past new, but comfortable and she kept it immaculate. She told him about school while they ate sloppy joes on burger buns with cheese covered broccoli on the side. The food was good and Draper enjoyed it.

Draper wanted to find a motel, but Gabriella insisted he sleep on her pull-out couch bed, a decision he regretted when at midnight his staring at the ceiling began to get old. Designed to cause misery to any occupant the four-inch mattress barely supported his back from touching the steel springs. When he woke in the morning, Gabriella was buzzing around in the kitchen fixing breakfast. The girl had suddenly become downright domestic, he decided, musing about his sudden entry into fatherhood without an ounce of preparation or proper training. When he thought about it he realized that's how most people approached the first one. His unofficially adopted daughter, kidnapped at fourteen and forced into prostitution by cartel drug dealers, had somehow gathered the strength to survive, escaping after three years into the desert where she stumbled into Draper and Bill DeCollado. He'd spent many hours training her to shoot until she could score near perfect at the Sheriff's department range. He included basic active shooter response in her training arsenal which he hoped she'd never have to use. Pulling on his pants and listening to her singing to herself in the kitchen, Draper couldn't help a twinge of pride; she stood smart, eager to learn, and proudly carried her concealed-carry permit alongside the unregistered 9mm Glock 19 he'd found for her; both hidden in her homemade purse.

"I want you to be careful Gabriella; I'm involved in something again that may involve the cartels." If it gets to sticky we may have to move you to a school further north," Draper said before mouthing a fork full of sausage and eggs.

"I can take care of myself," she said.

"I have no doubt, babe, I just want to make sure."

"Dad, I'm eighteen, I've seen more of the seamier side of life than most women see in a lifetime. Very little would surprise me. Besides, despite my past, I can act helpless and virginal before I shoot their asses." She grinned at Draper, jerking his chain just for fun.

"Be serious, girl, I don't want anything happening to you."

"I know," she said, no longer kidding, "I appreciate your concern and I will be careful and if I think there's a problem, I'll let you know."

"Thank you," Draper said, knowing he sounded like an over protective parent. "So, how are your grades this semester?"

"All A's except anatomy, because there is a lot to remember. I think I'm going to end up with a B. How's Molly?" Gabriella asked, changing the subject.

"She's fine."

"Are you guys sleeping together yet?"

"None of your business, girl."

"I'm going to take that as a yes. Good, I like her."

"Got any classes today?" Draper asked, attempting to change the subject.

"Just one, but not until four this afternoon; why?"

"Thought maybe we'd go fishing," Draper said, "It's a beautiful day for a drive."

"Fishing?" Gabriella said, her tone a bit incredulous, but willing to follow along. "You don't like fishing."

"Yeah, I do. I'm just picky about what I catch. We drive around, look for likely spots and see what happens. The fish I'm after are the two-legged kind."

"Ah," Gabriella said, "now I'm on board. Just what species of fish are we looking for, exactly, other than the asshole kind?"

"My, such language from a nice, educated young lady."

Draper enjoyed teasing her, watching her eyes sparkle when she realized he was poking fun at her. She'd come a long way from the scrawny dirt-covered waif he and DeCollado had rescued in the Mexican desert.

"Okay, smarty, where are we going and who we going to kill?" Gabriella said.

Draper gave her a brief rundown of events over the last few days leading up to the hoodlums looking through Alice Quinn's father's place and his finding the buy/sell agreement. "Alice mentioned to me an attorney named Goodsill called her about selling the place a day or so before the goons showed up and beat her up."

"Is she okay?"

"No, she's in the hospital in Tucson, St Luke's as I'm sure you remember, in pretty tough shape. Nothing fatal, but she might have some scars, both physical and maybe emotional."

"Does she live in Tucson?"

"No, actually, she teaches school here in Phoenix. She and her father have been on the outs for years." Draper found Gabriella's Phoenix metro phone book and looked under Attorneys, a large part of the A-section of the yellow pages, for a Goodsill. "Christ, there's too damn many attorneys," Draper grumbled.

"What are you grumbling about, you're one of them," Gabriella said.

"Please don't tell anyone, it would ruin my nice guy reputation," Draper said, still pawing through the hundred-plus pages of legal ads. Finally he jumped to the M's and looked for Randall Markham, who was currently the appointed replacement for the former Congressman Draper and DeCollado had disgraced a year earlier.

"Congressman Markham's Office," a cheery voice answered.

"Is the Congressman available? This is Charlie Draper."

"One a moment, Mr. Draper, I'll check."

After several minutes of pleasant music, Markham answered, "Who'd you kill now?"

"No one today, but then it's early yet."

"As long as you don't want me to bail you out of jail, what can I do for you? I owe you a lot, my friend."

"Just need the address of an attorney named Goodsill. You know him?"

"Unfortunately, I do. Him you could shoot and I'd probably help. Why do you want to talk to that scumbag?"

"His name came up on a buy/sell offered to the father of my current client."

"Tell him not to sign anything until I look at it."

"Her," Draper said.

"What?"

"My client is a lady."

"Whatever, Goodsill is not only a crook, he's a terrible lawyer."

"So, where do I find him?"

"He works 'Of Counsel' for the Brandenburg Firm in Tempe. They are a very big firm who uses him for shit jobs so the partners stay clean, but most of us think they're connected to organized crime."

"I was afraid of that. Any chance 'organized crime' might include the cartels?"

"You didn't hear it from me, but between us kids, I'd bet on it."

"Thanks, Randall, I appreciate it."

"No problem, call me sometime when I'm not in D.C. and I'll buy you dinner."

"You got it," Draper said, and hung up."

"Well?" Gabriella said.

"The fish are biting in Tempe today," Draper said.

Chapter Six

Phoenix-Tempe Metro Area

Draper drove the Malibu with Gabriella riding shotgun. She'd done something with her hair, though he hadn't a clue what; he did know she'd filled out and looked every bit the part of young woman who would attract suitors like bees in a tulip patch. He resolved that eventually one of them would steal her away, but not before he shot the first couple or perhaps wounded them a little. Likely, just as he was adjusting to being a father, he'd have to learn to be a father-in-law.

"I've got a dog," he said to stop the musing.

"Good, you need a dog, though I was hoping for a mother," Gabriella said.

"It's not really mine. I just have temporary custody until Alice Quinn recovers. It was her father's dog." Draper ignored the mother part.

"What kind?"

"Definitely part Border Collie and something else, trusts no one, but follows its master and bites assholes," Draper said.

"Other than the follow part, sounds like you," Gabriella said.

"Smart-ass," Draper said, "a little respect for your elders, please."

"Are you going to keep the dog?"

"I might unless Alice wants him."

"What's his name?"

"Dog."

"Figures," Gabriella said.

Draper pulled into a parking lot across the street from the offices of the Brandenburg Firm in downtown Tempe. The lot had a yellow driveway barrier and an automatic ticket booth. Draper pushed the button, retrieved his ticket and the bar rose. The sign said *Reserved for Clients of the Brandenburg Firm Only. One Dollar per hour unless validated by a Partner.* Draper decided that for a buck he could pretend he was a client. There wasn't much else for parking available. After selecting a spot he and Gabriella walked across the street to the offices, a large, modernistic building designed, or so it seemed, by an architect only partially recovered from a massive drug overdose. A tiny brass sign indicated the firm name and no list of partners. Apparently there was no need to advertize. Through the heavy front door they were greeted by a blond receptionist behind a cherry-wood desk sized to impress but with nothing on top except a telephone console with numerous buttons. The ceiling rose to a grand height with big glass at the gables.

"Can I help you?" the blonde asked.

"Yes," Draper said, "we are looking for Mr. Goodsill."

"Mr. Goodsill is of counsel with this firm and doesn't keep regular hours. I can leave him a message and I'm sure he will get back with you."

"There is somewhat of a deadline I'm afraid. My name is Charles Draper; I represent the daughter of Mr. John Quinn, deceased. Miss Quinn was contacted by Mr. Goodsill about the sale of

Mr. Quinn's property and she would like to discuss terms of the sale since she's had another offer."

"Oh, in that case, I could call Mr. Goodsill and I'm sure he would get in touch with you," the blonde said, assuming Gabriella was the client and they both were captivated by her stunning good looks, solid efficiency and the size of the building. Draper gave her his cell number and moved to retreat to the parking lot and wait.

The massive office door closed when Gabriella said, "My guess, she's sleeping with one of the partners."

"Now, why do you say that?" Draper said.

"Not the brightest bunny in the briar patch and many thousands of dollars worth of silicone cleavage."

"I don't know, I didn't notice."

"The hell you didn't," Gabriella said.

They sat in the Malibu thirty-five minutes indulging in father/daughter talk before Draper's cell rang. "Draper," he said into the instrument.

"Mr. Draper?"

"Yes."

"Goodsill, here, I understand you are representing Miss Quinn?"

"Yes," Draper said, letting Goodsill expand the conversation.

"Can you meet me at my office in an hour? I think I have a favorable number for Miss Quinn." Goodsill added an address near downtown Phoenix.

"We'll be there in a bit," Draper said, before hanging up and turning to Gabriella, "Fish's on the hook."

Downtown Phoenix is comfortably surrounded by Interstate Highways 10 and 17 forming an almost perfect square and making access into and out of the area convenient except during rush hour.

Tempe is east and a little south with Sky Harbor Airport in between, but the 202 Loop ties into the Interstate box at its northeast corner making the drive an easy one. Draper took Mill Road north to the 202 Loop and the N7th Street exit into downtown, pulling up to the building containing Goodsill's office forty minutes later. A stark contrast between the pretentious offices they'd just left and Goodsill's low-rent digs chimed loud. Surrounded by older warehouses, storage lots protected by chain-link fences topped with razor wire and abandoned retail buildings, Goodsill's Law Firm seemed out of place. No sign, brass or otherwise indicated its use and the building needed paint indicating considerable deferred maintenance. Draper tried the door, needing effort to overcome the swollen doorjamb.

Draper looked in and quickly lifted his arm up to prevent Gabriella from entering. "Stay outside and don't touch anything," he said. Draper stood in the doorway and scanned the small room containing an old Steelcase desk on its third coat of paint, scattered papers, surrounded by bookcases of law texts covered with dust. The vintage oak desk chair behind the desk held a dead body Draper assumed to be Goodsill, supporting a bloody hole decorating his forehead.

"Is he dead?" Gabriella said.

"Very. You stay put, while I take a look around for a second."

Draper stepped inside following his Glock and walked to the desk. After clearing the two-room office, he looked for anything that might have Quinn's name on it and found nothing. Taking out his handkerchief he carefully wiped the doorknob and anything he might have touched.

"Let's get the hell out of here," Draper said to Gabriella, "we lost the fish."

"What do we do now?" Gabriella said on the way back to the Malibu.

"Got to think about that one since it appears somebody is trying to cover up something; I'm just not sure what. How soon is school out?"

"Finals are next week," I should be done on Wednesday."

"Good, Thursday, I want you packed up and ready to move up to Aguila's place." Good friends of Bill DeCollado, Draper's old friend from their agency days, Sheila and Harry Aguila had a place up on the reservation northeast of Phoenix that served as a safe haven in the past. Harry had a security system that could detect an intruder while he or she only had thoughts of trying to enter.

"In the meantime, you are going to have to put up with me on your couch," Draper said.

"Doesn't seem too bad a deal to me," Gabriella said.

***

Javier Barajas stood scowling out the third floor window of the *casa de putas* he owned in Hermosillo, Son, México. The building and its occupants were part of the empire he'd built using violence, intimidation, fear and any other means available. The first two floors supplied income and the top floor served as his headquarters. Barajas oversaw a multi-billion dollar sovereignty including drug trafficking, human smuggling, prostitution, high-end stolen vehicles, guns, and anything else that would turn a buck. Known locally as *Los Pícaros*, the cartel's territory included most of central Mexico from Nogales on the east to Mexicali on the west. Barajas' Arizona *el Jefe*, his first cousin on his father's side, Ricardo Ortiz sat on the edge of the wood desk cleaning his fingernails. At thirty-six, Ortiz' murder list included Mexicans, Americans, women, children if necessary, and prostitutes who misbehaved. Javier Barajas knew without a doubt that the day would come when he'd have to kill his cousin. Ricardo was valuable up to a point, but undisciplined. His primary advantage was his American citizenship which allowed him to manage things north of the border.

"We are doing well, are we not, Cousin?" Ricardo said.

"We are," Javier agreed, "but that does not mean we can be careless. The project we plan is difficult and must be kept secret. It will be very expensive, but the rewards great. It means, *mi primo*, we must be careful not to alert the American Border Patrol. The elimination of the American rancher went well, but the three we sent to get the buy/sell bungled the job. Was it necessary to kill the *abogado?*"

"It wasn't. The idiots misinterpreted their orders. The lawyer Goodsill was useful and greedy, a nice combination," Ortiz said.

"That was a bad mistake, Ricardo, see to it that it doesn't happen again. I was told one of the dimwits that were supposed to retrieve the buy/sell survived the shoot out with the American police."

"That is true. He is in the County jail at Ajo. The shootout though wasn't with the American police." Ortiz hesitated, not wanting to tell his cousin that a single unknown shooter had spoiled their plan. "It was some American friend of the daughter."

"I don't care who the hell he was, just make sure he gets dead, *rápidamente,*" Barajas said.

"*Si, mi promo,*" Ortiz said.

"Give me some good news. I need something to cheer me up." Javier Barajas lit a slender black Cuban cigar and stared icy-eyed at his cousin.

Ricardo Ortiz knew that stare; he also knew he would be expendable should his cousin want it. He always planned good news to counter the bad. "There is much good news, Cousin; our plans in Southern Arizona are beginning to make fruit. We now control nearly all the gang activity in both Phoenix and Tucson, which will provide a continuous supply of young women for the *prostíbulos*, as well as a large market for drugs."

"Bullshit, Ricardo, tell me something I don't already know." Javier Barajas exhaled blue cigar smoke at his cousin, his eyes fired with irritation and stabbing the air with his cigar, "I want some action on securing that ranch. It's an integral part of the plan and you know it, Goddamn it! Now get the hell out of here and get it done."

An hour later, still smarting from the sting of his older cousin's words, Ortiz poured two fingers of Tequila and swallowed it in one swig. He waited a few moments for the burn to change to warmth in his chest, breathing slowly and gaining control of his anger. He stood taller than most Hispanics, likely from the introduction of foreign blood in an unknown relative's past. Secretly he enjoyed the dominance it afforded him in controversial situations since his stature and careful physical training intimidated adversaries. His few friends and employees knew him as short-tempered and a sadistic killer, a reputation he cultivated at every opportunity. His anger came from carefully guarded knowledge that Javier Barajas was only the male figurehead of the Sonoran cartel organization. The real person in charge of the outfit, with the killer instincts of an adult lioness was Javier's sister Marisol, a female assassin who Ortiz feared most.

After a few minutes of anger suppression and another shot of Tequila, Ortiz used his cell to call his right-hand gang leader and another family member, but only by marriage. He knew his Mexican cousins expected results and he intended to make sure it happened. The first order of business included finding out who interfered with the search for the land buy/sell documents.

***

Charlie Draper spent the next two days with Gabriella fending off questions about his past, details he'd stuffed into a mind box and closed a tight cover. She'd tried to pry the lid open a couple of times in the last year, pulled up short by Draper's negative response. He knew the time would come when she'd force the issue. For reasons he only partially understood, he hesitated telling her too much fearing it would somehow damage their relationship. He admitted only that he'd become fond of her and enjoyed having her around as long as she didn't prod him about his now distant past.

On Sunday, after they'd spent an hour shopping at a local grocery store, Gabriella cooked dinner in early afternoon. Later, when Draper found the couch planning a nap after the meal, she waylaid him.

"Charlie, why won't you tell me about it?"

"National security, my dear, can't. Sworn to secrecy, you know."

"That's B.S. and you know it. I want to be your daughter; don't you think I deserve to know a little about you?"

"Granted, I've never had anyone to tell before."

"What about Molly?" Gabriella said.

"She's never asked. Yet."

"You know she's going to, so why not practice on me."

Draper thought a moment about that possibility before starting at the beginning, telling a little about the best parts, leaving out the worst and editing the rest. He stopped when Gabriella came and sat next to him and put her arm around his neck, tears flowing down her face. She cried hard for several minutes while Draper held her.

"Thanks, Dad," she said, blubbering into Draper's shirt, "I promise I'll never ask again."

"What's your schedule for tomorrow? Draper said, gently sitting her up so he could see her eyes.

"I have a test first thing in the morning and then the next one is Tuesday afternoon. Why?

"Want to take a ride to Tucson after your test is over?" Draper said.

"What are we going to do in Tucson?

"I want to check on Alice Quinn. See how she's doing and maybe visit with her and see if she remembers anything new."

"I'd love a road trip, Dad." She hugged him and left to blow her nose.

They left at ten-thirty on Monday and reached Tucson just after noon. Draper regretted opting for the Malibu and his cramped legs forced him to decide he would go back to a larger vehicle the next time. They stopped and ate lunch before arriving at the hospital close to one-thirty. They found Alice Quinn propped by pillows sitting nearly upright in bed when they stepped into her hospital room. Her friend Bauer sat in an uncomfortable-looking straight-back chair holding Alice's hand. The right half of Alice's face was still covered with gauze, though she smiled and seemed more alert than when he'd last visited.

"Mr. Draper, this is Buck Bauer, on old friend who owns the ranch next to my Dad's place."

"We've met," Draper said. "How are you, Buck?"

"Good, "I took your advice," Bauer said, opening his cowboy-cut sport coat so Draper could see a leather shoulder rig and the black butt of a Glock.

".40?"

"Yup."

"Been practicing?"

"Yup."

"Good man; this is my daughter, Gabriella."

"There must be a mistake," Bauer said, beaming a big cowboy grin with teasing devils in both eyes, "you are much too pretty to be the daughter of this ugly customer."

Gabriella blushed, but came right back with, "Purely an accident of nature."

Draper turned to Alice Quinn, "You obviously need protection from this bum; do you want me to shoot him now or wait until later?"

"Tamp down the testosterone, boys," Alice said, grinning in spite of the gauze still covering her face.

"You know, Buck, in spite of your youth and obvious lack of decorum with ladies present, I'm beginning to like you. Fun aside; we stopped by to see how you were doing Alice."

Draper surprised himself warming up to someone who looked like a hayseed, walked and talked like an extra in a spaghetti western, but who's eyes confirmed strength coupled with a no-bullshit attitude.

He watched Gabriella's reaction and it confirmed his assessment. Only time would tell how he responded under pressure.

"Do you remember anything significant about last Friday?" Draper asked Alice.

"Nothing much, other than these men came to the door, forced their way in demanding the buy/sell agreement and started beating on me when I told them I didn't know where it was."

"They didn't find it," Draper said.

"How do you know?" Alice questioned.

"I know because I found it in with some other personal stuff I'm sure will interest you."

"Like what?" Alice asked.

"Personal items along with old pictures your father very cleverly hid in the bedroom. I'll show it to you when you get back home."

"That might be today or tomorrow," Buck said.

A nurse came in and interrupted wanting to change bedding and sponge bathe the patient. Gabriella elected to stay while Draper and Bauer went to the waiting room.

When they were seated, Draper said, "Have you talked to the doctor, yet?"

"Yes, yesterday. They are happy with how she's progressing. There's no brain damage, no broken bones other than her nose and a couple ribs, but she'll have some facial scaring, the extent of which remains to be seen."

"Does she have any plans when she gets out, someone to tend to her, like Home Health?"

"She's agreed to stay at my place, albeit reluctantly, until she's able to move around. Damned woman is determined to get back to teaching as soon as she can. I'm not sure that's wise until they find who did this." Bauer's forehead creased with worry lines as he talked.

"She's a bit independent I'd guess from my limited experience," Draper said, fully aware the cowman across from him carried a torch with a tall flame.

"Yup, been waiting around since high school panting like a puppy dog; not something I'm proud of," Bauer said.

"Appears to me she might be worth the wait, but then I'm no expert on women."

"I just want to keep her safe."

"We agree on that," Draper said, while his mind drifted in a different direction and silence spread over the waiting room. "Since we both have her interest in mind, how about as soon as you get her down to your place, we meet in Tucson and I'll take you on a little airplane ride. Let's fly every inch of Quinn's ranch and see if between us we can spot anything unusual. There's got to be a reason someone would pay that kind of money to kill old man Quinn."

"Don't have to meet in Tucson; I have a landing strip at my place. I built it years ago when I was taking flying lessons, but never used it much. It's still usable, the Fish and Wildlife Service uses it occasionally to count deer."

"Super. What day?" Draper said.

"Let me call you, it'll depend on when they let Alice out of here," Bauer said

Chapter Seven

Southern Arizona

O
n Thursday, after Gabriella finished her last test, Draper helped her pack a suitcase for a temporary move to Henry Aguila's place. Henry and his wife Sheila lived in a well-protected spread on the Fort Apache Indian Reservation. The Aguila's, friends of Bill DeCollado who had opened their home to Draper and guests he needed to hide the previous summer. Old as dirt, yet ageless, Henry retained fierce individualism common to his Apache ancestors. Draper knew Gabriella's safety was assured since old Henry's defense would include his last dying breath.

He stood at the gate, tall, stoic and unyielding, waiting as they drove up, his four-wheeler parked alongside. He knew they were coming since Draper called, but Henry's elaborate early-warning system, a techno wonder he designed and built himself, signaled their arrival in plenty of time to arm the cannon, or in this case, greet the guests.

"A long time between visits, white man," Aguila said, scowling at Draper. "Your forgiveness is only possible because you bring beautiful young maiden with."

"That's why I brought her," Draper said, "knew I'd never get through the gate without her."

Gabriella grinned and jumped out and hugged the old Indian. Draper watched considering the change that had transpired since he'd found her in the desert. In the distance he could see a Bell 205 A-1 helicopter sitting next to Henry's machine shed. A civilian version of the famous Bell UI-1 commonly known as the 'Huey," the 205's extended fuselage grew out of the military's desire to carry more troops. The aircraft belonged to William Alan DeCollado, Draper's half Spanish and half Apache friend from his covert operation days in Southeast Asia.

"Bill here?" Draper said.

"He flew up this morning when I called and told him you were coming. He's over in the shed messing with the whirly-bird thing." Henry maintained that anything that flew and wasn't covered with feathers had to be the creation of devil spirits. Draper knew the old Indian was blowing smoke, but never contradicted his belief.

"Tell Bill I'll come out to see him as soon as I say hello to Sheila," Gabriella said, climbing on the four-wheeler behind Henry. Draper watched them speed away before climbing in the Malibu and driving over to the machine shed.

At fifty-nine, and fifteen years senior to Draper, DeCollado had been his mentor, partner and friend during his struggling learning years as a covert operative. The old Apache taught him a love of flying and could do things with a helicopter that would terrify most pilots. The Bell 205 was the child he never had and he babied it the same. Draper parked the Malibu next to the Bell and wandered into the shed. DeCollado, bent over a disassembled magneto, filing a rough spot.

"You must be in trouble with Victoria," Draper said.

"How so?" DeCollado said, not looking around and continuing to file.

"You are here and she's not. You two have been joined at the hip for almost a year."

"Had to take Jennifer back east to a photography workshop; be gone several weeks."

DeCollado and Draper's client from a year past, Victoria Hollings, formed a relationship resembling oil and water. Victoria Hollings, a long-time monied, statuesque widow whose beauty belied her age though only a couple years younger than DeCollado, had stolen his Apache heart. Draper laughed at his long-time friend, certain the fire would die quickly, yet a year later it looked permanent. She'd moved into DeCollado's long-time bachelor home twenty miles east of Phoenix.

"Need your help," Draper said.

"Figured as much," DeCollado said.

"Nothing dangerous, just hear me out and give me your thoughts."

"I'm listening," DeCollado said, not letting up from gentle filing.

Draper sat on a five-gallon bucket and brought DeCollado up to date. The story didn't take long since there wasn't much to tell other than he had a new client and had failed so far to protect her.

"How bad is the damage to your client?" DeCollado asked when Draper left a moment of silence to see if he'd get a response.

"Hard to tell, the physical damage is serious enough but emotional might be another story. The beating was pretty brutal."

"You know you are dealing with the cartel?"

"Figured as much."

"We're going to hit them back?" DeCollado said. Draper noted the use of a plural pronoun.

"Likely," Draper said. "Possibly got some help this time."

DeCollado didn't say anything, so Draper continued, "Name's Buck Bauer, Army Rangers, appears capable. He's watching over her now."

"Who the hell names their kid 'Buck,' for Christ's sake?"

Draper's cell phone rang. He looked at the caller ID and received a small surprise. It read John Pérez.

"John, what's up?" Draper said.

"Draper, you remember when I told you to move to out of state?"

"Yeah. Why, were you serious?"

"Not as serious as I am now. I have a citizen in here, currently under investigation for shooting and killing a armed gangbanger here in Tucson. Says he knows you. He was in the company of one Alice Quinn who, as I understand it, is a client of yours. Says his name is Buck Bauer and he refuses to talk unless you are present, so you better dust off that moldy attorney license and get your ass down here," Pérez said.

"Shit!" Draper said, "Where's Alice? Is she alright?"

"She's fine, though from the look of her, someone did a number on her face. She the one you had in the hospital here?"

"That's her. Hang on a minute." Draper turned to DeCollado, "Can you fly me to Tucson?"

"Give me fifteen to get her ready and the old Bell will go anywhere. Take about an hour flight time," DeCollado said.

"John, I can have Bill fly me down so we'll be there in an hour and a half or so. We'll have to grab a rental car so say two hours."

"Make it quick as you can, I don't want to be here all night."

Draper hung up and turned to DeCollado, "Sorry, Bill, something's come up down in Tucson. That friend of my client had to shoot some gangbanger."

"You run up to the house while I get the old girl ready."

Draper hurried to the house, made his excuses and apologized for running out. Gabriella hugged him and pushed him out the door. "Go help your client, Dad, I'll be fine."

They entered the Tucson airport landing pattern just under an hour later and met a patrol officer waiting. The Tucson Police furnished transportation, driving them with lights, but no siren, to police headquarters. Pérez looked tired and not happy at their arrival. Draper felt sympathy for the man whose job ranked as dangerous, frustrating, and always exasperating coupled with long hours and embarrassing pay. He greeted Draper with a tired eyes and a weak smile. "About time you got here. Let's go to my office and I'll fill you in. I've got them in separate interview rooms."

Seated in Pérez's office Draper and DeCollado waited for Pérez to begin. Draper decided the Lieutenant had taken some shit from the brass judging from the man's attitude, but he couldn't fathom why. If someone higher up was applying pressure there had to be a reason and to Draper it stank of cartel activity. He knew from previous experience that the cartel had a heavy presence in over two hundred American cities and it made sense that Tucson, less than seventy miles from the border might be one.

Without saying a word, Pérez removed a small yellow pad and wrote something on it and slid the note in front of Draper. It read: *Conversation being recorded - follow my lead.* Draper looked at the note and said, "Your dime, Lieutenant, what do you want?"

"We have a woman in custody who says she is your client, Counselor. Her name is Alice Quinn. Her companion, a Ralph Bauer, who goes by 'Buck,' shot and killed a Hispanic young man who we believe is a member of local gang. We are considering charging Mr.

Bauer with second-degree murder, since he won't tell us what happened without your presence."

Draper decided to play along, saying, "Was the gangbanger armed?"

"He was, with a nine millimeter S&W automatic."

"So what's the problem, Lieutenant?" Draper asked. "It appears to me I have a smart client."

"We have several witnesses who say your client fired first."

"Are these reliable witnesses?" Draper said.

"I can't speak to that, but it's possible they might also be connected in some way to the deceased."

"Was the gun the gangbanger used in hand and threatening?"

"Seems likely, but the witnesses say no."

"I'd like to speak to Miss Quinn first and then to Mr. Bauer. Mr. DeCollado is my associate and he will need to be present also."

"Okay, follow me and I'll take you to them. I will be in the room also."

Alice Quinn, still with one side of her face bandaged, looked frightened and exhausted when Draper entered the room. She jumped to her feet as Draper rounded the interview table, took her arm and looked straight into worried eyes. "Don't say anything, only answer my direct questions and don't elaborate, okay? Everything is being recorded. Just sit down, it will be fine." She sat and Draper dropped in beside her with his chair turned toward her. Pérez and DeCollado sat across the table.

"Are you okay, Alice? No injuries, feeling all right, anything you need?" Draper asked.

"I could use a glass of water," Alice said. "I'm tired, we've been sitting here for hours."

"We'll get you out of here as soon as we can but first the Lieutenant would like you to answer a couple of questions." Alice Quinn nodded and Draper looked at Pérez signaling him to go ahead.

"Miss Quinn, please tell us what happened this afternoon."

Alice Quinn spoke in a soft voice, relating the afternoon incident that led to Buck shooting the gangbanger. Draper listened in silence. After she finished Pérez led Draper to a second interview room leaving DeCollado with Alice.

Bauer sat stoic behind a similar table with his hands clasped together on top. Draper gave him a speech similar to the one he gave Alice and then let him talk.

"The doctor okayed Alice's release this morning but it was almost noon before all the paperwork and fiddling around was complete," Bauer said, starting. His manner indicated slight nervousness, yet his words rang firm and truthful, not unlike someone finding himself under the scrutiny of a large police department for the first time and intimidated by the process. "I suggested we stop for lunch somewhere. Alice agreed. We found a small place on East Broadway and I pulled into the parking lot. When we got out of the car, this asshole came up with a gun. I shot him. There were a couple others who ran away." Bauer's delivery came easily, only the precise details with no embellishment. Draper could see his Army Ranger training at work.

"Did you touch the gun?"

"No, Sir. I did kick it under a parked car after I shot him. The cops retrieved it."

Draper looked at Pérez and said, "Go ahead and ask whatever questions you want, but it looks to be clear-cut self-defense to me."

Pérez took over and asked several questions that led nowhere. Draper could see no amount of intimidation would shake his military tight answers. He found himself liking the kid.

"I think you should release my clients, Lieutenant Pérez," Draper said, "If there are any other questions or issues you can contact me and I will make them available as necessary."

"Okay, get them out of here, but they should stay in our jurisdiction."

"I don't think that's a good idea. Their lives are in danger and I need to move them to a place that's secure. I'll have them available within hours of your call."

"Where?" Pérez asked.

"They will be at a place where I can have them available within hours of your call."

"You're not going to tell me, are you?"

"No," Draper said.

After they were out of the interview room Draper told Pérez his plan to fly his clients to Henry Aguila's place. Pérez wasn't happy about it but relented. An hour later they were in the parking lot of Police Headquarters waiting for a police cruiser to take them to the airport. Alice Quinn looked exhausted and Bauer had his arm around her for support. She didn't object which Draper took as a encouraging.

"Good thing I put the seats in the back of the chopper," DeCollado said.

"We are going to fly you two up to a friend's place for safe keeping," Draper said. "There's too much going on here we don't understand, so until we find out I want you two under wraps."

"What are we flying in," Alice asked.

"A nice roomy helicopter," DeCollado said.

"I've never flown before." Alice's statement wasn't a refusal, but Draper could sense hesitation, debating whether or not a helicopter ride was preferable to people shooting at her. It took a moment before the helicopter won, but it was close.

The patrolman who drove them to the airport chatted the entire way, pointing out the sights of Tucson as if they were tourists. Draper considered it useful because he didn't want his clients talking in front of the cop. The patrolman left them in front of the FBO terminal and Draper breathed a sigh of relief. His mind rolled with thoughts of what their next move should be without success. He was glad when helicopter noise made conversation impossible except over the headsets only he and DeCollado wore. DeCollado, busy with piloting said little until they were well clear of Tucson airspace.

"I'm going to track due north to Globe before diverting toward Henry's place," DeCollado said, while setting his autopilot.

Draper looked back at Alice Quinn. Her eyes clamped shut, she had both hands gripped tight on Bauer's arm and the little Draper could see of her face looked ghost white. He found a plastic barf bag in the chopper's door pocket and handed it back to Bauer in case the need arose.

Long shadows broke over the Arizona landscape as DeCollado guided that Bell north toward the Mogollon Rim. Draper could see the sharp escarpment looming large in the distance. Globe passed underneath with Draper's mind puzzling over the events of the last week.

"Okay, now what?" DeCollado said through the helicopter intercom.

"Damned if I know," Draper responded.

Sonoran Justice by Dave Folsom

Chapter Eight

Tucson, Arizona

T he next morning, with Alice Quinn and Gabriella safely stowed away at Henry and Sheila's place, Draper made up his mind. The decision was based in part on anger and a good deal on a lack of a better idea. He shared his thoughts with DeCollado, Bauer and Henry Aguila over coffee strong enough to refloat the Titanic and laced with Henry's homemade brew. They sat on five-gallon buckets in the machine shed, full to the gills on Sheila's breakfast. Draper outlined his plan to the others knowing the critics would pick it apart, chew it up and reform it in a way that might make it work. He was right.

DeCollado, a master at covert operations, outlined the dangers, of which there were a considerable number. "The definition of *gang*," he said, "in case you don't remember, is a group of bad-asses who operate as one for protection. Getting one alone is problematic."

"How do you know if the gangbanger you pick is connected to the cartel?" Bauer asked.

"We find out from John Pérez. I suspect he knows which gangs do most of the drug trafficking. It's likely that group is funded or at least supported by the cartels. That was certainly true in Phoenix and I doubt Tucson is any different," Draper said. "I think we need to rattle the cartel and since we don't know who they are and most probably they are in Mexico, let's shake their operation a little and see what drops out."

"There's likely a bunch of new leaders since we did damage to the health of a couple of top dogs last year," DeCollado said.

"That's what I figure, also. The problem is the higher echelon tends to keep a low profile and lets the underlings take all the risks," Draper said. "We need someone to give us a name to start with."

"How about we start with a street worker and work our way up?" Bauer said.

"There's that," Draper said, "but it could get messy and difficult to determine if the info is reliable. Tucson is John Pérez's town and I've sort of promised him I'd try to keep from spilling too much blood inside the city limits."

"Cops sometimes have CI's, maybe John Pérez could get us in contact with one," DeCollado suggested.

"What's a CI?" Bauer asked.

"Confidential Informant is someone on the street who works with the police, either willingly or unwillingly. The willing ones are most reliable because they do it for the money and an occasional pass," DeCollado said. "The unwilling ones do it to get out from under a minor beef."

"I think you should call your friend John Pérez," Bauer said.

An hour later the three men sat strapped into DeCollado's Bell 205 a couple thousand feet over the surrounding mountains on a direct track to Draper's desert hacienda outside of Ajo. He'd left the rental Malibu for Gabriella to use in case she needed it. The hour long flight afforded time to solidify the plan. Pérez had promised to set up a meet with one of his undercover narcotics cops. For the rendezvous they'd need an inconspicuous vehicle. An older Lincoln Town Car painted basic black was the favorite choice of drug dealers and other assorted assholes everywhere. One sat covered with a canvas tarp in the back of Draper's hanger. Its battery saved by a trickle charger from a local hardware store, guaranteed it would start. DeCollado set the 205 down on Draper's concrete run-up slab and shut down the engine. Draper stepped out running with his head down under the rotor. At the walk-in door he keyed the lock and stepped inside. In moments, he had the Lincoln uncovered, battery hooked back up and the engine started. He drove it out, parked near the house and moved to help the others drag the Bell inside before closing the doors.

"Looks like a black pimp-mobile," Bauer said.

"That's what it's supposed to look like." Draper had a local body shop darken the side windows, a look favored by gangbangers and useful in disguising occupants. Draper secured the place for long term absence knowing Rachael, Molly's dispatcher, would ensure one of the deputies stopped by every few days and make sure Dog had food and water. Driving, with Bauer riding shotgun and DeCollado in the back seat, Draper pointed the car up the Interstate toward Tucson. The trunk rode full of armament, including sniper gear, automatic weaponry, handguns and an assortment of body armor.

"Judas Priest," Bauer said, "you must be planning a war!"

"That's what it is; the fucking Sonoran wars," DeCollado said from the backseat. "The cartels are armed to the teeth and if we are going to mess with them, we'd better be also."

They arrived in Tucson in late afternoon when the sun was behind them working its way into the western mountains. They had plenty of time because their meeting with the undercover cop wasn't until after dark. DeCollado suggested dinner at Juanita's so Draper called and asked Pérez to join them.

"What's your plan?" Pérez asked after he seated himself and ordered. "I hope like hell I don't regret getting involved in this."

"I'm not going to sugar-coat it John; we plan to hit them hard and fast, tonight if possible. We want them to think there's a new bunch in town wanting to take over the territory," Draper said.

"For Christ sake, try to keep the body count down," Pérez said. Draper could see Pérez wasn't comfortable with his role in the evening's activities. He was curious, yet he didn't want to know too much.

"The count will be what it is," Draper said, an answer that made Pérez squirm.

***

Kemen Razo rolled over in bed searching for his delight of the night and found her absent. He'd picked her up during the afternoon at a bar and they'd spent a couple of hours exercising between the sheets. He'd talked her out of her clothes with a baggy of coke, a small price since he had a supply large enough to buy all the women he wanted with nose candy left over. He watched the girl, barely twenty, standing at the table across the room cutting white powder in preparation for inhaling. At nearly forty years old Kemen rarely used drugs and when he did, only Mary Jane. He'd dealt in them, buying and selling in large quantities for years, yet he'd kept his distance. His plan, once he had enough cash, included a place on an island somewhere, a rotating bevy of young women and all the fine food and drink he could handle when he wasn't painting. Kemen dreamed of traveling around to art galleries and showing his paintings, none of which he had finished yet, but he felt he was getting close. He could almost smell the salty air tantalizing his nostrils while he created his soon to be famous art. The drugs were simply a means to an end.

"Come on, baby, hurry up, gotta go to work soon," Kemen said, knowing it wouldn't have any effect until she was finished, dancing an excited state, eyes dilated to the max, wanting to play.

"Hold your horses, will ya, I'm coming," she said, between snorts, planning a high that would last a couple hours.

Kemen relaxed, thinking about the shipment tonight, a big one that would add nicely to his island account. It was a system he'd used for better than ten years, though the border crossing was getting more difficult. The new Border Patrol efforts had made sending through a couple small dummy loads first essential and then, while BP was busy tearing apart the dummy vehicles, their real shipments could sail right through with the mass of daily border crossers. It was easy and cheap to recruit expendable drivers, both male and female desperate to cross the border into the land of opportunity though many ended up deported back to their home country. The cartel listed them and the drugs they lost under the cost of doing business column. For every trick Customs and Border Patrol tried, the cartel was ready with two counter measures. Kemen heard through the grapevine that the cartel planned a bigger, more effective way of moving the drugs, but he hoped he'd be long gone. The girl came to him in the middle of his musing, singing with her eyes wide dilated, dancing onto the bed like a gazelle. Kemen promptly forgot painting, islands, money, and the drugs that would come yet tonight.

***

The black Lincoln Town Car sat in a dark alley in downtown Tucson exactly where Pérez had indicated, waiting. Draper's watch indicated half-past ten pm, a half hour past the appointed time and he was getting edgy. Finally, there was a tap on his driver's window. He pushed the button to crack the window. "Draper?" the voice in the dark said.

"Yeah, you're late." Draper said.

The back door behind Draper opened and Bauer slid to the opposite side allowing a slight man in ragged dark clothes to slip in. A hooded sweatshirt nearly obscured his face and the undercover cop could have passed for either a buyer or a seller. "Name's Ramos, been watching you, had to make sure you were okay," he said. "Pérez tells me you are looking for info."

Draper struggled to turn around so he could face the new occupant. "We need some help," Draper said. "We want to hit a big drop and mess them up a bit, you get the shipment off the streets and we get someone we can get info from."

"You guys Feds or just damn fools looking to get dead?" Ramos said.

"Sort of," Draper said, noncommittal. You don't need to know who we are."

"Okay, I guess if Pérez says you are clean, I won't ask," Ramos said. "The big fish around here and for most of south Tucson is a bad-ass named Kemen Razo. Always has a couple of bodyguards with him; big Columbian bruisers that enjoy hurting people. They've got a warehouse on 32nd where they split up the shipment for distribution up north."

"You can't stop it?"

Believe me, we've tried. It's like they know we're coming and all we get is an empty warehouse. All the judges in town have been stung so many times we almost have to have pictures and samples to get a warrant. They breakdown the shipment and move it out before we can get back." Draper could hear a high level of frustration in the cop's voice.

"Okay," Draper said, "here's the deal; you get the drugs and we get Razo. Once we are done with him you can have him back. We'll leave the door wide open and you can walk right in. What's the address?"

"Wait just a minute, I can't do that. I have to be in on everything that happens."

"No, you don't," Draper said. "When you get there, it's likely there'll be some bodies and you need to be able to convince the powers to be that some other bad guys did the deed and this meeting didn't happen. You give us the address and then hang out somewhere close by where somebody can vouch for your presence. I'll call you when we are done. A neighborhood bar that's not too busy so staff will remember you would be perfect."

"Sounds risky to me," Ramos said.

"You think a shipment is coming in tonight or not?" Draper said, impatient.

"Fuck you, man, the only reason I'm risking my ass is because Pérez said you were okay. I've spent years wheedling my way into the drug underground and I'm not going to risk having a bunch of wannabee Feds messing up my game."

"Fair enough, Ramos, the last thing we want to do is throw a monkey into your play," Draper said, softening his tone, he'd been trying to push the young cop to see how he'd react and liked the response. "We only want you to be off the location somewhere close in case something goes bad. As soon as we are done I call you and you come in with the troops and clean up. You get the drugs and your friend Razo with his dick in the cookie jar. He may be little worse for wear though."

"You can shoot the son-of-bitch if need be," Ramos said.

An hour later, armed with the address, Draper eased the Lincoln into a dark alley behind a downtown warehouse. The larger entrance doors faced the street allowing anything up to a small semi-truck to back into a single dock. Smaller vans and delivery-sized units could drive straight in a street-level 12x12 foot-sized overhead door. Deserted at night, the alley only provided access for city sanitation and utility workers. The three men donned vests, head gear, and backup weapons, before selecting a M-4 carbine set on three-round-fire option with two extra magazines. Dressed in all black, a light-weight black mask left only their eyes exposed. Draper didn't want any of their opponents recognizing them or remembering a face.

The walk-in door in the alley was locked and alarmed, a problem Draper liked since the occupants wouldn't expect interference from that direction. The alarm, a thirty-year old analog system a ten-year old could disable, took DeCollado less than a couple of minutes. Draper tackled the lock, a recent eight-pin deadbolt but not yet refitted to the more sophisticated electronic versions. He raked the pins with his pick set and only got one which meant a new still-stiff model and the other seven would be work. It took him four minutes, when an old model with more use would have been considerable less. When he was finally able to roll the cylinder it responded with a satisfying click. Draper filled his right hand with his Glock and pushed the door open a crack and listened. When silence reached his ears he moved it enough to pass through and stepped into a dark room. He clicked on a small LED flashlight and found himself in a storage/utility room that controlled all the building utilities.

Signaling DeCollado and Bauer with a finger pointed at the electrical disconnects, Draper felt lucky. They had night vision goggles and if necessary they could pull the disconnect switches and leave the bad guys in the dark.

"I'm going to check what we're up against. If you hear any gunfire or anything else put them in the dark," Draper whispered to DeCollado. He looked at Bauer and continued, "Follow close, if it goes bad, shoot to kill."

Draper tried the door into the main warehouse and the knob turned easily with only a slight squeak. He slid inside and stopped, waiting for any sign that they'd been heard. Silence ensued and he could feel Bauer move in behind. The main part of the warehouse lay dark except for security lights. The illumination was enough to keep them from running into things and dark enough to mask their movements. On the far side, toward the front, ventilation noise veiled any sound. Beginning a systematic search, they cleared each area before moving on. Near the front, through a lighted office window, they could see two men playing cards at a table.

"Watch those two while I clear the upper rooms," Draper said.

Bauer nodded and Draper started up the stairs to what looked like two offices on a second level balcony. The wooden stairs looked noisy so Draper stepped close to the side stringers while keeping his M4 pointed at the two upper doors. The first room, a small office with a desk and a single four-drawer metal file cabinet showed empty through the window. The second office didn't have a window so Draper tried the knob. It turned without noise and the door opened. Draper stopped its movement and listened. The sounds reaching his ears were obvious. A female voice squealed, giggling over the sounds of male grunting and creaking bedsprings. Draper stepped across the room and the woman screamed an instant before the barrel of the M4 touched the side of her companion's head.

"Tell her to shut up and clasp your hands together behind your head or it'll be the last thing either one of you hear," Draper growled.

When the man complied, Draper said, "Bill, there are two downstairs and a guy and a women up stairs. Help Buck secure the two downstairs and bring them up to the upper level. We'll do our thing up here."

"On my way," Draper heard DeCollado say in his wireless earbud. He mentally appreciated the advanced technology DeCollado had talked him into after last year's adventure. It made communication during an operation easy.

"You're a dead man, asshole," man said.

"Perhaps you don't understand, my friend, what you feel is the barrel of a M4 carbine set on three-round auto. That means if either of you make the slightest wrong move you will both see hell long before I do." Draper shoved the M4's barrel into the sheet where he figured the man's side would be, not gentle.

"Ow! Jesus Christ, that hurts, man."

"It'll hurt a lot worse if you make another sound. You lie still and enjoy whatever's left of what you were doing. It's either that or a quick trip to hell, whichever you prefer."

The woman stared at Draper with hate eyes dilated with cocaine fever and a longstanding habit. Draper guessed her age at around twenty and not too much longer she'd look twice that as the drug habit ate away her looks. She already appeared wasted, her features hardened by abuse. Draper wondered if her companion was the infamous Kemen Razo until the woman whined, "Do something, Kemen," and the man replied "Shut-up, bitch!"

Draper heard footsteps coming up the stairs, a noise creating a sense of urgency. Draper cracked his male prisoner alongside the head with the M4 barrel figuring pain would keep him occupied.

Striping the sheet off his captives, he threw pillows across the room while checking for weapons leaving the two naked on the bed.

Pointing the M4 at the man's forehead, Draper said, using the gun's barrel for emphasis, "You both get up and move over by the door and sit on the floor with your hands behind your head. Move!" Draper followed, standing alongside the door, M4 ready. He knew it was likely DeCollado, but wasn't taking chances.

Chapter Nine

Tucson, Arizona

The door opened a crack and DeCollado's voice said, "Charlie, I'm coming in." DeCollado entered barrel first scanning the room and seeing the two on the floor, stopped. "Friends of yours?" he said.

"Join the party," Draper said, relaxing a bit.

DeCollado entered followed by the two Hispanic card players from the main level. Behind them Bauer held his M4 on them, looking totally unscathed and pleased with himself. The two captives were zip-tied, hands behind their backs.

"Nice work," Draper said. Set them on the floor so they can watch.

Draper walked over to his two captives. "You," he said, indicating the girl, "put some clothes on."

While she dressed, Draper searched around the bed for weapons and found a 9mm Beretta stuffed between the mattress and box spring. "This your toy?" he asked the girl.

"No," she said, staring at Draper while she slipped into a plain cotton dress.

"Lie face down on the bed and put your hands behind you," Draper said, zip-tying her hands together when she complied. "Lie quiet and you might survive the night. We're going to have a

95

discussion with your boyfriend and if he doesn't cooperate, we'll have the same discussion with you and believe me, it won't be pleasant."

By the time Draper finished with the girl, DeCollado had her boyfriend zip-tied to the one straight-back chair in the room, his arms straight down so he could grip the chair seat and his wrists secured to the chair back. "I assume we're going to use the gook persuasion method?" he said, loud enough for everyone in the room to hear it.

Bauer looked surprised and said, "That what I think it is?"

"Worse," DeCollado said. "It takes a real tough asshole to survive it, but not before they spill their guts out. Since we don't have any goat hide we'll have to use a zip-tie, but it's just as effective."

"Goat hide?" Bauer asked.

"Yeah, you take a strip of goat hide and soak it in water and then tie it tight around a man's neck and when it dries, well, suffice it to say it makes breathing rather difficult and is usually fatal. Takes about twenty minutes to half an hour, but the subject will spill everything they know before the end."

Draper watched Kemen Razo develop fear sweat on his forehead while DeCollado and Bauer chatted as if they were alone in the room and talking sports. He walked over to where Razo sat tied to the chair and pulled a zip-tie out of his leg pocket and held it in front of the man's eyes. "Know what this is?" he said.

Razo didn't answer, but squirmed against his restraints.

"Here's how this works," Draper said, "I'm going to ask you a couple of questions and you are going to give me truthful answers or I'm going to put this around your neck and you will get one more chance before I kill you very, very slowly. That's after we remove some very important parts of your body and make you bleed from a lot of holes, *entender?*

"I demand a lawyer! You can't do this!"

"Oh, but we can because we're not cops. We are the competition."

Draper saw fear develop in Razo's eyes where it hadn't been before. Strapped naked to the chair, his defenses broke quickly. "They'll kill you for this," he said, trying to retain his macho, but followed with, "what do you want to know?"

"Tell me about your operation."

The man jabbered, a mixture of Spanish and English, trying to give the impression of limited English understanding. After several minutes of beating around the truth and revealing little, Draper slid the zip-tie over his head pulled it tight enough to be uncomfortable. "Tell me something useful or I'll finish you and continue with your friends."

"Wait a minute," Bauer said.

Draper looked at him hard. "What?"

"You aren't going to make the girl watch this, are you?" Bauer said.

"Why not?" Draper said.

"You want her barfing all over? Why don't I take her in the other room or downstairs?"

"I don't care what you do with her, just don't bother me again. I'm going to carve this one up some."

Bauer helped the girl up and walked her out onto the balcony and closed the door. "What the hell's with him?" Draper said, drawing an eight inch knife from a leg scabbard and waving it under Razo's nose. The man clenched his teeth and closed his eyes determined not to give in.

Draper knew from experience that torture was more a mental process than anything else since the mind and the body will shut down in response to extensive physical abuse to a point that further action only results in either unconsciousness or the death of the subject. Effective torture that extracts reliable information takes time, something they didn't have. He was stalling convinced that Razo wouldn't spill a word.

"Cut him and let's get on with it," DeCollado said, playing his role.

The scream came then, long, loud and with only slight muffling by the closed door. The female cry peaked and dropped suddenly, followed by a gurgling choke.

"What the hell'd you do to her?" Razo said.

"Guess she didn't want to cooperate," Draper said.

Bauer came in the room, "Got what we wanted. The drugs will be here any time; had to kill the girl though."

"I doubt she'll be a loss to anyone. Kill the other two and I'll take care of this one," Draper said.

Bauer and DeCollado pick up the two card players and forced them out the door, leaving Draper alone with Razo. He stared hard at his prisoner while extracting a clear fluid-filled pen-like object from his pocket.

Razo stared back as two muffled gunshots echoed through the warehouse. "Jesus Christ, man, what are you going to do"?

"What do you think asshole? Give me your boss's name or you're dead like the others."

"Ricardo Ortiz!" Razo screamed, and Draper stabbed the auto-injection pen into his neck.

"Sleep tight," Draper said leaving the room and taking the stairs two at a time.

Bauer and DeCollado met him at the bottom of the stairs. "How's the girl?" Draper said.

"She's fine," Bauer said, "performed like a pro. Damn, did you hear that scream? I was standing right next to her and she damn near blew my eardrums out. She's in the utility room. I left her tied 'cause I didn't want her running out. She's pretty scared."

"Good idea. How we doing for time?"

"Cutting it close," DeCollado said. "They should be arriving any minute."

"Okay, take your places, I'll cover you from out here," Draper said.

They waited in the dark about a half hour during which Draper called Ramos' cell. Ramos answered with a gruff, "What?"

"It's Draper. Everything went as planned. We're waiting for the trucks to arrive."

"Lilly okay?"

"Yeah, she's a good actress. She's safe and sound."

"Thanks, I appreciate that."

"Hang in there a little while longer and with any luck we'll give you a nice bust," Draper said.

Draper roamed the warehouse in the dark, his mind taking inventory of its contents. The big containers turned out empty, mostly for show he decided, and the lower office where the two played cards held his interest longest. It made sense in an operation this large there would be a hidden stash of cash. It took diligent searching to find it but under the counter incased in concrete was hidden compartment, secured by a ten-dollar Master lock. Draper almost laughed. Apparently they weren't too concerned about theft. He had it open in under a minute. The lid raised to expose a three foot by three foot half-inch steel plate-lined box stacked to the top with bundles of one-hundred-dollar bills. Without hesitation Draper selected a single bundle with his gloved hand, slipped it inside his shirt and re-secured the lock, closing the cabinet door. He had no qualms about making the cartels cover expenses. The feds could have the rest.

At ten minutes after one in the morning, Draper was back in position when a horn honked outside. DeCollado activated the electric door opener and as it raised high enough for a pickup to enter, two Ford F-250 Crew Cab pickup trucks with cab-high bed covers on them drove in. As soon as they were clear, DeCollado reversed the opener to close. When the door hit the floor, Draper and Bauer pounced on the two trucks.

In minutes the two occupants in each truck were kissing concrete with their hands and ankles zip-tied. Once the men were secure, they turned their attention to the truck's cargo. Draper opened the rear canopy door and what he saw stunned him. The pickup beds were stacked floor to ceiling with plastic wrapped bundles of various sizes, some small and some large, packed so tight it left little room for any other cargo. Behind the front seats, a brown tarp covered more plastic wrapped packages piled level with the windows.

"Holy shit," DeCollado said. "I think we struck the mother lode."

"Does appear that way," Draper said.

"What do you suppose its worth?" Bauer said.

"Varies," Draper said, "the Mary Jane, right here and now, probably about four hundred a pound. By the time it gets to Chicago or New York, more like two grand a pound. Lot's of markup in distribution." The hard drugs a bunch more. I'd guess well over a million dollars in each truck, street value."

"Easy to see why they kill over it," Bauer said.

"Good thing to remember," Draper said, "we're playing a dangerous game here, these guys are in a kill or be killed business and won't hesitate to protect themselves and their cargo."

"So, how do they get it across the border?" Bauer said.

"Think of it like this, son," DeCollado quipped, "you throw enough wet shit at the side a barn, a little will fall off, but most of it will stick. Runners bring it across on foot to a stash house somewhere on this side of the border. Then, when it's safe, they reload the bundles and bring them here for distribution."

Draper laughed, "Buck, Bill's analogy is a bit graphic but there is truth to it. Consider that the government estimates that we have operational control of less than forty-five percent of our southern border between the U.S. and Mexico. Since that border is nearly two thousand miles, the drug cartels have thousands of square miles of rugged, unforgiving territory to bring anything they want into the U.S. I'd guess most of the drugs coming through the checkpoints are a ruse.

"I thought they'd substantially increased the number of agents along the southern border," Bauer said.

"True, they have, especially since 2000, but consider the border includes thousands of miles of coastline along the Gulf of Mexico, Florida and even the eastern seaboard, not to mention the northern border. That's a lot of territory," Draper said.

"It's likely they catch less than ten percent of the drugs and maybe a little more of the illegal immigration," DeCollado added.

"I'd best call Ramos, I think he'll be pleased," Draper said, changing the subject. He didn't want to dwell on how hopeless their task appeared.

Ramos answered with, "Shit, I thought you'd never call; everything alright?"

"It's fine. Come join us, but don't call in the troops until we get the hell out of here. We need to get Lilly out of here also."

"Yeah, it's important the cartel thinks she's dead. Be there in minute."

Ramos beat on the overhead door less than five minutes later.

DeCollado punched the button to the opener and stopped the door as soon as Ramos ducked inside. He saw the open door on the second pickup and whistled. "You guys done good," he said.

"Like it?" Draper said grinning.

"Damn right. Where's Lilly?"

"Back in the utility room. We didn't want anyone to see her," Draper said.

"Can you guys hold the fort for about an hour, while I take her somewhere safe? She's been my CI for a couple of years and I don't want her getting hurt."

"We can probably arrange that, but make it a half hour. We need to be clear of here before you bring in the troops. We don't want any time discrepancies to mess up the case."

"I agree, in fact, I know somewhere I can stash her and be back in fifteen."

"Better yet, go, use the back door," Draper said. "You got a story for all this? It better be a good one."

Ramos headed for the utility room, shouting back at Draper, "It's a dandy, been putting it together while you and your friends were screwing around in here."

Ramos returned in less than fifteen minutes and Draper showed him the locked steel cover in the office cabinet. "With any luck that's the cash storage box. A bundle of cash would make this bust really sweet," Ramos said.

Draper stood silent, noting that the Tucson Police Department should be willing to overlook of a few of his past transgressions. Maybe he could get Pérez to buy them dinner. He doubted it, but might be worth a shot.

"Drugs go north, money has to go south," Draper said.

"I owe you one for this," Ramos said.

"Damned straight you do and I intend on collecting one of these days. A nice thick steak would be nice."

"You got it, and your friends, too."

Leaving Ramos to call in the troops, Draper, DeCollado and Bauer loaded up the Lincoln and pulled out of the alley under a lightening sky. The mountains surrounding Tucson carried long shadows and dark outlines scraping a blazing red sky colored by high thin clouds. The picturesque morning relieved the weariness clutching at Draper's bones. He felt good even though they likely hadn't put a dent in the cartel's operation. But shaking the tree would anger the boys down south and with any luck they'd make a mistake. Draper intended to be there waiting.

"Is anybody besides me hungry?" DeCollado said. Seems I remember a restaurant out by the airport that is open all night."

"Always thinking about your stomach," Draper said, turning toward the airport. Now that DeCollado reminded him, he realized they hadn't eaten since dinner.

"Damn right, no one else does," DeCollado said.

After they ate, Draper dropped DeCollado off at the airport so he could fly Draper's 182 home for a couple days and drove Bauer to his ranch. The young rancher sat silent until the Highway 85 turnoff and Draper assumed he was asleep. It turned out he wasn't.

"What'll happen to the girl?" he said, and Draper knew instead he'd been musing.

"Nothing. She'll rest, suck up some blow and be back on the streets working tonight."

"You sound a little callous about it. Isn't there something we can do for her?"

"Reality is she's the only one that can help her. As long as she continues to use drugs she'll have to be a working girl to afford it," Draper said.

Bauer stared out the windshield watching the painted lines flash by without seeing them. Draper knew he was wrestling with knowledge of life's underbelly, a not so pretty picture when it's right in front of you. Draper's former occupation exposed him to the seamier side of life, leaving him with the nightmares and a cynical attitude to prove it. It was something only cops and spies really understood and Draper doubted he could explain it to Bauer, despite the fact he'd been an Army Ranger. Bauer hadn't learned it was one thing to kill because the other guy is shooting at you, and quite another to kill because the enemy deserves it.

He dropped Bauer off and drove to his place fighting sleep and bone-weary. Dog greeted him with a waging tail and soft barks. The car parked in front of his porch was a newer Ford Police Interceptor unmarked except for the hidden light bars. As he walked by he felt a cold hood.

In his bed, she stared back, a single sheet tucked under her chin. "You're late, cowboy,"

"You got a gun under there?" Draper said.

"No," she said, "I'm totally defenseless."

Chapter Ten

Southwestern Arizona

Draper woke to the sound of his cell ringing. He peered around the room though sleep-filled eyes, finding himself alone and wondering where the hell he'd left his phone. Three rings later Molly walked in, looking two clicks above gorgeous wearing a thin housecoat with nothing underneath. Draper determined that fact when it gapped open in front.

"Don't get used to this," she said, holding the phone behind her back and sitting on the bed. If I'm going to be your secretary I want some payment."

"Bribery is illegal," Draper said, "and you're a sworn officer of the law."

"Keep talking and I'll get more expensive," Molly said.

"I thought you had to go to work?" Draper noted the phone quit ringing.

"Not until this afternoon and with lights and siren I can make it in under an hour. I'll let you check the phone or I can put it on the table."

"On the table works," Draper said.

Much later, nearer to noon, Draper lay in bed watching Molly doze beside him. She'd aged gracefully, at almost forty she still turned heads. Even her County Sheriff uniform couldn't hide her feminine curves on the few times she had to wear it for formal occasions. While not a classic beauty in the Hollywood sense, she drew male second glances without trying, unconsciously emitting sexuality in a subtle way mixed with confidence and a tough exterior. Draper had trouble explaining it, but he knew he liked it.

"I've got to go to work," she said, eyes popping open, bouncing out of bed and heading for the shower.

"Sure, go to work, leave me here alone," Draper said.

"Poor baby," she said from the bathroom door and disappeared.

Ten minutes later she was back, scrubbed and toweling her short hair in preparation for a finger comb. She started to dress in clean clothes she'd begun habitually leaving at Draper's place. He considered it a sign of progress and emptied out a couple of dresser drawers six months earlier.

"Stop staring at me," Molly said.

"Why?" Draper said, "I like staring at you."

"It embarrasses me," she said. "You shouldn't embarrass a woman with a Glock 19 in her purse."

"The view is well worth the risk," Draper said, ducking the small pillow she threw at him.

"Coming back tonight?"

"Can't, duty calls, Commission meeting tonight. It'll last late."

Minutes later she was gone, leaving him with the memory of a promising kiss and a pot of hot coffee. Draper dressed, poured himself a cup, added a little brandy on top of flavored cream and walked to the front porch. The sun up for hours, only Dog waited for him. He sat and surveyed the desert with Dog's head on his lap. It would be easy, he decided, to forget everything bad by concentrating on the memory of his night with Molly. He couldn't because of dog eyes burning into his soul. It seemed the animal was asking, "What have you done so far today to find out who killed my master?" His answer, "Nothing today, but we had a good day yesterday" appeared lame. Dog's silence made him rise to roam the house looking for his unanswered cell.

Back on the porch with a now approving canine companion, Draper scanned his messages finding two, one from John Pérez and another from Buck Bauer. He punched Pérez's number first.

"Pérez," the Tucson cop said.

"John, its Draper, you called?"

"Christ, yes, you read the morning paper?"

"No, my place is a long walk for the paperboy; he hasn't arrived yet."

"Smart ass, don't you have internet?"

"What's that?" Draper said baiting the Tucson cop because it was early in the morning and he'd had an enjoyable night.

"Well, I know you're innocent, but we busted a huge load of drugs last night, over four million dollars worth and as an added bonus of two million dollars in a hidden cache. Ramos is running around here crowing like a rooster with new hens. I don't suppose you know anything about this?"

"Not a thing."

"Well, here's an inventory. The surprise was fifty pounds of pure heroin. That alone was a million and a half street value. The rest was marijuana and cocaine. ATF is still counting the cash but we're sure it will be a couple million. The Chief is having a press conference in about an hour trying to make as much political hay as possible. There is one little tiny hitch," Pérez said.

"What's that?" Draper said, not caring, but playing along.

"One of the bad guys is claiming there were a whole bunch of cops and they tortured him. We found him bound and naked."

"Too bad for him; you know drug dealers will say anything when they're caught."

"Well, thanks anyway, you don't have to bullshit me, Ramos ratted on you, but only to me. You know I can't condone your involvement, nor can I share it with anybody."

"I know that, but you could buy us dinner, if not on your generous cop expense account, then out of your own pocket."

"You know I don't have an expense account," Pérez said. "You should hope the day doesn't come that I have to arrest your ass."

"You could come down to Ajo and I'd introduce you to the best-looking Sheriff this side of the Pacific Ocean. We're real modern here, restaurants and everything."

"I'll think about it," Pérez said.

"You know don't you, you'd be a lot less grouchy if you were getting it oftener," Draper said and Pérez hung up on him.

"Guess that means he's not buying dinner, Dog," Draper said. Dog cocked his head, but had no comment.

Draper's second call went to Bauer. The phone rang six times before dropping into voicemail. He left a message and hung up. Draper sat on the porch with Dog, nursing his coffee and admiring the desert. He felt a little at loose ends, as if he should be doing something, a feeling accented by Dog's continuous stare. Normally he would have opened the hanger and played with the 182, tinkering or polishing, but DeCollado had his Cessna.

Draper dozed, still recovering from the long night when his cell woke him. "Draper," he said, fumbling with the flip-phone.

"Charlie, this is Buck, I was thinking maybe we could take a couple of my horses and do some exploration of John's place and see if we can find anything that might tell us why somebody wanted to kill him."

"That seems reasonable, but how about we fly it first maybe we can narrow down the ground search.

"You got a plane?"

"I do, the one DeCollado took in Tucson is mine, but I'll give him a call and maybe he can fly down since his Bell 205 is here. He can go with or take his 205 home. Let me call Bill and I'll let you know what the plan is."

Draper called Bauer back twenty minutes later. "We're on for tomorrow morning. Bill wants to pickup his chopper anyway since he's got a job for a couple days."

"Great, my little runway is just south of the house and I'm a couple miles southwest of John Quinn's."

"See you in the morning."

Draper spent the remainder of the day sweeping blow sand out of the hanger and off the run-up pad, one of the continuous necessary chores required when living in the desert. He tried to keep busy to take his mind off Molly and the night's activities. The thought occurred to him that having her around permanently would be a good thing, except he didn't know if she was ready to give up the Sheriff thing.

The next morning early Draper heard the 182 before he saw it. He sipped a swallow from his second cup of coffee, patted Dog's head when his ears perked, and followed with the comment, "Friendly's coming, Dog." The view from his porch faced north allowing a restricted view of the brilliant blue morning sky. In his narrow scrutiny there wasn't a cloud, testifying to the likelihood that it would be a nice day flying. After a few minutes he spotted the plane turning on final toward his hard sand-packed runway. The plane flared and settled to the ground guided by the soft touch of Bill DeCollado who undoubtedly thought landing in the middle of the desert without buildings, trees, crosswinds, or active gunfire ranked right alongside child's play. He maneuvered the 182 off to the side of the hanger into a small tie down area Draper used for rare guests. There they tied down the plane temporarily while they dragged the Bell out of the hanger because it would be out of the helicopter's rotor wash.

"Hey there, young feller, nice plane you got," DeCollado said stepping out of the 182.

"You like it, huh," Draper said.

"Well, it's ok, but the propeller is in the wrong place and damn thing needs a lot of runway."

"Come on, grumpy, got time for a cup?"

"Not this time, sonny, got a well-paying client waiting Phoenix."

Draper had known DeCollado for nearly twenty years and they'd worked covert ops in Southeast Asia for most of that time and the older man rarely called him by name, opting instead for references to his youth with "young feller," "sonny" and similar phrases. Draper resented it at first, and had long ago accepted it, determining it likely his older friend would never change.

Draper helped DeCollado pull the Bell out onto the run-up pad and watched while he did his pre-flight, lifted off, spun it around on the ground cushion, and gained altitude before turning northeast toward Phoenix. A few minutes later he lost sight of it in the morning sun.

Draper taxied the 182 up on the run-up pad, grateful he'd installed the fifty by fifty concrete slab. Even though the cost had taken a bite out of his savings, it more than paid for itself in convenience, maintenance, and safety.

He went to the Lincoln and moved the tactical equipment from its trunk to the baggage compartment of the 182. He viewed it a precautionary move, but he'd been too long in covert ops not to always be prepared. It was unlikely the cartel would be able to discern responsibility for the other night's events. They'd been very careful to keep their identities under wraps but in the back of his mind the fact that Ramos might have somehow learned his name was a worry. By the time he'd finished loading the plane it ate at him to the point he dialed Pérez.

When Pérez answered, Draper said, "Did Ramos give you any indication he knew my name?"

"No, he referred to you as my 'friend" and I told him you weren't my friend. Why?"

"No reason, just checking. Even when we bailed Bauer and Alice Quinn out I figured everyone there assumed I was his lawyer."

"I made sure no one thought any different. Been very careful about that," Pérez said.

"Would you get a hold of Ramos and make sure? And if he does know my name somehow put a clamp on him, will you?"

"He'll be my next call."

"I'm probably being paranoid but I'll feel better if you do. Thanks, John."

Draper hung up and went to the house and made sure Dog had plenty of food and water, petted the animal with instructions to "guard the place," packed a small ditty bag just in case and returned to the 182.

Since the wind blew from the east at about ten knots, Draper taxied to the far end of his sand runway and started his into-the-wind takeoff roll aimed at the hanger. At rotate speed he lifted the Cessna off the ground and began a gentle climb to two thousand feet. It was a short flight, less than seventy miles and Draper ignored the autopilot, instead electing to hone his dead-reckoning skills. Prior to autopilots, radio navigation aids, GPS technology, and inertial navigation systems (INSes), aircraft navigation was a seat-of-the-pants skill, using calculated bearings, visual landmarks and continuous correction based on estimated wind speed, and reference maps. Dead-reckoning, used extensively by early flyers, was still practiced by good pilots. Following Highway 86 southeast until it turned west Draper picked a mountain peak in the distance that would take him into the vicinity of the Quinn/Bauer ranches. Within a total of thirty-two minutes of flying time Draper spotted the Quinn buildings and began searching for Bauer's runway. When he saw it the windsock indicated a light northerly wind he set up an into-the-wind approach from the south. Draper flew parallel to the little dirt strip until he'd passed the end, chopped the power, set the flaps at twenty percent and turned into his final. As he neared the ground and started to flare he could see a pickup waiting at the other end. After touchdown he taxied to where the pickup sat, cut the engine to idle and popped open the passenger side door. Bauer joined him.

"Nice," Bauer said, admiring the instrument panel and its variety of techno-gadgets cluttering it. "You instrument rated?"

"Yup," Draper said. "You said, I think, you had some flying experience."

"Yeah," took a few lessons a couple years back."

"How many hours have you logged?"

"About fifty in a Cessna 172 Skyhawk, Bauer said."

"Soloed?" Draper said.

"Not yet. I was about there a couple years ago and then the economy tanked and I had to concentrate on the ranch."

"I hear you," Draper said. "The 182 has similar flight characteristics with more power, range and speed. I have an instructor's ticket also. You want to try a takeoff?"

"Sure!" Bauer said.

Draper spent a few minutes talking flying a 182, a subject dear to his heart, concentrating on those refinements the 172 didn't have. Bauer did a reasonable job of getting the 182 into the air and then Draper took over while they flew at low altitudes over the mountains.

"I share a common boundary with the Tohona O'Odham Indian Reservation that runs along the mountains south to the border and from there east to Quinn's place. His place lies adjacent to mine and I believe they are about the same size," Bauer said, pointing at the landmarks that delineated his property. They flew south along Bauer's property line to the international border. Nothing on the ground below marked the boundary forcing Draper to rely on his GPS and the terrain. Flying the border with Mexico, Draper stayed well into U.S. airspace but could see a small range of mountains paralleling the border on the Mexican side. It looked innocent enough and he couldn't see signs of suspicious activity, but decided he'd give a lot to sneak a peek at the other side of those hills. They flew the boundaries of both ranches without seeing anything out of the ordinary. Draper used the landmarks to fly parallel east west lines while they both studied the ground below.

"This might turn out to be a waste time," Bauer said, looking out the window and seeing nothing but the rugged Sonoran landscape.

"Flying is never a waste of time," Draper said, "it does, however, appear unproductive so far though."

Draper decided to fly the border again and take a second look at the small range of mountains that had caught his eye earlier.

Taking one last sweep Draper pointed out the range of low mountains surrounded by a relatively flat desert landscape. The upthrust probably not over a thousand foot difference from the desert floor looked about five miles long and less than a couple miles wide.

"How far do you estimate the far side of that little group of mountains is from the border?" Draper said, putting his own estimate at a couple miles, tops.

"I know the ranch main house is four and a half from the border so I'd say no more than two."

"That's an easy six and a half miles, seven at the most," Draper said, talking more to himself than Bauer.

"What's your point?" Bauer said, trying to follow along and failing.

Draper pondered a couple of seconds before deciding to share the tunnel theory with the younger man. "Last year, Bill and I came into possession of a tunnel plan indicating the construction a very sophisticated tunnel from Mexico into the U.S. A tunnel that would be large enough to drive big trucks through, although I think a tram system would be more likely because there wouldn't be any way to turn trucks around on the U.S. end without considerable extra excavation."

"Where at?" Bauer said, "You mean around here?"

"It seems the most logical place. Let's say they start digging a small tunnel over behind those mountains, they take it down to one hundred feet below the surface and dig straight at Quinn's house and it was big enough to allow two pickups to pass. Let's say a twenty-four foot roadway. A pickup can carry two million in drugs on the average depending on what kind. For arguments sake let's figure they only

114

work a twelve-hour shift at night. It looks to me that they could ship something like $35 billion dollars worth a year with little chance of losses.

"Holy shit," Bauer said, "that's three billion a month!"

"Give or take, we are making a lot of assumptions here and I have to admit none of the powers to be I've mentioned this theory to have given it much credibility," Draper said.

"How could they terminate the tunnel in the U.S. without someone seeing it?"

"Easily," Draper said. "Hypothetically, let's assume Alice decides to sell the ranch. Neither she nor her sisters want it and it's not worth all that much right now. Some investor picks it up that has connections with the cartel. They build a metal building, say a hundred by fifty, or maybe bigger and raise horses. The building is for an indoor riding arena, supposedly. Install two freight elevators down to the tunnel and now you have a perfect re-loading area for our two pickups full of drugs and they have easy access to both I-19 and I-10 with little chance of getting caught. And if one pickup load does get caught, likely the Border Patrol will assume it slipped through at Nogales."

"Son of a bitch," Bauer said, "I'm not sure why, but that makes sense."

"There's one tiny flaw," Draper said.

"And that is?"

"You," Draper said. "If both ranches were included, there'd be little chance of anybody seeing anything."

"But I wouldn't sell," Bauer said, "And nobody has approached me."

"Never the less," Draper said, "I think it would be prudent for you to never go out unarmed and watch your back. Remember the asshole that got Quinn did it from over a thousand yards. He's a pro."

Chapter Eleven

Southern Arizona

Draper dropped Bauer off at his ranch and flew a direct line to his home. Worry nagged at the back of his mind. The scenario he'd outlined to Bauer made sense in too many ways, yet his gut told him without proof or solid confirmation he'd play hell convincing anyone. He knew the politics of the southern border issue demanded hands off. The nonsense of jurisdictional control between the state and Washington bureaucrats interfered with any real progress. Draper felt regret that dedicated people fighting for Sonoran justice put their lives on the line everyday when there was no clear direction to win.

Draper set the 182 on his sandy runway and taxied to his concrete run-up pad, spun the plane around tail toward the hanger door and killed the engine. Dog waited until the prop stopped and trotted over to the plane his tail wagging in greeting. Stepping out, Draper petted the dog saying, "I wouldn't mind if your mistress decides she doesn't have room for you, Dog, I'm beginning to like having you around."

Draper fixed himself dinner and ate on the front porch sharing with Dog and watching the Arizona sun drop behind the western mountains. A magnificent display of crimson shades danced on the evening sky. The brilliant hues lasting only a few minutes, Draper

117

watched as they faded into blackness. He cleaned up his supper dishes and went back to the porch to watch the stars. His phone rang and the caller ID indicated John Pérez.

"Charlie, I don't know if there's a problem or not but we've lost contact with Ramos. His handler hasn't heard from him for twenty-four hours and he's supposed to check in every day."

"Has that ever happen before?" Draper asked.

"No, never, we've got everyone out looking but he's not at his place or any of his usual haunts."

"Do you think it's related to the other night?"

"That's just it, I don't know, but until we find out otherwise, I'm assuming so. You'd better watch your back just in case," Pérez said. The Tucson cop's voice sounded even, yet Draper detected concern in his voice when he added emphasis to the 'watch your back' part.

"Thanks for the warning John, I'll keep it in mind," Draper said and closed his phone. He sat petting Dog for a few moments before getting to his feet.

"Looks like we need to make a few preparations, Dog," Draper said.

Draper walked to the hanger with Dog following behind, unlocked the walk-in door and stepped inside. With the Lincoln parked in the back, Draper had to turn on a light in order to see what he needed to do. A few minutes later he stepped out of the hanger, shut off the lights and relocked the door. Dressed in a bullet-resistant vest, dark clothing, and armed with his Glock and an M4 carbine he began a slow cautious tour of his property. The Sonoran Desert, because of its location, is inky black dark in the period between sunset and moonrise. Dark comes suddenly and completely on moonless nights, an effect that surprises tourists and traps unprepared travelers. Without night vision goggles Draper wouldn't have been able to move safely among the thorn infested desert flora. He knew running headlong into a buckhorn cholla or an Ocotillo in the dark would be a very painful and long remembered experience. He walked until he estimated he was fifteen hundred yards from the house. He'd left a single sixty watt light bulb on the porch glowing and used it as his guide. He began a slow purposeful circle maintaining his distance from the house until he'd completely circumvented the buildings. Throughout the trip he watched the ground for signs of foreign visitors but found none. Satisfied there was no immediate danger he walked back to the house. It was likely that if anyone came it would be after the moon rose which gave him a couple of hours to prepare. He had plenty of extra ammunition in the house and the thick concrete walls made it a veritable fort. He felt certain he and Dog could hold off an army if necessary and a couple of assholes would be easy. His preparations complete, he brewed a fresh pot of coffee, poured a cup into some flavored cream, retired to the front porch and sat in his favorite chair to wait.

Draper heard the dog growl and realized he'd dozed off. He sat up slowly and studied the dark desert. The moon's nightly journey across the black star-filled sky only beginning, the desert radiated an eerie glow casting long moon shadows across the landscape. Draper could see the first two or three hundred yards down his driveway but beyond that nothing. Dog growled again. Draper slid to the porch floor while aiming the M4 over the bottom rail. He scanned the desert through the night scope. At first the view looked quiet then suddenly a body ran between two Saguaros carrying a weapon. Draper knew the giant desert cactus afforded poor cover because of its fleshy interior was held upright by a thin woody skeleton near the surface. He felt certain a three shot auto burst chest-high would take the man out, but hesitated wanting to know how many he faced. So he waited figuring that any game would include at least two or three with an up close and personal agenda. Draper decided to give them the chance. Over the next half hour he counted three moving ever closer, cautious, but expecting him to be in bed. He wanted at least one alive for some intense interrogation later but it wasn't an absolute necessity. While he waited Draper assessed his position. He'd cleared the area around the house out about a hundred and fifty feet or so just for such an occasion. That meant for a short time during a frontal assault they'd have to be in the open. Unless they were entirely stupid, an option he doubted but had high hopes for, probably only one at a time would come straight in, with the others waiting or coming from the sides. He felt confident he would pick them off one by one.

Minutes went by while Draper held his hand on Dog's head to keep him quiet. The first invader stepped out from behind a Palo Verde and sprinted toward the porch. Halfway he dropped, scoped the front of the house for a bit before rising and coming the rest of the way. He looked heavy, muscular and capable in a sleeveless t-shirt and a dark do-rag on his head. "Gangbangers," Draper thought. He didn't take any chances and killed the man silently crushing his larynx and closing off his carotid artery. He let the man slide quietly to the porch floor hoping the other two hadn't seen a thing. Presently the other two came, running bent over with weapons leading. Draper let them get within twenty feet and shot the right hand runner center mass. The other man let loose a short burst in the general direction of the house and when Draper fired, careful to miss, the man dropped his weapon and turned and ran. "Get him, Dog," Draper hissed and the Border Collie leapt off the porch and sprinted after his quarry. The runner made it about thirty feet before the dog hit him knocking him to the ground growling ferocious and biting. Draper ran up to the downed man who was screaming loud and trying to fight off the dog and yelled, "Hold still, asshole, and he'll stop biting."

"Okay, Dog, we got him," Draper said, petting the dog to let him calm down.

"What's your name, asshole?" Draper said.

"Fuck you," the man said.

He looked in his mid-twenties, Hispanic, arms and neck tat-covered, dressed in a sleeveless black t-shirt with black shorts. Draper searched for weapons, finding a chrome Beretta 96 and a heavy switchblade knife capable of sticking a good sized hog in addition to the AK-47 he'd dropped during his race with Dog.

"Tough guy, huh," Draper said, bitch slapping him across the nose. "Turn over and put your hands behind your back or I'll let the dog eat on you a while."

Draper zip tied the man's hands and marched him back to the porch before making him sit on the sand walkway. "Guard him, Dog, and if he moves, bite him." Dog sat on his haunches and growled baring his teeth into a vicious smile.

Draper investigated the other two gunmen. Both dead, Hispanic, with gang tattoos, they came armed with handguns and AK-47s and switchblade knives. By the time Draper gathered it all up he had quite a stash of armament. That done, he left the bodies where they were figuring he had all night to take care of them and slipped a black cloth hood over his captive's head before marching him over to the hanger. Inside Draper pushed the man to the rear of the dark building where he sapped him just hard enough to render him unconscious for a few minutes and guided him to the floor. Touching a hidden button caused his heavy workbench to slide sideways four feet revealing a steel trap door in the concrete. Lifting the door exposed steps leading down into a small concrete block lined hole and turned on a small ten-watt light. The bulb only partially illuminated the area. The floor consisted of Sonoran sand. Draper dragged his unconscious captive down the stairs and laid him on the sand. Back up the stairs into the hanger, Draper retrieved a single wooden chair and returned to the hole. He propped the man in a sitting position and zip tied him securely to the chair.

The gangbanger started to come around and Draper removed the hood. He starred at Draper silently, his defiance obvious but unsure of what his captor intended. Draper said nothing while he worked.

"Comfy?" Draper said when he'd finished and received no response.

"There's one thing you need to know, asshole," Draper said, "when I leave the light will go out leaving you in complete darkness. You will be able to feel if a scorpion runs up your leg, though, so be sure to sit very, very still my friend, because if you don't..." Draper hesitated for a moment, "well, I guess you know that a scorpion sting can be fatal, especially if you're allergic. You aren't are you? I take from your silence you aren't so you should be fine for a couple days, maybe a week. After that you'll get a little thirsty but don't worry about it." Draper talked in a soft, easy conversational voice, while his captive stared, not believing any of it. "Now, the spiders are a problem, especially the black widows. Did you know the female black widow mates and then kills and eats the male? Kind of weird, don't you think? There are lots of black widows in the desert; they like dark moist places, like down here for instance. But don't you worry unless of course, you move around and let them know you're here."

"What the hell do you want?" the man spit out.

"A very good question; the truth is I need information. If you feel like telling me now, fine, otherwise I'm going to leave and come back maybe in a couple of days to see if you are still alive. If you die on me well, I'll take you out and plant you alongside your buddies and let the coyotes feed on you. Did you know a pack of coyotes can completely dispose of a body in less than twenty-four hours? They surely can and scatter the bones over miles of territory. Want to talk now?"

"Fuck you, asshole!"

"Okay, friend, it's your funeral," Draper said and started up the stairs. He didn't stop and didn't turn around. When he got to the hanger floor he closed the trap door and pushed the button sliding his workbench back into place.

Draper knew from his experience in Southeast Asia, total darkness can have a strange affect on a man's psyche. Suggest some creepy, crawly creatures and the mind will do the rest. The enemy in those days used tunnels and hollowed out caves, but Draper figured his little hidey-hole would produce the same results. Besides, he needed time to dispose of the other two. Draper wondered just how tough the little bastard would be after twelve hours in the dark.

The next hour consisted of disposing of the bodies. In a lean-to behind the Quonset hanger Draper had a 1948 Farmall M tractor with a wide frontend modification and an aftermarket loader. The old thirty-horsepower M tractor was an amazing piece of equipment. Designed for row-crop faming, over two hundred forty thousand were built between 1939 and 1954 and many are still in running condition. Other than sun-faded red paint, Draper's M looked as if it had never been touched mechanically, had a four-cylinder engine that started on the first crank, a five speed thunder-mesh plus reverse transmission that would pull a four-bottom disk plow six hours on a tank of fuel.

Draper fired up the old tractor and drove it around to the front of the house using the aftermarket lights he'd installed. He loaded the two bodies into the loader bucket and proceeded toward the huge volcano chimney that sat a mile beyond his property line. The chimney had an eroded fault on one side that made it look like a giant fist and a thumb sticking out of the desert. Draper liked it sitting like a guardian in the distance. About halfway to Thumb Mountain as it was called on local maps, a large mostly dry wash cut across the southwest corner of his property. Draper dumped the bodies in a side wash knowing the desert coyotes and other scavengers would make short work of them. In a couple a few weeks there'd be nothing left but bleached bones scattered for miles. He returned home in under an hour. The night wind would eliminate any sign the tractor had been moved. His last effort concentrated on finding the vehicle his unsuccessful assassins had used to disturb his peace. That issue required a quarter mile walk down his driveway where he located an unoccupied black Lincoln Town Car with darkened windows. The three dickheads had conveniently left him the keys. Draper drove it back to his house, locked it up, went to bed and slept soundly until almost ten the next morning.

When he did get up he made coffee and taking a half slice of bread for George, he found the gecko waiting impatiently for breakfast. Dog lay sleeping beside his chair as if the canine had experienced a hard night. George stood on his hind legs, accepted the morsel and scampered away. Draper sat balancing his coffee cup on the chair arm disappointed that he'd missed the sunrise by several hours.

At one-thirty in the afternoon, exactly twelve hours after he'd secured his captive in the hole, Draper pushed the button that slid the workbench away from the steel trap door. He lifted the lid to his hidey-hole and peered in. The prisoner blinked his eyes unaccustomed to even the faint light thrown by the 10 watt bulb. Draper called it Cellblock 9 after the infamous German concentration camp cellblock at Terezin during World War II, now in the Czech Republic. This was its maiden voyage and Draper knew he would be pleased with the results.

"How we doing down there?" Draper said.

When the man didn't respond, Draper moved down the steps and looked his prisoner over. Normally, Draper knew from his own training, disorientation and confusion doesn't get severe until twenty-four to forty-eight hours depending on the mental strength of the subject. Of course, those training tests he'd been subjected to didn't include the mental stimulation of crawling critters. Draper could see wet tear streaks on the man's face and his pupils were dilated searching for light.

"What's your name?" Draper said, using a quiet, even voice.

The prisoner looked confused, squinting as if he was trying to remember. After several minutes, while Draper waited, he said, "Hector."

Draper knew the interrogation would be slow while his captive recovered.

After an hour the man began to talk and within another half-hour he'd spilled his guts. Draper recorded the whole thing for future use with a miniature pocket recorder. When he was certain he had it all, he slipped the black hood over the man's head. He considered rendering him unconscious but that meant carrying him up the stairs so Draper elected to let him walk. Once they were in the hanger he closed up the hole and led his captive outside and across the yard to the front porch where he removed the hood and cut the zip ties.

In Draper's mind he had little choice; the man had outlived his usefulness and was an uncomfortable liability. Even though the man was a cold-blooded killer, intent on ending Draper's life, the courts would take years to levy justice. Draper considered the options and rejected them all. He took the man's chrome-plated Beretta and threw it over next to Lincoln.

"There's your piece. Take it and leave before I shoot you where you stand."

"Fuck you," he said, and as Draper suspected he would, he went for the gun.

"Dumb-ass," Draper said, as gunman picked up the Beretta and spun around. He made it three-quarters of the way before Draper's Glock .40 barked twice and slammed him back against the Lincoln's door.

Draper sat in his porch chair, listening to the dog growl at their dead guest while he pulled out his cell and called the Sheriff's Office in Ajo.

Chapter Twelve

Southern Arizona

U ndersheriff Tom Pickett arrived forty minutes later followed by the coroner's wagon. Draper watched from his porch chair with his hands in plain sight and didn't move when the Sheriff's right-hand man stepped out of his pickup cautious. His hand rested on the butt of his sidearm.

"What exactly is going on here, Charlie?" Pickett said, standing behind the pickup's door.

"As you can see, the asshole is dead," Draper said, indicating the gangbanger's body lying next to the Lincoln with an outstretched hand a foot short of his chrome-plated Beretta. Blood oozed from a large hole in his forehead with most of the back missing. "My .40 does a lot of damage at close range."

The shooter's AK-47 lay beside him in the dirt with a half-empty magazine. Draper knew searching the body would turn up a large switch-bladed knife. His own Glock lay on the table beside his chair. "Check my doorjamb and I'm sure you'll find at least one slug that will match the AK on the ground."

Draper handed Pickett his gun butt first and the Undersheriff racked the slide ejecting the loaded round and dropped the magazine. "Casing?" he said.

"Somewhere over there on the porch," Draper said.

"Only one round?" Pickett said.

"Two. I was in a hurry and missed one. It's a shame to waste good ammo on a gangbanger asshole."

"Who'd you piss off this time that would bring a such a person clear out here?" Draper knew Pickett pretty well and there wasn't a more honest, dedicated cop around anywhere. Molly had hesitated and thought long and hard about making him Undersheriff, an administrative job that required management skills plus top notch investigative ability. Pickett had both and went at his job in a thoroughly capable way proving her right. Draper liked his dry, no nonsense personality and slowly they'd come to respect one another. Because of that, he'd staged the scene as close as he could remember so there wouldn't be a lot of fabrication necessary.

Pickett waved up the coroner's wagon and they went about taking pictures and generally investigating the crime scene. It took two and a half hours.

When the crime scene boys were done, Pickett stepped up on the front porch. "Can I ask you some questions, Charlie?"

"Sure, Tom, ask anything you want," Draper said, "grab a chair and sit."

Pickett sat heavily, as if he wasn't sure how to begin. He took off his hat and wiped sweat off his brow before starting. Draper recognized it as part of his 'aw-shucks' interrogation technique. "Now let me see if I've got this right; this gangbanger, so far unidentified, driving a car from Tucson," Pickett said, "whose ownership is listed as 'Tucson Imports, Inc.' drives up to your front door and starts shooting at you for no reason with an AK-47, two rounds from which the boys retrieved from your doorjamb. Correct?"

"That's about it," Draper said.

"And you shot him once in the forehead?"

"Appears so."

"That's a pretty lucky shot," Pickett said.

"No, I was aiming for center body mass, but it was a hurried shot."

"Where'd the Beretta come from?"

"Don't know, I didn't see it until after he was down," Draper said. "I didn't want to touch it and mess up your investigation." Draper hadn't moved the Beretta near the man's hand on purpose. He didn't want the scene to look too perfect. Pickett, good cop that he was would be more suspicious if the answers were too pat. Crime scenes are rarely perfect. There's always something that doesn't fit. Draper knew Pickett would stew about the gun for a while, but eventually he'd be satisfied. By the end of the week he'd have a dozen other crimes to worry about. Draper counted on it." "Maybe he had it in his other hand and just dropped it," Draper suggested.

Pickett rose from his chair and said, "For a retired government guy, you sure seem to stir up a lot of trouble."

"All I've been doing is rattling the cartel's cage a bit."

"Well, try not to bring it home, we'd prefer you keep it outside Ajo County.

"I'll do my best, Tom."

Draper spent two days planning his next move. His captive in the hole under the hanger floor had given him the names of two cartel higher ups, one of whom matched the name volunteered by the drug runner in Tucson. While the dead man had never met either one, gang rumor had it that these two ran most everything south of the border between Mexicali and Nogales. Draper also had two bonuses;

the first being the name of the *jefe* or "boss" north of the border and the second information on the Quinn assassin, facts, but no name.

On the second afternoon, Draper gathered the box he'd packed at the Quinn's ranch containing the mementos he'd found secreted in the hidden drawer. He spent an hour reading through the documents and sorting out the relevant from personal items. He left the crimson diary untouched figuring only Alice Quinn should decide what could be shared if anything. The unsigned buy/sell was for one hundred fifty thousand. Draper guessed that amount was probably close to right considering the market, yet highway robbery compared to the land's worth in the early part of the decade. There wasn't much that he could use and he was about to pack it up when his cell rang. He looked at the number and it took a second to recognize the main number into the Sheriff's Office.

"Charlie," Rachael's voice came through an octave higher than normal, "the Sheriff's been shot! And Tom, too; by somebody with a high-powered rifle from a building across the street!"

It took all of Draper's training to control his emotions before he said, "Slow down, Rachael, have they been taken to the hospital?"

"Yes, I think so."

"Okay, I'm on my way, call me if you hear anything."

Draper pulled his third Glock .40 backup gun out of its hideout compartment, checked it before shoving it into his shoulder holster and ran for the door. His mind racing, he figured he knew who the shooter was and it was likely he'd hang around long enough to ensure the kill before disappearing. With any luck he could catch the son-of-a-bitch before he had a chance to escape. He ran to the hanger, unlocked the hanger doors, pushed both doors open enough to get the 182 out and jumped into the plane. He started the engine and taxied out on to the run-up pad and glanced at the limp wind sock. He stopped momentarily after lining up on the runway for a quick magneto check. Thirty seconds later Draper applied full power and took off without a pre-flight, something he'd never done before in his entire flying career. He looked at his watch realizing only fifteen minutes had elapsed since Rachael's call. The 182 could put him the Ajo Municipal Airport's pattern in another twenty minutes, maybe in time to catch the bastard who shot Molly. Up to that point he hadn't had a chance to get angry, but suddenly it was there and it took all of his long time training to control it. "Treat it like any other mission, dumb ass," he said out loud, competing with the plane's engine noise. He called the tower and requested a straight in approach.

"No problem, Cessna 18, traffic is light, use runway two-nine'r, wind is five to ten and variable," the air traffic controller returned.

"Hey, you don't happen to have had a twin jet with Mexican registry come in the last couple of days?" Draper asked, "He's a friend of mine and I was hoping to catch him."

"Sure did, came in yesterday. You better hurry; he's filed a flight plan to leave for Cancun in about forty minutes."

"Hey, thanks!" Draper said. His gangbanger prisoner had said the guy had a twin jet and flew up from Mexico somewhere. Draper felt himself go cold, a feeling he'd been trained for whenever a mission started. Until it was over nothing else mattered.

Draper would deny later that his landing fell short of perfect since he hurried it, braking hard as soon as his wheels touched to make the first taxiway turn. Lined up on the taxiway he powered up to a fast taxi speed and headed straight for the Cessna Citation Mustang sitting on the asphalt. He'd spotted the executive jet during his final approach, since its unique size and shape stood out like an elephant in an ant hill. When he was close enough, Draper spun the 182 around so his right wing was within twenty feet of the Citation's windshield. He could see the pilot trying to wave him off as he cut the power on the 182, set the brakes and pulled the keys. The only way that plane was leaving would require running over the 182 and if he tried neither plane would end up flyable.

Draper stepped out of the 182 and walked toward the Citation's door and waved casually at the pilot who shook his fist in return. He counted on surprise and considerable arrogance on the part of his quarry and by the time he reached the closed door, the Glock lay in his right hand alongside his thigh with the safety off. He took his fist and beat on the door, yelling "Hey asshole, you're in my spot!" The plane door dropped open exposing an angry well-built man about thirty-five. "What the hell are you doing, fuck-head," he growled, "move that piece of shit or I'll move you, prick!"

Draper, glad the man was leaning forward out the narrow doorway since it gave him the advantage. He reached up and grabbed the man's shirt front and jerked as hard as he could. The heavier man propelled out the door, scraping hair and hide off the top of his head on the low metal door header. His forward motion propelled him forward to land face first on the hot asphalt. He clawed at a shoulder holster when Draper took aim and shot him deliberately in the right knee and the fight ended.

Draper kicked the little .32 Auto away when the man dropped it and knelt down beside him shoving the .40 Glock under his chin. "Give me an excuse asshole, please."

"You'll die for this; you ruined my knee," the man said between clenched teeth, "I'll get you if it's the last thing I do."

"Maybe," Draper said. "The knee was for shooting the Sheriff and if she dies so help me God, I'll find you and make you wish I'd killed you today. Give me any trouble and I'll ruin the other knee."

Sonoran Justice by Dave Folsom

The man looked at Draper with ice cold hate eyes, "I'll make you pay if it takes the rest of my life, I'll kill your mother, father, all your kids, your wife, all of them before I kill you, asshole!"

Draper pressed his .40 against the man's forehead hard and said, "Same to you my friend give it your best shot."

Within minutes a Sheriff's department marked cruiser slid to a stop nearby and a deputy jumped out and crouched behind the driver's door covering Draper and his captive with his sidearm.

"Put the gun down and show me your hands, do it now!" a deputy shouted, all business.

Draper knew him casually, but couldn't remember his name. He set the Glock on the asphalt and raised his hands where the deputy could see them. "The man bleeding on the ground is a hired assassin so watch him close. I haven't completely cleared him for weapons."

A second Sheriff's Department vehicle screeched to a stop containing two more deputies. On the passenger side Draper was glad to see Tom Pickett, his left arm bandaged from wrist to shoulder and cared in a cloth sling.

Pickett walked over and said to Draper, "I'm seeing a lot more of you than I care to. Who's your friend?"

"He's the one who shot you and Molly. How is she?"

"Not good, Charlie, she was hit hard. She's in surgery last I heard; going to be there a while."

"I should have shot the asshole in both knees," Draper said. "What about you?"

"Bullet just scratched my arm, but I ended up with a bunch of concrete shrapnel in my arm and some in my back. Sore as hell, but no big deal. You want to shoot him again, I'd turn by back, but those two deputies would probably shoot us both."

"Might be worth it," Draper said.

"God, I need a doctor," the wounded man said, "You have to help me."

"Hey, Eric, come frisk this guy and cuff him," Pickett shouted at one of the deputies, "and call for an ambulance." Turning to Draper, he said, "Think we should do something to stop the bleeding?"

"Not as far as I'm concerned," Draper said. "Okay if I holster my piece? I hate having it lying on the hot asphalt."

"Sure, go ahead," Pickett said. "Sounds like the ambulance will be here shortly. They'll take care of the leg."

Draper noticed that the shooter had fainted. "Pansy-ass, I think he's gone out on us," he said.

Two hours later, after the ambulance left with two deputies on board followed by time wasted waiting for an emergency search warrant, Draper and a partly disabled Pickett found a M98B Super Magnum sniper rifle, chambered for .338 Lapua carefully hidden in a custom compartment along with a high-powered rifle scope, several magazines of .338 ammunition packed in with an array of other weaponry.

"We got him," Pickett said, "by now the forensic boys have dug some slugs out of the Court House door and I'll bet money they match this piece." Pickett held the M98B with gloved hands, turning it over and examining the weapon. "How the hell did you know, Charlie?"

"Lucky guess, Tom," Draper said, "though we'll probably never be able to prove it court, I'd bet my left nut he's the one who killed Quinn as well.

"Lucky for you we should able to match rifle with the slugs in the Court House door," Pickett said, otherwise we'd have a problem with probable cause at the airport."

"Frankly, Tom, I don't give a rat's ass about probable cause; I'm more interested in Sonoran justice."

Sonoran Justice by Dave Folsom

Chapter Thirteen

Southwestern Arizona

D raper arrived at the hospital a little after five with Pickett in tow. The Undersheriff offered him a ride and Draper accepted since it was that or another rental. They stopped at the nurse's station and learned Sheriff Henderson was still in surgery.

"At least she's still alive," Pickett said trying to put a positive spin on an otherwise dreary announcement.

They retired to a waiting room and at six Draper said, "Why don't you go home, Tom. You have family waiting."

Pickett nodded and said, "I will if you promise to call me as soon as you find out anything."

Draper agreed, knowing Pickett would be back before the night ended. Whatever the outcome with Molly, Draper knew it wasn't over. He sat alone in a taupe colored room staring at an abstract oil painting on the wall plotting how he would slice and dice the ones responsible. The painting consisted of slashes of different crimson shades and splattered with large and small red dots. It seemed appropriate to his mood, resembling a cup of blood thrown at a wall. Above the painting, a wall clock dawdled, moving between numbers at a sluggish pace.

"Mr. Draper?"

A tall woman in green scrubs stood in front of him and Draper realized he'd fallen asleep. "Yes," he said.

"Miss Henderson is out of surgery. She's in recovery and she'll be there about an hour before they move her to a room. I'll come and get you when she's ready."

"How is she?" Draper said.

"I can't tell you because I don't know. The doctor will be in shortly to visit with you."

The surgeon arrived after another half-hour. "Are you a relative?" he said, entering the room.

"No," Draper said, "but I hope to be someday. She doesn't have any close relatives in the area. How is she?"

"Your friend is a very sick woman as the result of a large caliber bullet that lacerated her liver, damaged the lower left lung lobe and fractured a couple of ribs. She's lost a lot of blood and she probably wouldn't have survived had we not gotten her into surgery as fast as we did. We are considering her in critical condition. If she survives through the next forty-eight hours she has a better than even chance of making it. We were able to stop all the bleeding and repair everything, she's being given blood, antibiotics to ward off infection and baring complications she should be fine. As soon as she's moved to a room, the nurse will come and get you and you'll be able to see her. It'll be morning or later before she'll be able to converse much. She's also getting pain medication."

The doctor's cryptic description reminded Draper of a surgeon on daytime drama TV, cold, analytical and disinterested. He wanted to take the man by the throat and shake him. When medical man turned and exited, Draper realized his fists where clenched.

***

When Molly opened her eyes she saw Gabriella staring close and holding her hand. "Hi," she mumbled, trying to sit up but couldn't for some reason and pain raced through her chest.

"Easy, Mom, you can't move around much, you'll pull stitches loose." Gabriella started calling Molly 'Mom' shortly after Draper introduced them and it wasn't long before Molly adjusted to the new title. She'd found herself amazed at Gabriella's ability to blend into new surroundings and situations with relative ease. Molly wasn't sure exactly when it happened but she'd become fond of Charlie's adopted daughter.

"Aren't you supposed to be in school?" Molly said, grimacing from pain when she tried to move.

"I'm done for the summer. Bill flew me down when you were shot."

"Shot?" Molly looked around and then back at Gabriella, "I don't remember. What happened?"

"You were shot outside the Court House four days ago by an assassin hired by the cartel. Tom Pickett was wounded also but only superficially. He and Charlie captured the assassin shortly afterward. You were in surgery almost nine hours and pretty much out of it for the last four days." Molly couldn't help noticing how mature Gabrielle looked, leaning over the bed as if she was in charge and the adult in the room. She'd become a beautiful young woman almost overnight, and a bossy one at that.

"Where's Charlie?" Molly said.

"He's out in the hall talking to the Doctor. He'll be back in a minute," Gabriella said.

***

The next month ran a blur in Draper's mind. The hospital released Molly after a week to a rehab hospital where she spent another two weeks followed by a slow trip to Draper's place. He and Gabriella hovered over her to the point she finally rebelled. They watched while Molly tried to get out of bed struggling, yet refusing assistance.

"Dammit," Molly grumbled, sitting on the edge of the bed exhausted, while her two caregivers stood nearby, "you two keep nursing me I'll never get up."

Draper stood silent, while Gabriella chided Molly, "Mom, you are as stubborn as the Missouri mule you sleep with. You were almost killed for cripes sake, and lucky to be alive. It's going to take months for you to completely recover and in the meantime you are going to have to put up with a grumpy nurse if you don't behave." Gabriella put her arms around Molly's neck and kissed her cheek. "So there you go, take it or leave it."

"I think I'll take it, Sweetie," a chastised Molly said.

Draper exited the room while Gabriella attended to the Sheriff. Stopping in the kitchen he grabbed a beer out of the refrigerator and headed for the front porch. Dog trailed behind and when Draper moved his chair to the sunset side of the porch, the canine followed. "I'm going to need you to watch over those two, Dog," he said, pulling out his ringing cell phone.

Draper packed his guns the next day. On-body weapons included his favorite Glock 23 in .40 caliber, a Glock 28 in 380 ACP caliber and a second Glock 23, the last two both in ankle holsters as backup weapons. He considered the .380 a throw away in case he had to and not much good for anything serious.

"You're leaving aren't you?"

Draper started at the voice, breaking his concentration. He turned to see Gabriella standing behind him with her hands on her hips. "Yeah," he said, turning back to his packing.

"When is it going to stop?"

"Not until the demand for drugs in this country stops."

"Why can't you let law enforcement take care of it?"

"Good as they are, they can't," Draper said. "You should know that."

"Why not?" Gabriella said, demand in her voice.

"It's complicated, but the short answer is because law enforcement is handcuffed by rules that give criminals all the advantages. We have a complicated court system that allows crimes to go unpunished for months and sometimes years because of crowded dockets and insufficient evidence. Living in a free society is great, but taken to extremes causes its own problems. The long answer requires understanding the cartel mentality. It's all about money, politics, power and control. The ones in charge will go to any lengths to get what they want and anyone standing in the way is eliminated without prejudice, including family, friends and enemies.

Gabriella stood silent for a long moment staring at Draper while mentally trying to comprehend his words. Draper waited, watching dew form in her eyes. "People who would enslave fourteen-year-old girls deserve killing," he said, softly.

Not satisfied, Gabriella pressed on, "What about the guy who shot Molly?"

"I'm counting on the cartel to take care of that," Draper said.

"What do you mean?"

"The cartel controls the prisons in this state. It's likely he'll be punished for failure. Those boys down south aren't very forgiving."

Gabriella stood determined, her expression worrisome and eyes misty. Draper stepped to her side and pulled her close. He held her long moments while she dampened his shirt front. The slap of rotor blades vibrated the rafters when Draper said, "Got to go, Babe, I'm counting on you to take care of Molly. The Sheriff's department is sending two deputies to guard you two and they will be here shortly."

***

The next day at a few minutes past nine am, Draper and DeCollado walked into the back room at Juanita's. The room smelled of fresh tortillas, simmering *pollo* and *ternera* mixed with green peppers and onion. Draper couldn't help feeling hungry and it was a long time to noon. Detective Lieutenant John Pérez sat at the usual table staring into a steaming cup of black coffee.

"Sit," Pérez said, without looking up.

Draper and DeCollado sat taking two chairs at the opposite side of the table.

Juanita came into a silent room and said, "You going to drink, eat or just sit there starring at one other?"

"Bring us some coffee, loaded, please, would you Juanita?" DeCollado said. "They need it to improve their humor."

Like a flash, the old Mexican restaurant proprietor slipped back into the room with steaming hot cups of black coffee with real cream on the side. Draper could tell from the wafting odor that the liquid contained enough brandy to choke an elephant. Pérez looked as if he needed every drop. Draper and the Tucson Detective weren't exactly friends since Pérez frowned on Drapers methods, but had to concede they were mostly effective.

"Your dime, John," Draper said, waiting for Pérez to start the conversation.

"How's Sheriff Henderson?" Pérez said.

"Lucky to be alive and facing months of rehab," Draper said. "The good news is we got the asshole that shot her."

Draper waited, certain Pérez had more on his mind than Molly's health.

"We found the bodies of Detective Ramos and his CI yesterday, dumped on the street in downtown like garbage. It wasn't pretty," Pérez began, his voice strained and low, staring into his coffee as if it was a crystal ball.

"I'm sorry, John," Draper said, trying not to show the anger he felt.

The room fell silent as Draper could tell Pérez was wrestling with his long-held law enforcement ethics. When faced with a situation that screamed for revenge at any cost, he didn't like the options. Worse yet the man felt guilty because he wanted to find the perps and personally execute them.

"You know I don't approve of your methods and at times in the past I've wondered if I shouldn't be arresting you," Pérez continued.

Draper smiled but didn't respond. He knew his methods tended to challenge Pérez's friendship even when the results turned out positive.

"What do you plan to do about Sheriff Henderson's shooter?" Pérez said.

"Nothing."

"What do you mean by 'nothing'? Don't bullshit me. I know you better than that."

"It's the truth, John, I figure the cartel will take care of him and if they don't, well, we'll cross that bridge when it happens." Draper looked squarely at Pérez. "Now if you ask me what we are going to do about the people who hired him, that's a different matter. We suspect the people responsible for the deaths of Detective Ramos and his CI are one in the same."

"Can't argue that," Perez said.

"The question is," DeCollado injected, "why would the cartel risk the wrath of local law enforcement by executing an undercover cop and dumping his body in a way that smacks of cartel retribution? It seems as if they would be asking for Federal involvement."

"As an example of how tough they are. Scare tactics, I suppose," Pérez said. "We need someone on the Mexican side that is tired of all the killing and crime; someone who is fed up and wants to take their country back."

"Good luck with that," DeCollado said. "A large percentage of the population lives mostly hand to mouth just to survive. The drug industry is big business, well-funded, and income- producing in a staggering way that makes even honest citizens consider it, or at least ignore it. The others are living in fear."

"So, what are you going to do?" Pérez said.

"We are going to snoop around Tucson and listen until we can get a line on who ordered the hit on Molly. When we find out you can rest assured we will make them very sorry." Draper decided not to reveal that he already had a name.

144

"Jesus, I didn't want to know that, so I'm going to pretend I didn't hear it." Pérez shook his head staring into his now empty coffee cup.

"Look, John, I respect your convictions as a member of law enforcement, but you also know that your hands are tied. The people we're after have no conscience. They will do anything necessary to protect their business. You know it as well as we do." Draper spit out the words with more intensity than he'd intended, his words fired by the anger roaring inside him when he thought of Molly.

"Charlie, revenge isn't the answer either," Pérez said looking straight into Draper's eyes.

"It isn't revenge, John; it's no different than killing termites attacking my house. These people are destroying my house, metaphorically speaking, and deserve to be eliminated without prejudice."

"Termites and people aren't the same, Charlie."

"They are when they attack my house. Molly Henderson is part of my house. We may have caught the shooter, but I want the ones who sent him."

Pérez sat quiet for several minutes, looking at the two men across the table from him. The tall one's eyes were like slits of hard granite, determined and enraged. The older one sat quietly, unmoving, watching, dangerous in a different way and reminding him of a sidewinder ready to strike. "Okay," he said, "how can I help?"

"To your knowledge, who is running the southern Arizona operation now?" Draper asked.

"We don't know for sure. The big boys have gone underground. We catch a few of the underlings who are more in the dark than we are. Mostly they are trying to make enough to send back to their families in Mexico. Their mouths are clamped shut by threat to their families back home. The feds deport them and a week later they're back with another load of drugs."

"We all know the border is undermanned, trying to guard a revolving door akin to trying to stop a leaking dam with chewing gum," Draper said.

"So what's your plan?" Pérez asked. "I know you have one and if you don't want to tell me that's okay. All I ask is to keep the body count down inside the city limits if at all possible. Beyond that I don't give a shit what you do as long as it slows the drugs down puts away bad guys. I just don't want to know too much about your methods."

Chapter Fourteen

Southwestern Arizona -

Detective-Lieutenant John Pérez left Draper and DeCollado sitting in the backroom at Juanita's. Neither man said a word until they were certain the Tucson policeman was out of the building.

"I have a feeling he doesn't like us much," DeCollado said.

"He's a cop, a dedicated one and he has a strict line of conduct that leaves him conflicted when he can't just go out an arrest somebody," Draper said. "I don't think we could ever be friends, but there is a level of anger in him because he can't go knock some heads together."

"Like us?"

"No, not exactly, but I believe he thinks about it."

"So what's next?" DeCollado said.

"You remember when that sleazebag thought we were going to kill him that night in the warehouse?"

"Yeh, he gave us the name Ricardo Ortiz."

So? There's got to be a hundred guys in Mexico with that name."

"True, but how many are high up in the Cartel ranks?"

"It would depend on how high up we're talking about."

"A couple of days before Molly was shot I got a visit from three Tucson gangbangers intent on shortening my life expectancy. I took out a couple of them and captured a third. We had a little sit down and he told me there was a first-class shooter the cartel was using who flew up from Mexico. The guy didn't know his name but when Molly was shot I guessed it had to be him. When I called the tower in Ajo I found out there was a Cessna Citation there with Mexican registry."

"That's how you were able to stop the asshole." DeCollado said. "Now tell me how you were able to get your captive to talk, *amigo de confianza*."

"Best you don't know. Suffice it to say he blabbed his head off. I also got two names, one of which was our common acquaintance, Ricardo Ortiz."

"I trust you gained this very valuable information by perfectly legal means and not by, *¡no lo permita dios*, torture?" DeCollado said, his face twisted in mock disbelief.

"Of course not," Draper said.

"I've been thinking about something Pérez said about needing someone on the Mexican side. I have a cousin that lives down in San Bartelo, a little burg east of Hermosillo. Haven't seen him in a couple years but I could send out some feelers and see if he'd be willing to help.

"Can we trust him? The cartel's influence is widespread and dangerous." Draper voice belied his reluctance to involving others.

"I'm sure we can but let's do it this way. He's an American citizen by birth so he can cross the border anytime. Let me invite him up for a visit, you can meet and talk to him and judge for yourself."

Two days later, after Draper and DeCollado made a quick trip to Ajo to checked on Molly and Gabriella, they stood on the American side of the Nogales International Border crossing watching a constant flow of bodies, cars, and trucks of all sizes. Most of the foot traffic was a mixture of tourists carrying Mexican treasures back home, and Hispanics crossing both ways on personal business or visiting family. Nearby, hundreds of vehicles sat in line waiting their turn for inspection. Vehicles and walkers alike were subjected to identification checks and searches, the extent of which depended on a complex screening process known only to Homeland Security. Draper hated it; convinced it did little to stop illegal activity since there was no real penalty other than deportation and mostly just inconvenienced the innocent.

"There he is," DeCollado said, referring to a taller than average Hispanic man who waved at them. Draper watched the man walk toward them, assessing him as he was prone to do. He liked what he saw on first impression. With coal black hair, dark eyes and a solid build, he looked to be in his mid-forties and capable of holding his own if necessary.

"Meet my cousin Diego Ferrez; Diego this is Charlie Draper," DeCollado said.

Draper shook the man's hand noting his hands were large, work-hardened and capable of a firm grip. "Glad to meet you," Draper said.

"My pleasure, *mi amigo*," Ferrez replied.

"Let's go somewhere quiet where we can talk," DeCollado said.

They walked following the crowd to the short-term parking lot. Ferrez and DeCollado began to jabber in Spanish of which Draper could only pick up an occasional word and scowled at DeCollado.

"We should probably use English since the white-boy here is lacking in education," DeCollado said, noting Draper's look.

"Sorry," Diego said, "sometimes I forget when I'm thinking in Spanish."

"Not a problem," Draper said, "I can follow along if you slow down a bit."

"I'm fluent in English so we'll use that."

At the parking lot they located Draper's black Lincoln. "We've got rooms at the Best Western in Green Valley, we can talk there. I'll drive, Bill, while you bring Diego up to speed."

The forty-two mile drive from Nogales to Green Valley took just under forty five-minutes on Interstate Nineteen. Green Valley was one of the many small towns that popped up along Arizona Interstate highways as bedroom communities to Tucson, Phoenix and smaller population centers. The residents were a mixture of retirees and younger working-class families wanting small-town living and the availability of higher paying jobs in the bigger cities. Draper listened without comment as DeCollado explained their problem to his cousin. Listening to details of Molly's near death by a hired gunman raised anger in Draper that he'd thought he'd tamped down. It took some tongue-biting to keep his mouth shut.

They reserved three rooms at the motel, but for the first several hours they camped in Draper's room. When they were settled in, Draper spoke first. "Diego, as Bill has told you, our situation results from an attempt, not only on my life, but on someone very close to me by the cartel. They murdered a local Tucson undercover cop and his CI who helped us take down a large drug shipment in Tucson. Bill and I have some experience with these people and it's unlikely they are going to forgive and forget. A preemptive strike would discourage further harm to us and the ones around us. We'd like to strike them hard in upper management, hard enough that it will cripple their activities for an extended period of time. I know that sounds optimistic, but we see little choice. We have names of members of the cartel hierarchy and our intention is to eliminate them. This is an extremely dangerous game and if you don't feel comfortable playing, say so now and we'll take you back to Nogales with no hard feelings."

Diego Ferrez sat straight-backed in a motel quality chair worn deep by years of service. His eyes hardened under a furrowed brow. He appeared to digest what he'd been told, but Draper sensed the man's mind wasn't totally on the conversation. His face mirrored wheels turning in his head, grinding the words he heard and matching them to some prior knowledge. A long moment went by in silence. "You two seem to have a bit of a predicament," he said, just before Draper was ready to call the whole thing off.

"That's an understatement," Draper said.

"Thank you for bringing me into this," Ferrez said, "I've been wondering how to eliminate those *hombres* who have made my country a haven for criminals and left our people fearing for their lives. Perhaps I should tell you what I know and some of what I suspect and then maybe we can be on the same table."

Draper smiled, but didn't correct Ferrez's misplaced idiom. Instead he waited for the man to continue, saying, "Please do."

Diego Ferrez stared hard at Draper measuring his worth Draper supposed, as he would most certainly do. He didn't want to push the man, yet he felt impatience rising in his chest. It joined a measure of anger frosted with deep frustration whenever he thought of Molly and how close he'd come to losing her.

"It's rumored the cartel is receiving funding for a special project from the Russians," DeCollado's cousin said in a voice so soft

Draper might have missed it had the room not been silent. It took a moment for this new information to sink in.

"The Russians? Why are they involved in this?" DeCollado said, mimicking Draper's thought.

"What better way than to create of nation of drug addicts. The US is a huge country, rich in resources trending toward a socialistic society. They are consuming expensive illicit drugs at an alarming rate while demanding more government services. Your entertainment and sports elite stand around using drugs like it is some sort of recreational sport while pretending to know it all. Take a hard look at those industries, and your government and tell me what you see. The news media is filled every day with people caught with drugs, prostitutes or fingers in the cookie jar. The way you are headed, fifty years and you'll look like Mexico does today, a two-class society, the very rich and powerful and the desperately poor. I'm sure you can guess which class will be the largest."

"What proof do you have that the Russians are involved?" Draper said.

"Proof? None at all. Only that there have been new strangers about, rumored to be Russian, and that they are negotiating funding for some sort of huge construction project in this area."

"Any idea what kind of construction project?" Draper asked.

"No, but a great deal of heavy machinery parts have been trucked into Hermosillo lately, mostly at night and without any fanfare or reason," Ferrez said.

Draper looked at DeCollado knowingly, and said, "I think you and I should take a trip south and visit your relatives."

"I was thinking the same thing. The question remains, what's the best way?" DeCollado said.

"What about flying into Mexico with my 182?" Draper said. "It's a little bit of a hassle, but not an insurmountable one. We could also get a look at that ground south of Quinn's place."

"Sounds do-able; then what?" DeCollado said.

"Then we kick some ass," Draper growled.

"Sounds like a plan," Ferrez agreed.

Flying into Mexican airspace had long been problematic for private pilots due to inadequate flight control facilities, scarcity of aviation fuel or more correctly the requirement that fuel needs had to be ordered and approved ahead of entering Mexican airspace, a dubious attempt by suspicious customs officials trying to control the drug trade. Mexican officials also required Mexican-issued insurance on the aircraft which Draper knew about and considered a non-issue since it was easily obtainable from local agents. The fuel rules had gone away in recent years and while Draper hadn't flown into Mexico in years, DeCollado did it routinely as part of his flying business.

"The bigger hassle is U.S. Customs who demand one hour prior notice of entry into U.S. airspace," DeCollado said as they were driving back from Nogales the next day after dropping Ferrez off at the border.

"And?" Draper prompted.

"It means we have to file our destination and return flight plans before we leave. We'll need to determine what day we are coming back and there is no changing it."

"Well, I'm thinking this is going to be more of a reconnaissance trip than an action one. Let's figure on finding out everything we can without stirring up any trouble. Once we get what we need we come back the same way we did the last time."

"Charlie me boy, this isn't like going into Nogales a couple of blocks, this is two hundred miles into interior Mexico. Not the same thing."

"Don't I know it," Draper said.

In spite of Draper's impatience, getting Mexican insurance, making sure they had all their proper papers, passports located and some minor maintenance on the 182, burned up four days. On the third morning just after sunrise while he sat on the porch drinking coffee, Draper called the Ajo Sheriff's office. After two rings Rachael answered.

"Hi, Charlie," the dispatcher said, rolling Draper's name seductively, jerking his chain. How's Sheriff Henderson?" Rachael's informality didn't extend to her boss, who she had a pedestal ceiling high.

"She's coming along very well, Rachael. Still not out of bed much but Gabriella's pushing her to get up more." Changing the subject, he continued, "Is Tom Pickett around?"

"He is, hang on."

Several minutes elapsed before Pickett came on the line. "What's up?" he said, without a greeting.

"Tom, I've got to be out of the country for four or five days. Is there any possibility you could spare a deputy to come out and stay with Molly and Gabriella. I'd be willing to stand for their salary."

"Let me talk to the guys who are off the next few days, see if I can get some volunteers and call you back. Give me a half-hour," Pickett said and hung up.

Draper sat on the porch, petting Dog's head, drinking coffee and thinking about what they would do in Mexico. He knew whatever they decided came fraught with danger. The people they were going after were likely unforgiving and ruthless in a country overrun with high-priced criminals. Anything they did would be looked upon with extreme prejudice and getting out unscathed appeared unlikely. He was on his second cup when his cell phone rang.

"Draper," the voice said, "It looks as if I'm the only one in the Sheriff's Department that doesn't like you."

"Now, Tom," Draper said, "you know you like me, you just don't want to admit it."

"You wish," the Undersheriff said, "in any case, I've got eight deputies off during the next five days and every damn one volunteered. They want to double team considering the people we're up against."

"See," Draper said, "there you go."

"Like hell, they're all are in love with the Sheriff."

"I suppose that's some of it," Draper admitted, "but I appreciate it. Have the first team here on Wednesday morning at 6 am and I'll brief them."

"There is a rumor about that you have access to automatic weapons and if that's true you might make them known just in case."

"Already done," Draper said.

Wednesday morning dawn rose crimson with the sun peaking between the fingers of Thumb Mountain and casting a velvet purple glow on Draper's small piece of Sonoran Desert. Saguaro Cactus laid long shadows and hid the furious activities of desert creatures. Draper's third cup of coffee sat nearly empty when a black Ford 250 pickup drove up pulling a travel trailer. He felt some relief that he knew casually the driver, a seasoned Deputy and one of Molly's best hands. The passenger was newer with less experience, but one of the best marksmen on the force according to the Sheriff. The two cranked down his anxiety level a couple of notches as he indicated an insulated coffee carafe and two mugs.

"Appreciate you coming, Lyle," Draper said.

Both men poured themselves coffee. Lyle Morrison, the older deputy, sat while his partner leaned against the porch railing. Draper had met the younger man once, but couldn't for the life of him remember the kid's name.

Morrison came right to the point. "Pickett says you have automatic weapons, but we're not supposed to know about it. That true?"

"It is if you need them. I have two Colt USM4s sequestered in the living room closet. Use them to protect Molly and Gabriella as necessary, but I'd appreciate it if you forget about it afterwards."

"Jesus, I wish we had the budget for a couple of those," Morrison said.

Draper spent nearly an hour bringing the two off-duty deputies up to speed on the potential for attack and his defensive perimeter. In mid-sentence Draper realized Gabriella stood in the doorway.

"What's going on?" she said.

"Gabriella, meet Deputies Lyle Morrison and ..." Draper hesitated a moment as he grasped for the kid's name. He stumbled through and added, "They are going to hang around while I'm gone,

The younger man stepped forward with his hand out and said, "Brad Gutierrez, Miss, very glad to meet you."

"Nice to meet you, Brad," Gabriella said, smiling and Draper would have sworn she blushed. He looked into her dark eyes as if seeing her for the first time, amazed at how she'd suddenly blossomed from the skinny dirt-covered waif he'd plucked away from cartel killers after Jennifer Hollings only a year earlier. She stood taller, confident and morphed into a beautiful young woman almost overnight. He wondered why he hadn't noticed the change before. She looked directly at Draper and said, "Mom knows about this?"

"I haven't gotten around to telling her yet. I didn't want to bother her and I only found out they could come yesterday."

The 182 ready to go, Draper walked out to the plane to begin his pre-flight and Gabriella followed.

"You be very careful," she said, like a mother hen protecting her chicks from a fox.

"I will, Babe, this is just a recon mission."

Gabriella wrapped her arms around Draper's neck burying her face into his shirt. She held on tight and Draper could feel dampness spread across his chest. "Come back safe," she said before turning and running back to the house. Damn, Draper thought, the girl makes it hard for a man to be an asshole.

Draper made a quick explanation to Molly with a longer goodbye. Finished with his pre-flight, and after a magneto check, Draper pushed the throttle hard against the firewall. The plane jumped forward lifting him into an azure sky. An hour later he turned downwind at DeCollado's ranch and landed to pick up his friend.

Flying into Mexico had, in the past, been a frustrating experience. , however, changes both in Mexico and primarily in U.S Custom's requirements, it was now easier to fly into Mexico than to fly back. Draper and DeCollado elected to file flight plans both for the entry trip and the return trip because of Customs requirement that incoming traffic notify Customs at least one hour prior to entry into

U.S. airspace. Since Mexican telephone service, especially long distance out of country was problematic at best, made it necessary. The hitch was the return date couldn't be changed and to miss it would risk months of bureaucratic problems. After making sure they had all the necessary paperwork including proof of Mexican insurance on the 182, passports, plane ownership, and personal identification they were in the air.

As soon has they'd crossed the border, Draper detoured west to explore the low range of mountains south of Quinn ranch. Despite an hour of search they couldn't see anything out of place. The low hills, covered with Saguaros, Palo Verde, and the usual desert flora, looked the same as they had for thousands of years.

"Shit," Draper said, "I was certain there had to be something there."

"Maybe there isn't a tunnel and there's some other explanation for Quinn's death," DeCollado suggested.

"You don't believe that any more than I do."

"Just saying," DeCollado said.

Forty minutes out of Hermosillo, Draper called approach control and notified them of their departure point and destination. Approaching the airport Draper slipped into the landing pattern and when they were on the taxiway the tower directed them to the Customs area. After parking they walked into the Customs and Immigration building. A visit with the *Commandante* resulted in a sixty dollar landing and entry fee which Draper paid without question. A blizzard of paperwork followed including filling out forms and obtaining stamps. In all though, the process was uneventful and took less than an hour. Customs didn't seem interested in searching either their luggage or the 182 for which Draper was grateful. Their guns and other helpful hardware were secured in a specially built compartment in the 182's fuselage that looked riveted but could be opened with a special tool.

Draper asked if he had to move the airplane and was told it wasn't necessary. They exited the building into a warm tropical sunny day without a breath of wind. Diego Ferrez waved from a short distance away standing next to a French Peugeot automobile that looked abandoned.

DeCollado's cousin leaned casually on the roof with his arms crossed. "What you think of my new automobile, not bad for *un agricultor pobre, si?*

"Poor farmer, my ass," DeCollado said.

The Peugeot, long since devoid of its original paint, had treadless tires with radiating weather-checks. Part of the side window glass and both sides of the windshield carried spider cracks. Draper thought it best to shoot the wreck and put it out of its misery. Because of his height Draper claimed the front passenger seat while DeCollado folded himself into the back. To both of their surprise it started and ran.

"My home is near San Bartolo about eleven kilometers away. No so far, we'll be there soon."

Draper doubted that watching the dirt road running under his feet. He'd elected to place his left foot on the car's frame while his right rested on the thin remnants of the floorboard. In between there was nothing. The driver's side looked little better covered with several layers of faded once multi-colored linoleum.

Ferrez grinned at Draper and pointed at the open floor saying, "Mexican air conditioning."

Draper directed DeCollado's cousin through a turnstile and into the customs parking lot where the 182 was tied down. Heat waves reflected off the hot asphalt made the one hundred degree air temperature feel hotter than its reading. DeCollado loaded their scant luggage into the Peugeot sweating buckets while Draper exposed a large aluminum case sequestered in his special compartment.

"That what I think it is?" Diego said.

"Yup," Draper said, "If we're going to hunt assholes, we've got to have proper tools."

Chapter Fifteen

Hermosillo, Son, Mexico

The drive to Diego Ferrez' small farm meandered through the eastern half of Hermosillo onto a barely paved roadway following a range of low hills. Sparse vegetation, rugged sandy outcroppings and thorny flora afforded little cover for desert creatures. Draper couldn't help noticing the resemblance between interior Mexico and many parts of the Middle East. Mexico lies roughly on the same parallel above the equator as does Egypt, Libya and many other Middle Eastern countries. Construction favors concrete buildings, flat concrete roofs with protruding rebar and hanging stairways to an uncompleted upper level. It brought to mind long ago memories of similar buildings. Draper closed his eyes and tried to blank out the vision of high stone and mortar walls guarding massive estates. The skeleton homes outside the walls stood dirty, blistering hot and stuffed full of half-starved children sleeping on soiled mattresses and dirt floors. Even Ferrez' car reminded Draper of the Middle East. It wasn't hard to understand how the cartels could recruit drug runners as easily as terrorist groups recruited suicide bombers. Likely the sign-up line extended a considerable distance.

"The government has tried to curtail cartel activities, but murder, corruption and intimidation seem to have an effect. The

161

people are afraid and the military is no help," Ferrez said, his voice saddened, "Those who have tried to resist have either been killed or driven out of the county."

"Aren't you concerned you could be targeted?" Draper said.

"*Si*, it's a worry, but I have an advantage that most don't. I'm an American citizen and I suspect the cartel doesn't want American's murdered unless they can make it look accidental. They are still cautious, but not as much as before."

"Why not?" Draper asked.

"I'm not sure. It's probably because no one cares about a few dead Mexicans. I suppose because it appears the U.S. has enough problems without worrying about us *peons*."

They drove in silence for a couple miles, the Peugeot fishtailing in the loose sand responding to Ferrez' Mario Andretti driving technique. "So how'd you end up an American citizen?" Draper asked.

"My mother went into labor early while she and my father were on a harvest crew across the border. They took her to a hospital in Yuma, Arizona and thanks to your convenient law my parents made sure they got all the paperwork showing I was born in the U.S. Mexico is my country, I've lived here all my life, my wife is Mexican, and all my kids were born here so why would I want to go to the U.S?"

"Land of opportunity?" Draper said.

"Maybe, but my country could be the same if we could get rid of the drugs and all that goes with them. I'm hoping to learn things from you and William."

"You know this is a war and in war people die." Draper emphasized the last word.

"My friends and I are ready for that. Many innocents have already suffered death at the hands of the cartel. What would be different?" Ferrez' words posed a question for which Draper had no answer.

Diego's home included an obviously self-built structure using scavenged materials painted with leftover primary-colored coatings mixed together. The result was a mysterious light-brown hue that tended to mask the building into the surrounding landscape. Despite its questionable beginnings the home itself stood large, cozy and environmentally tight. A tall thick masonry chimney on the north facing side served as winter heat and summer air conditioning.

"Built it all myself," Ferrez said before Draper could ask.

"Nice job," Draper said, admiring the smooth clean plank floor and hand-built kitchen cabinets. Ferrez' wife stood proud in a corner of the room, her hands together at her waist and awaiting introductions. When she smiled, her dark eyes sparkled looking at her husband. Hard work and children had only confirmed her natural beauty and Draper guessed her age at mid to late thirties.

"Welcome, *Señores*," she said.

"Maria, you know my cousin, William and this is his friend Charlie Draper," Ferrez said.

The woman stepped forward and on tiptoes kissed DeCollado.

When she stepped back she nodded to Draper, "Señor Draper," Maria said.

"Call me, Charlie, please."

Dinner consisted of enchiladas with rice and refried beans on the side. The conversation ran light and casual. After consuming enough to stagger a water buffalo, the men moved outside into the cool evening.

"I suggest we hide your special case in the barn for safe keeping," Ferrez suggested.

"Good idea, but first I need to retrieve my Glock. I feel like an antelope that stumbled into a lion's den without it" Draper said.

"I must remind you to be careful. Possession of firearms carries stiff penalties in Mexico unless you are a cartel member and even they keep them under wraps unless making a point," Ferrez said.

When the silver case found a home under a pile of loose straw and he had the Glock tucked into a shoulder rig under his shirt, Draper relaxed a little until the barn door creaked and a man stepped into the dimly lit barn. His hand went automatically for the pistol.

"Relax, it's my friends," Ferrez cautioned. "They've come to meet you both."

Over the next half-hour five more men slipped quietly into the barn to join the expanding group. Each was introduced and took a place on a circle of rough benches in the barn's walkway.

Draper stood leaning against a six by six roof pillar assessing the new arrivals. As a group they were all middle-aged, dressed in rough work clothes and sturdy boots, all serious, but talking amongst themselves. The last one in, didn't sit and stood behind the group staring at Draper. His expression questioning, he stood taller and heavier than the others and Draper guessed in a fight he'd be a handful. Draper didn't doubt he could take the man, but realized the possibility he wouldn't come out of it unscathed. Ferrez introduced him as Carlo Escar and the man ignored Draper's outstretched hand.

"Don't mind Carlo, he doesn't like *Americanos*."

Draper thought about a response, but decided to hold his tongue. It hadn't escaped him that without help they weren't likely to succeed. Instead he lowered his hand and stared back until the other man dropped his eyes.

DeCollado did the talking, using Spanish, while Draper watched the various responses from each man. "The cartel sent a hired killer to kill the Sheriff of Ajo County who is a friend of Mr. Draper.. They've also sent *asesinos* to kill Mr. Draper."

"What's the cartel have against this man?" a seated listener asked.

"It's a long story, but suffice it to say, Mr. Draper and I, with help from others, have been a nuisance to cartel activities on more than one occasion. We were able to intercept a sizable drug shipment in Tucson, which made them very angry," DeCollado said.

A number of questions followed, which DeCollado answered. The discussion went on several minutes until Draper stepped away from the pillar, looked directly at Carlos Escar and said "You may not like *Americanos* but I don't much like *gilipollas*."

Silence dropped into the barn like a heavy curtain when Draper called the man an asshole. It took only a second or two for him to react, charging at Draper with his arms outstretched and fists clenched. Using the man's forward motion Draper grabbed one arm, tripped him and chopped him across the back of his neck. By the time the man's face hit the straw covered dirt, the muzzle of Draper's Glock touched his left ear.

"You, my friend are dead, because you didn't think before you attacked," Draper whispered coldly. "Your first lesson is *never underestimate the enemy*."

"And you just passed the test, *mi amigo*. You can let me up now," Escar said in perfect English. "Diego said you were tougher than a Sonoran sidewinder. I had to find out for myself."

Draper didn't move and continued to threaten the man lying face in the dirt, "You are lucky I didn't shoot you."

"Don't I know it," Escar said, holding out his hand. "I'm damned glad to meet a fellow attorney. Harvard Law, '96."

"Take it easy, Charlie, he's okay," Ferrez said.

"If I'd known you were a lawyer I sure as hell would have shot you." Draper said, slipping the Glock back in its holster and accepting the man's hand. "What the hell are you doing here?"

"Same as you, I'm trying to find a solution."

By one a.m., only Draper, DeCollado, Ferrez and Escar were left in the barn. The others had quietly slipped away one by one disappearing into the night. Draper noted there had been no sounds of vehicles either coming or going.

"We've been meeting for almost a year. Our progress has been mostly recon, gathering names of cartel leaders, enforcers, and other players. We have a long list but they are mostly minor players."

"You are doing something, that's a good start," Draper said.

"Yes, but these men are farmers, with families, who know nothing about fighting." Ferrez said.

"What about you?" Draper asked Escar.

"Me? Army Rangers, Desert Storm and Somalia, though mostly many years ago; but I'm still good with weapons and I know how to kill," Escar said.

"Good to know. You stick around us and you may get some new practice."

"I think we should take a tour of town and let you see what goes on in Hermosillo," Ferrez suggested.

They took Escar's vehicle, not because it was any newer or better than the Peugeot, but it was larger and roomier. A four-door Dodge sedan of dubious age, sat sun-faded, on similar bald tires, with body work by a runaway stamp mill. The fenders were rusted through and the floorboards required wood inserts. At one time the paint was canary yellow. Escar lifted the hood and exposed a shiny clean Hemi V-8 looking showroom ready.

"Sweet," Draper said. "If we get in a car chase, at least we know the engine will get away."

"You didn't look at the suspension. It's all new and the body disguises half-inch armor plate that will stop anything under .50 caliber." Escar grinned, proud of his work.

"All right, let's go take a look-see," DeCollado said.

The Dodge purred like a cream-fed kitten, emitting only a slight rumble as it sped down the dirt roadway racing toward Hermosillo. Draper sat shotgun with Ferrez and DeCollado in the back. Ferrez and DeCollado had sawed-off Remington 870's, 12 gauge pumps with the plug removed, loaded with double-aught buckshot in addition to handguns. Between Draper's knees lay his favorite, custom-built M4 chambered in 5.56 NATO. Draper liked the M4 in close quarter situations because of its lighter weight and recoil as compared to the AK-47. It's lighter bullet resulted in increased wounding capability. Most men knocked down with the M4, stayed down. Escar's AK-47 lay between the two men.

Escar drove slowly through deserted streets lit only by an occasional red *burdel* light or a forgotten porch lamp. The town seemed quiet with little movement. As they approached the industrial area, Escar stopped at the top of a small hill overlooking a fenced storage facility.

"This is the activity I was telling you about," Ferrez said. "It started about six weeks ago. The crates are shipped in by sea to *Puerto de guaymas* and then trucked overland to this place."

Draper took out a pair of night-vision binoculars and scanned the area Ferrez indicated. A tall chain-link enclosure surrounded about ten acres filled with large crates, cargo containers, and palleted materials. The open pallets held materials that looked like gears, structural steel pieces and boxes of large bolt fasteners. Draper estimated they were over five hundred yards away which made details problematic. Armed guards patrolled the perimeter indicating the interior contained some value.

"*¿Qué te parece?*" Ferrez said from the back. "What do you think?"

"I think we need to get closer," Draper said, looking at Escar. "How about you and me do a little recon?"

Donning body armor and night vision goggles, Draper and Escar made their way down the hill keeping to the shadows. Draper let Escar lead watching him closely to see if he remembered his Ranger training. Halfway he began to feel more comfortable since there was little doubt the man hadn't forgotten anything. At two hundred yards they stopped and timed the guard's movements to discover a period when both guards were out of sight. They watched for three cycles to ensure they were correct.

"Looks like we have at least five minutes, maybe a little more if we're lucky," Escar whispered. He took a sixteen penny nail out of one pocket and tossed it at the chain-link. The nail bounced off a link with a tiny spark barely noticeable in the dark. "Hmm, electrified," he added.

Carefully timing themselves, they began exploring the fence line and memorizing as much as they could of the materials within. Much of what Draper saw reminded him of common building materials, confirming what they'd suspected. He studied the diamond shaped gear-like materials finally concluding they were in fact segmented cutter head pieces that when bolted together made up a circular head for a boring machine. He stood puzzling over his estimation of the size when Escar touched his shoulder and motioned that they had to drop back into the surrounding vegetation. The two guards returned and stood less than thirty feet away sharing a smoke. Draper and Escar could hear their voices jabbering in Spanish and caught the distinctive odor of marijuana, but neither man dared move. Fifteen minutes dragged by before the guards resumed their routine and finally disappeared again.

"Were they talking about anything interesting?" Draper said.

"No, only about *putas*, though one mentioned the houses were run by a woman."

"That's not unusual, is it?"

"It is in this country."

"How so," Draper asked.

"Mexican society is generally patriarchal, especially where criminal activity is concerned. It's common to have a madam, but the money goes to someone else, usually a man who's the real person in charge."

"You're saying the boss of the cartel here is a woman?"

"That's what it sounded like. The leg-breaker around here is a genuine asshole named Riis, a low-level bad boy and a cold blooded killer. But the real kingpin is Javier Barajas. My understanding is he controls all of Sonora. I'm just not sure where this woman fits in.

"Maybe those two are the ones we should go after. I've heard of Riis, but Barajas is new.

They're cousins, but only by marriage. Watch out for Javier Barajas; he's unpredictable, and he likes to inflict pain. The story is he beat a man half to death for talking to one of his girls and then shot him in cold blood while he was lying on the floor. The *policía* came and took the body away and tried to question the witnesses but no one admitted to seeing a thing. That's what we are up against."

Draper led climbing back up the hill with Escar behind. They carefully picked their way through the thick brush trying not to leave evidence of their presence. They reached the top just before three a.m. The moon had risen to its full height in the sky letting its waning crescent afford enough illumination that the two men didn't need night vision goggles. Both were breathing hard.

"Well?" DeCollado said.

"Didn't find out much except there's a definitely a major construction project planned and there are segments for a cutting wheel, but they don't look big enough," Draper said.

"How big would they have to be?" Escar asked.

"On the plan we saw, the tunnel diameter was over twenty-four feet. The segments down there are not much more than twelve or fourteen.

They climbed into the Dodge and Escar began to pick his way through deserted streets back through Hermosillo toward the Ferrez farm. Conversation settled into silence as the four men withdrew into their thoughts. Draper knew he was tired because he couldn't stop his mind from churning the day's events into a jumbled mess. He tried without success to logically select a reason for the small size of the cutter segments and it refused to come. By the time they reached the farm DeCollado and Ferrez were asleep with Draper close to it. He hoped Escar had enough strength left to get home.

When Escar dropped his passengers off he said, "Meet again tomorrow night?"

"Yes," Draper said, "I need some time to figure out where to go from here."

Draper watched the old Dodge disappear into the night darkness wondering about the driver. He hadn't quite figured the man out as yet, so he reserved judgment. He seemed capable but only time would tell. It was different with DeCollado; they'd worked closely before and they could move together like a precision team; each knowing exactly what the other would do in any given situation. Both knew that the other would kill without hesitation. Not so with a new team member and Draper found it a little disconcerting.

"What do you think of Escar?" Draper said, standing in the Sonoran gloom.

"The surface looks good, but we won't know for sure until we see him in action. Old Apache aphorism, *warrior must look into the eyes of his enemy before he knows where his strength lies.*"

"Hope that isn't too late, Draper said.

"Escar is a man on a mission," Ferrez said. "Carlos and his younger brother were brought up by their grandmother. There was about a ten year difference in their ages. Carlos went to the U.S. sponsored by a scholarship, joined the army and went to Harvard. His brother became a gangbanger and murdered a man when he was sixteen. He's been in a Mexican prison ever since. Carlo doesn't talk about it but I'm sure his goal is to make sure other young boys don't go down the same road. It looks like a losing battle to most of us. The youth of this country are doing drugs and destroying themselves before they even out of their teens. Even the girls cover themselves with gang tats and think it cool." Ferrez shook his head and Draper could see he was having trouble with the words. "I worry about my own kids. Maybe I made a mistake bring them up here."

"If things get too bad let me know, I know a place in the U.S. we can stash them and Maria, too," DeCollado said.

"Thanks, I hope it doesn't come to that." Ferrez said.

Chapter Sixteen

Hermosillo, Son, Mexico

On the following night, the same group arrived at the barn in the hours just before midnight. Escar poked his head in first, dressed in heavy clothing covering body armor. The others came one by one, spacing out their arrivals by ten or fifteen minutes. They were all dressed similarly in dark clothing and body armor. Draper and DeCollado did an inventory of their weapons finding an assortment of antique pieces consisting of mostly revolvers with rusty bores and sloppy actions. The best of the bunch was a Colt Model 1911 in .45 ACP caliber that looked like a range weapon with a half-million round count and all the bluing worn off.

"This piece was a hell of a weapon in its day," Draper said, holding the .45 above is head for all to see. "It would stop angry gorilla if you were brave enough to let him get within fifteen feet. Any further out and you'd have to count on scaring him to death." Draper's humor fell on deaf ears, so he turned to Ferrez, "We need to find these men some decent weapons."

Escar stepped forward setting a small suitcase on the end of one of the benches. "Thought we might, just don't ask where they came from." He looked at Draper and said, "I also have a couple of Uzi's and an AK-47 in my car."

The rest of the night until early dawn included dry-fire practice, stalking the enemy, and weapon maintenance. "Your weapon is your friend," Draper said, "keep it clean, loaded and safe. Practice shooting until you arm feels like it will drop off and then practice more. When you shoot, shoot to kill. A dead enemy can't shoot back. Aim for center body mass and keep firing until he goes down. Practice double tapping, which means every time you pull the trigger on an enemy, do it twice to make sure."

By two a.m. the clicks of dry fire echoed in the barn as the men practiced. Draper watched, his face unreadable, when Ferrez asked, "What do you think?"

"They are willing enough; the true test will come when they face some asshole trying to shoot back."

"Amen to that," Ferrez said.

"What about you?" Draper said. "Think you can kill someone when the decision has to be made in a nanosecond?"

"I think so."

"Work on it until you know. Then consider: what if the enemy is purely evil and deserves killing and if you don't do it they'll keep on destroying innocent lives with impunity?"

"You mean murder?"

"No, I mean killing someone who, because of their actions, deserves to be killed."

"I don't know if I could do that," Ferrez said.

"You need to think about it, because it may come up and you have to decide what you are going to do."

"I don't think I could just shoot someone in cold blood."

"Consider this," Draper said, and told him Gabriella's story. "I have an adopted daughter I found in the desert a year ago She'd escaped after three years in a Mexican *burdel* beginning when she was only fourteen. Do you think I had any hesitation when the opportunity arose to shoot the asshole that put her there?"

Ferrez looked at the dirt mixed with old straw under his feet and drew a small square with his foot before answering, "My oldest girl is just now seventeen. I can see where you probably didn't."

"Diego, these people are not nice folks trying to make a living. They are destroying lives, both here in Mexico and in the U.S. After what they did to Gabriella, I didn't and won't have a single qualm."

At 3 a.m. the barn emptied down to Draper, DeCollado, Ferrez and Escar. They sat in a circle on the rough wooden benches and Ferrez brought out four classes and an open bottle of Tequila. *"Beber a la salud de"* Ferrez said when each man had a full glass, "to our American friends."

Draper opened the door to his sleeping quarters in the barn where he and DeCollado had been lodging, since there was not room in the house. His high-end, multi-function, no glare watch read near ten in the morning. He peered out at a hot sunny day, covered by a cloudless azure sky that seemed to go on forever. The monotony of the weather unchanged, he realized his mouth felt dry as cotton, a bit of a Tequila headache rose between his eyes and his body screamed for coffee.

"Buenos días, Señor Charlie," Maria said when Draper entered the kitchen.

"Good morning, Maria, I sure hope you have some coffee," Draper said.

Maria turned to the young girl beside her and said, *"Café con brandy, rápidamente."* "Sit," she said to Draper.

"This is our daughter, *Calliste*," Maria said when the young girl returned with Draper's coffee.

After the introduction, Maria shooed the young girl out of the room and sat across from Draper. "This thing you do, it is dangerous?" She framed it as a question, but it came across as more of statement.

"Yes, Maria, I'm not going to lie to you. It is very dangerous." Maria Ferrez gazed deep into his soul with beautiful dark eyes Draper found mesmerizing. He felt tested as if she was measuring his worth.

"I only ask one thing and that is to do the best you can to see no harm comes to my Diego. Promise me, and then if something does happen, I will know you tried."

"I will, I promise, and if something goes wrong, William and I will take care of you and the children."

"*¡Gracias, Señor Charlie*, I know you will."

Draper took his second cup back to the barn where DeCollado sat outside looking at the town of Hermosillo in the distance.

"It looks so peaceful basked in the morning light" DeCollado said.

"Had a talk with Maria."

"Thought you might."

"She's concerned and has every right to be. I told her we'd take care of her and the kids, if things went bad."

DeCollado sat silent for a moment. "Got it covered, but I'd say we should make sure that doesn't happen."

After the noon meal, Draper and DeCollado borrowed the Peugeot and drove into town with DeCollado in the driver's seat. They scouted the streets, getting a feel for how it was laid out, what businesses there were and any other activity. They saw nothing overtly suspicious, just a normal Mexican town with mostly small businesses and shoppers milling about. Finally, they drove by the enclosed yard they'd investigated the night before. In daylight, nothing changed. The portion of the yard they could see contained similar materials to what they'd spotted the night before."

"See those cutter segment's?" Draper said.

"So?"

"They're small, too small to cut a tunnel the size we saw on the plans."

"Maybe they've decided to go with a smaller tunnel."

"I suppose that's possible, but why would they? The distance is short; a big tunnel is well within their financial means, they have the manpower and possibly additional financing from the Russians."

"So which variable would be the most likely to change?" DeCollado said.

"I suppose the distance, depending on where the start portal is and we assume the end portal is somewhere on Quinn's place."

"So, let's presume they go with a smaller tunnel, say one the size of a common railroad tunnel; is that feasible?"

Draper didn't answer right away because his mind raced over the possibilities and the probable problems. He silently wished he knew more about engineering such a project. "The biggest problem with a small diameter tunnel is ventilation."

"How so?" DeCollado asked, priming the pump and making Draper think.

"In a small tunnel some interesting things happen. A train moving through a tunnel at high speed pushes the air in the tunnel ahead of it leaving an immense vacuum behind. These forces have dangerous effects on both the tunnel and the train."

"So what do they do in railway and subway tunnels?"

177

"Subway tunnels, especially shallow ones, are fairly easy. Vertical ventilation shafts to the surface release the pressure ahead pushing it up to the outside and the ones behind draw air in to equalize the pressure as the train moves. You remember the famous picture of Marilyn Monroe having her skirt blown up standing on a subway vent grate?"

"Sadly, I do," DeCollado said.

"Railway tunnels use automatic doors at each end to force the air around the train to relieve pressure," Draper continued. "The door ahead keeps the air in the tunnel from being pushed out and creating the vacuum behind the train. The hitch is it requires a large enough tunnel to allow the air to move around the train"

"How much larger would it have to be?"

"Don't know. But I bet we can find out when we get back to the states."

Driving back to the Diego Ferrez farm, DeCollado held the steering wheel silent, his eyes straight ahead telling Draper the man's mind rolled with action scenarios. They were almost back before DeCollado said, "I don't know how or why, but I'd bet my ass there's a smaller tunnel going in somewhere. Think about it; if they had a tunnel into the U.S. similar to a railway tunnel they could move drugs or contraband of any kind with minimal losses and the rewards would be staggering."

"Okay, so tell me why the Russians are here? The cartel could, I suppose use the extra funding, but wouldn't they be giving up a big chunk of their profits?" Draper said.

"It does seem strange, I admit, but why else would they be here?"

"Christ!" Draper said, slapping his forehead with an open hand. "Neither one of us can see the forest for the freaking trees!"

"What?" DeCollado said, twisting toward Draper and hitting a hole in the road that bounced them both into the unpadded ceiling.

"You watch the road and let me do the thinking. It's the engineering! The Russians are providing the engineering!"

"I was waiting to see if you thought of that," DeCollado said, "It took you long enough."

"Yah, right," Draper said, smiling.

"Besides, if you didn't have me to get you thinking, you wouldn't be able to find your way out of a wet paper bag."

Members of what Draper was beginning to think of as the probie patrol, began their nightly entrance early and were all in place by nine thirty. Escar took them through basic hand to hand combat and self-defense before letting them practice as teams. Draper and DeCollado watched without comment. After the teams started practicing, Escar walked over to where the two American's stood.

"I don't know how many will live through a real mission. There isn't enough time to train them right," Escar said.

"We have to be out of Mexico by tomorrow, so it's going to be up to you to get them ready. When we go for real they stay in the background and don't make a move unless we call them in. Diego should be their leader and you, DeCollado and I will do the dirty work. You will be our backup. You don't make a move unless Bill or I get into trouble. Understood?"

"I understand and I'll follow your lead, but I don't have to like it."

"Carlos, I know you're capable, but neither Bill nor I have worked with you before and we don't want to have to worry about you. Let's get through the first sortie and then we'll see."

"Agreed," Escar said. "How long do we have before you come back?"

"Only about a week or two."

***

Gabriella awoke startled. Her heart pounding with fight or flight, gut wrenching fear filling her body; a feeling she hadn't had for almost a year. She lay quiet for several moments, listening, dreading she'd hear something, but only silence ensued. Rising beside the bed, she stood in her night dress feeling for her robe and slipped into it. Her hand went next to the second drawer of her dresser grasping the butt of her 9mm Glock. Walking into the dark living room she held both hands on the gun at her side. The living room lay empty, so she moved to check on Molly. The Sheriff slept and hadn't moved. Gabriella listened to her quiet breathing until she was satisfied nothing disturbed her charge. Tiptoeing across the living room she stopped beside the open front door secured by a locked heavy screen. Again she listened and again there was nothing. She checked the porch as best she could before turning the lock. Pushing on the door, she stopped when she saw movement outside. The Deputies; if not where were they? Suddenly the security screen flew open and a man in dark clothing with a dark mask stepped in holding an automatic weapon. Gabriella stumbled back and tripped, landing on her butt still holding the gun. She didn't know what kind weapon the intruder had, nor did she care. Without a thought the Glock came up and pushing the safety in one smooth move she pulled the trigger twice. The masked gunman grunted, rocked back against the screen and slumped to the floor. Outside, almost at the same instant, automatic gunfire rang out and Gabriella scooted behind Draper's desk. Heart pounding, she waited with the Glock ready.

"Gabriella?" a voice shouted. "It's Deputy Gutierrez. Are you okay?"

"Yes, I'm okay. Come in."

When the Deputy stepped through the door he looked into the barrel of Gabriella's Glock. "Tell me why I shouldn't shoot your ass where you stand, otherwise next week you'll be pushing up daisies like your friend," Gabriella said.

"Easy girl, I just shot the one outside."

"How the hell did this one get by you?" The Glock didn't waver a hair breath.

"I was out on hourly patrol, when I spotted these two clowns coming up on the house. No excuses, I was too far out. I'm glad you are alright."

"Lower your gun, Gabriella, I'll deal with Deputy," Molly said from her bedroom door. She also held a Glock albeit shaky. At almost the same time Deputy Morrison entered still tucking in the shirt of his uniform.

"What the hell?" he said, seeing the body bleeding onto Draper's living room floor.

"You two get outside and make sure the area's secure, I'll call this in. Gabriella, I'll need your gun," Molly said, holding a phone to her ear.

"Not until these two convince me there's no more threat." Gabriella said.

An hour later, Tom Pickett arrived following two more deputies. Draper's front yard looked like a law enforcement convention along with the county coroner's wagon. Another two hours passed before the women were finally alone again with Morrison and Gutierrez. Gabriella convinced Molly to go back to bed, hiding the fact her own nerves raced at peak levels. In her mind's eye she could still see the dark figure in the doorway following the image of a weapon and for many minutes she thought she was going to be sick.

"I'm going out for a looks-see," Morrison growled at Gutierrez, "you stay close to the women."

"Yes, sir," Gutierrez said.

Gabriella couldn't help feeling a little sorry for him, despite the fact he'd almost gotten her and Molly and killed. It was a tactical error she was certain he'd never make again, but one she wasn't ready to forgive just yet.

"I'm really sorry," Gutierrez said, standing at the door.

Gabriella's first instinct was to strike back at the man, but she softened a bit and said, "You'd better be or next time I'll shoot you."

"There won't be a next time," Gutierrez said.

Alone, Gabriella couldn't go back to sleep. Her heart slowed, but it beat far from normal with adrenalin still cursing through her veins. Whenever she closed her eyes she could still see the man in a dark mask. Finally, getting out of bed, she wandered out into the living room avoiding the front door by going into the kitchen. She opened the refrigerator and looked inside. After a moment she realized she didn't know what she was looking for.

"Can't sleep?"

Gabriella jumped; her already runaway emotions at their limit. "God, you scared me," she said, looking at the Sheriff standing in the doorway. "What are you doing up again?"

"I might ask you the same thing. Having a bad time?" Molly stepped forward and put her arm around the younger girl. "Come in the living room, let's talk."

Gabriella tried to choke down her thoughts without success and tears began to flow in rivers. She squeezed her eyes shut tight and let the Sheriff lead her to the couch.

"It's okay, sweetie, let it out, none of this is your fault," Molly said, the front of her pajamas absorbing new wetness.

"God, I thought it was finally over," Gabriella sobbed. "Maybe I could meet someone and they wouldn't know about my past. Now the news media will be digging into it and everyone will know."

"Are we talking about Deputy Gutierrez here?"

"No. Well, maybe someone like him."

"Gabriella, honey, I've only known two men intimately in my life. The first one when I was your age, who dumped me when he found out I wanted to be a cop. The second one you know. He's not perfect, but he makes me happy and that's all that counts. You have lots of time. Don't worry about it. In the meantime you have Charlie and me."

***

Ferrez drove Draper and DeCollado to the airport the next morning through a sleepy Hermosillo only starting to wake up. The morning sun began to invade the darkness leaving long shadows behind the towering Saguaros. Flight plan already in place, the plane fueled and ready, Draper did his preflight walk around while DeCollado loaded baggage. At the end of the runway Draper waited for tower clearance before initiating his takeoff. The 182 jumped forward in response to his forward push on the throttle and shortly they were airborne. The plan Draper and DeCollado decided on was to generally follow Highway 15D threading north toward Nogales. Their decision, based on the assumption that if a tunnel had been started it would be somewhere close to the only major highway in the area, dictated that route.

"What's that?" DeCollado said, indicating an area north of the highway. They'd been in the air about an hour without any indication of new construction.

"Don't know," Draper said, but let's go see."

Draper banked the 182 to the left and let the nose of the plane drift west off their previous course until they were heading a little west by northwest. They both watched as a large lighter-colored area on the ground grew in size in front of them. The plane's altimeter sat at fifty-five hundred feet, enough height, Draper figured, to mask them from inquiring eyes. Both men could see three large dozers, D-8 class or bigger with elevated sprockets pushing scrapers accompanying a couple road graders and an excavator. They appeared to be leveling a spot close to the toe of a small range of mountains running east and west. The mountains themselves, large hills in Draper's mind, were the brush and cactus covered formations typically found in the Sonoran Desert. The activity appeared to cover several acres at the north end of a small valley surrounded by similar mountains.

"There's some big iron down there," DeCollado said, referring to the construction equipment.

"You've got that right," Draper said.

They both studied the activity, watching puffs of black smoke as the dozers pushed dirt filled-scrapers out onto a haul road toward a dump site a short distance away.

"How far you think we are from the border," Draper said. He was sure he knew but wanted DeCollado's confirmation.

"Not over thirty miles, probably a little less," DeCollado said.

"So, as the crow flies, about the same distance to Quinn's place?"

"I would say so. Do you think that's the portal?"

"I'd bet my ass on it."

"Not much there to give up," DeCollado said.

Once past the new construction, Draper corrected his course to take them over Quinn's ranch and eventually into Tucson.

Chapter Seventeen

Southern Arizona

D raper could see his house and the county travel trailer sitting next to it when he turned on final at his packed sand landing strip. He felt glad to be back, though what he'd found in Mexico weighed heavy on his mind. They'd stopped in Tucson long enough to pass customs and top off the fuel tanks before heading for DeCollado's place. Draper flew the last leg home alone, thinking about what they'd discovered in Mexico and his two women. He played with the idea of moving them both up to Henry and Sheila Aguila's secluded home on the reservation. He'd been turned on to the Aguila's by DeCollado and they'd welcomed Draper and his teenaged charge with open arms. The best part was Henry had the finest security system this side of Fort Knox.

Draper touched down and taxied to his Quonset-style hanger. Gabriella and a now vertical Molly waited. He parked on the concrete slab, spinning around so the tail of the 182 faced the hanger doors and shut down the engine. As soon as the prop stopped, Gabriella ran to the door. When Draper stepped out she grabbed him around the neck and buried her face in his chest."

"I'm glad you're back," she murmured.

"I see your mom is up and moving around."

"Taking nourishment, too," Gabriella said into Draper's shirt.

"So what happened?" Draper said. He could tell from Gabriella's greeting and the look on Molly's face that he was about to hear something he wasn't going to like.

"They took another run at us night before last. Gabriella had to shoot one and Brad Gutierrez took care of the other; both dead. Tom called me earlier this morning and they've been identified as a couple of drug enforcers from Tucson," Molly said.

"Shit! I'm sorry Babe," Draper said, tightening his grip on Gabriella, and looking at Molly.

"She needs her Dad. I can wait."

"How are you?" Draper asked.

"Fortunately, I'm still alive, thanks to your daughter. Despite all the excitement, I'm up for a few hours more each day."

They walked to the house with Gabriella still hanging on to Draper and Molly walking on the other side. By the time they were halfway, Draper made up his mind. "I'm going to take you and Gabriella somewhere safe. Some friends of mine have a place on the reservation north of Phoenix. An army couldn't find you up there."

"I can't leave," Molly said. "I've got obligations and I need to get back to work."

"Like hell you do," Draper said, "I happen to know the doctor won't even think of releasing you back to work for another month. Tom Pickett is more than capable of running the department and all the political bullshit you do will just have to wait."

Gabriella turned her head away from Draper's chest and said, "You better do as he says, Mom, he gets really grouchy when his women disobey."

"Don't I know it," Molly said, "I mostly just ignore him."

"Besides, I can't afford a dozen deputies to follow you two around," Draper said, pushing the women toward the house.

It took longer than Draper expected for Molly and Gabriella to ready themselves and when they did he had doubts about the plane's weight limit. He loaded baggage watching Gabriella talking to the young deputy whose name still escaped him. "What's going on there?" Draper said, noticing Molly was watching also.

"Not sure, but I suspect there may be a little spark there. Gabby and I had a talk the other night. It was partly a reaction to the shootings, but she mentioned something I hadn't thought of.

"What?"

"Don't be obtuse, Charlie, she's almost twenty years old. She's thinking about men and having a family someday. I think you need to talk to her when you get the chance. And by that I mean let her talk and you listen. Are you listening?"

"I always listen to you."

"When did that start?" Molly said.

Draper called the Aguila's to make sure they were receptive to company and talked to Sheila. She sounded excited at the prospect of visitors which is what Draper expected. He'd spent under an hour securing the hanger and the house before loading the two women into the 182. Molly chose the back so she could stretch out leaving Gabriella sitting shotgun.

"You should teach me how to fly someday," Gabriella said.

"No better day than today," Draper said, tickled his charge might have an interest in flying.

"You mean it?"

"Certainly, see the wind sock on the hanger?" Draper said. "You always take-off into the wind and today it's blowing from the east, which means we have to taxi down to the other end of the runway. So push the throttle forward until the plane starts to move and steer with your feet"

"What's the wheel do?" Gabriella asked.

"Nothing, until you begin to take off. For now only worry about keeping the nose of the plane pointed at the other end of the runway. The brakes are on the top of the rudder pedals, which also steer the nose gear when you taxi. Draper continued explaining the plane's operational features until they reached the runway end.

"Now I'll turn the plane around until we are lined up with the runway and you can do the takeoff."

"Really?" Gabriella said.

"Nothing to it, first set you flaps at ten percent." Draper showed her how before continuing. "Push the throttle full forward and keep it going straight down the runway. Watch your speed until you get to sixty miles an hour. That's called rotate speed. Then pullback gently on the stick until the nose gear lifts off; then let your speed increase up to ninety as you climb out."

As the plane sped down the runway and started to fly, Draper corrected a slight left wing drop but otherwise Gabriella did an acceptable first-time takeoff.

"Can I open my eyes yet?" Molly said.

"Of course, our girl just did her first takeoff."

"Wow," Gabriella said, "there's a lot to think about."

"Lot's more to learn, also, but you are off to a good start."

Draper called the Prescott FSS, filed a flight plan and set the autopilot when they reached their assigned altitude. For the next hour Molly slept and Draper answered a barrage of questions posed by Gabriella on all aspects of flying until his cell phone rang.

"Draper," he said.

"You've been a busy boy, Charlie," a voice said.

"No more than usual," Draper said.

"We understand you just returned from Mexico," the voice said. Draper wasn't surprised they knew as his former employer had an entire department that did nothing but keep track of former operatives.

"Your intel is accurate, as usual."

"We would like to propose an assignment, if you are interested."

"I'm listening."

"It has come to our attention that you have irritated the Mexican drug lords and they've put a bounty on your head."

"How much?" Draper asked, not interested, but curious.

"Half a mill for one of your ears."

'That much?" Draper said.

"Since you seem to be a target, we thought you might be interested in an assignment to eliminate without prejudice."

"Okay, I'm listening." Trying to gather information, Draper wasn't interested in the agency's problems.

"The head of the Sonoran Cartel is a woman named Marisol Barajas. Don't underestimate her because she's a woman. They don't come any more vicious. She has a kill list longer than your arm."

"The name I had is a Javier Barajas. I assume a relationship."

"You are quite right; Javier is her younger brother, but she's the one in charge. The brother, however, is every bit as dangerous as his sister."

"So, what's the offer," Draper said.

"Half-million, payable on confirmation of her death; an eight by ten glossy would be nice but a newspaper article would do."

"You guys are getting cheap."

"Budget cuts, you know how that works. Are you in?"

"Let me talk to DeCollado and I'll call you back."

"Don't take too long."

"I'll take as long as I need to," Draper said and hung up.

Draper saw Gabriella looking at him. "What was that about?" she said, worry lines spreading from young eyes.

"Just a job offer, Babe, nothing important."

"You forget I've been bull-shitted by the best, Pops."

Draper did forget; this beautiful young lady sitting next to him was a delicate butterfly morphed from the dirty-faced, scruffy-dressed wildcat he'd lassoed in the desert running from cartel bad-asses. "I'm sorry I wasn't there the other night."

"I don't think I've ever been so scared. Before you found me in the desert, I didn't care because I didn't have anything to lose. Death would have been a relief. But, now, it's different. I want a normal life."

Draper watched a tear roll through his adopted daughter's freshly applied make-up leaving a black streak on her face. He wanted to hug her but couldn't because of his seatbelt, so he took her hand. "I'm proud of you, Babe," he said, "I can't promise you that things will always be easy or that it'll turn out perfect, but as long as I'm around I'll make it the best I can."

"Brad Gutierrez told me he was going to ask you if he could call on me."

"No shit! That went out of style fifty years ago. I thought you modern women did whatever you wanted."

"I thought it was kind of nice."

"I'll tell him if he doesn't treat you right, I'll shoot his ass."

"Somehow, I think he knows that already. The real test will be when he finds out my history."

"Your 'history' is nobody's business", Draper said. "You can tell him or not, that's your choice, but if you do and it bothers him, then he isn't worth your time."

Draper made a straight in approach to DeCollado's runway after noting the wind direction indicated by the orange windsock on the hanger. He walked Gabriella through the landing checklist and he was letting her bring the plane in while correcting her as necessary. "You want it to stall just before touchdown," he said.

On the ground, he let her taxi up to DeCollado's hanger. Since there wasn't a runway at their destination, Bill would fly them the rest of the way in his Bell. DeCollado had his chopper sitting outside ready to go. They transferred baggage, pushed the 182 into DeCollado's hanger and climbed into the helicopter.

"You want to sit up front with me?" DeCollado said to Gabriella, "We'll put the old folks in the back where they can't hurt anything."

Draper sat in back next to Molly and when they were belted in, hung his arm over her shoulders. "How are you doing?" he said.

"I'll be glad to get wherever we're going. Don't have much stamina these days."

***

Marisol Barajas screamed at her favorite lieutenant, who she kept in line with a combination of sex, withholding of same and fierce intimidation. Ten years younger than his boss, Pablo Castillo knew in his heart that she would not hesitate to kill him without a second thought if it became expedient to do so. When angry, which had become more often of late, she would belittle, throw any handy object, holler, scream, and drag him into the bedroom for an hour of carnal knowledge which occasionally went on all night. He felt like he was on a merry-go-round without the strength to get off. The woman used her body like a tool and Pablo was acutely aware that he wasn't her only workbench. Along with everyone else, he was also afraid of her. She killed without thinking and more than once he'd been forced to clean up after one of her rages. Her brother Javier, a first-class asshole in his own right, treaded lightly around his sister and Pablo had no doubt she'd kill her brother if circumstances warranted. Trapped in a life he couldn't get out of; not knowing for sure if he wanted out, the one thing he did realize was that it would end with violence.

"*Jodido imbécil!*" the boss yelled, her dark auburn hair highlighted with blonde streaks almost matching the red in her face. "Where the fuck was he?"

"We don't know; his daughter and the Sheriff's girl friend were there alone protected by a couple of county deputies. The girl shot one and one of the deputies got the other. Both are dead."

"Find that asshole Draper and find those women. I want them all dead and I don't care how you do it. Better yet leave their bodies in the street for all to see! No cowboy asshole, I don't care who he is, fucks with my organization and lives. A million *pesos* goes to the one who kills Draper. Now get the hell out of here and get it started. Come back when it's arranged. I'll be waiting."

***

Draper and DeCollado used up two days spending time in Henry Aguila's shop, planning, re-planning, abandoning plans and planning again. In the end they settled on two goals: The first was to hit the Sonora cartel hard by eliminating as many of their upper management, including and especially the Barajas sister/brother team, and as many of their closest associates as possible. The top echelon gone, the Mexican army and the police could probably handle the rest. The second goal was to put a stop to the tunnel, although as Henry suggested the first might make the second unnecessary. Draper hoped he was correct.

He mentioned the offer from Langley to DeCollado and the older man said, "To hell with them, make it a half-million each and we'll consider it. I'm getting old and need a retirement fund."

When Draper called back, his handler accepted the uptick in price without comment which told him they had more than one reason for eliminating the Barajas'. Draper and DeCollado both knew without question that if things went awry there wouldn't be anyone trying to get them out of a Mexican prison.

On the third day, they packed the Bell with everything they would need; a small pile including clothes and not much else other than a side arm and a backup each. They wouldn't be able to take anything more into Mexico since they had to walk part of the way. Neither man wanted a record anywhere of this trip into Mexico. DeCollado called his cousin Diego and made arrangements to be picked up on the Mexican side of Nogales two night's hence. The plan hinged on using the same pathway through the Nogales drainage tunnels they'd used the year before. There'd be no way to know for sure that access was still open until they got there.

"You know this plan borders on crazy," Henry Aguila said, "which is good since they won't be expecting you and it just might work. Who else could possibly be in those drainage tunnels?"

"It could be Border Patrol, smugglers, illegals trying to get to the U.S. or any combination of the bunch. It's like a maze down there," Draper said.

"Very easy to get turned around or lost," DeCollado said, "only crafty Apache able to negotiate white man's tunnel."

"Can't argue that," Draper said.

"Why can't you just let it go, let the authorities take care of it?"Aguila argued.

"You want me and mine to be permanent boarders? I don't think so. What are the authorities going to do? I have enough trouble trying to keep them from arresting me. Besides, I'm fairly certain the cartel will continue to come after us. We did them too much damage in Tucson and they found out my name. Fortunately the Tucson cop they murdered didn't know DeCollado or the other guy with me." Draper knew Henry would take Gabriella in a nanosecond and Molly also, defending them to his last dying breath.

"Just making sure you knew what you were getting into," Henry said.

"We've arranged some help in Mexico. They're green as grass but they want their country back and this might be just the seed to get them started." DeCollado said.

Bill DeCollado fired up the Bell 205 just after dawn the next morning. Draper sat drinking his second cup of coffee watching his friend prepare for the day and thinking about the previous night.

Molly had slipped into his bed still hurting nearly everywhere when she moved, but much improved. She lay quiet in his arms whispering in his ear until falling asleep. In the early morning shadows, Draper had risen trying not to wake his woman, dressed and moved to the maintenance shop to help DeCollado.

"Thought you were going to lie around in bed until noon." he said.

"Considered it," Draper admitted.

"We get back; you should make an honest woman out of that lady."

"You don't have a lot of room to talk, my old friend. Besides, she's the stubborn one."

The first leg of their flight was to DeCollado's place where they exchanged the helicopter for Draper's Cessna and flew it to his home on the desert. Once there, Draper drove out the black Lincoln and hangared the 182.

By late afternoon, Draper parked the Lincoln in one of the tourist parking lots on the U.S. side of the border in Nogales, Arizona. From there, he and DeCollado packed up their needs and walked into the narrow strip of the city that lies along the border. West International, a narrow street lined with older boarded up buildings and closed businesses lay parallel to the border. The street was empty with long shadows darkening the way. Their destination was a one story stucco building that had once been a thriving business but now sat forlorn and deserted. They slipped through the rotting wood fence and stepped into a junk-filled storage yard. The new dark steel border fence stood like a warning sentinel a little over a block away. Draper knew that, as intimidating as it looked, the tall metal barrier only slowed the smuggling of drugs and people temporarily. Draper carried a two foot long piece of iron bar with a short angle bent on one end.

The opposite end had been hammered flat like an oversized straight-blade screwdriver. In the back of the yard, Draper studied a sun-warped and weather-grayed four by four piece of three-quarter plywood which he knew hid a cast-iron manhole cover.

"I don't see any signs of disturbance. This year's crop of weeds look healthy so it doesn't look as if anyone's been through here," Draper said. "You agree?" He knew DeCollado could track a rattlesnake through a herd of nervous cattle and trusted his opinion. A skill the older man had learned as a young boy on the reservation, he'd honed it to a lofty level in the jungles of Southeast Asia.

DeCollado stood silent, studying the ground and the debris surrounding them. The Apache had sharp eyes and wouldn't voice an opinion until there wasn't any doubt. Draper waited knowing not to proceed until his friend cleared it.

"Go ahead and pull the cover," DeCollado said, whispering, yet unhurried even though in just minutes it would be dark.

The sun in Arizona, as Draper knew, didn't set, it crashed, leaving a pitch black world until the moon rose later in the night. They didn't dare use lights which meant they should be in the tunnels before the sun went down. Lifting up the plywood, Draper set it carefully aside trying to make it look as if nothing had moved it. He exposed a round cast manhole cover and the top of a concrete ring. Using the iron bar he inserted the bent end in the lift hole and tugged. The cover, rusted in, didn't move.

"It's stuck, that's a good sign." Draper said. DeCollado handed him a dirt-encrusted wooden six by six about five feet long and Draper bounced it a couple of times on the cover until he could see the cover move. The effort resulted in a muffled noise they both hoped wouldn't travel far. Draper handed the six by six to DeCollado and tried the cover lifter again. This time the heavy cover moved and Draper was able to slide it to one side far enough so they could enter.

Draper dug into his backpack and extracted a personal hazardous gas monitor. DeCollado looked questioning and Draper said, "It's a confined space. We got away with it last time but I picked up a couple of miner's self-rescue packs just in case. The self-rescue packs will give us each twenty minutes to an hour of oxygen."

"What if takes more than an hour to get out fearless leader?" DeCollado whispered.

"Then I guess we're dead."

"I know a couple of women that are going to be pissed if that happens."

Draper went in first, shining a small halogen flashlight in before climbing down the steel rungs the twelve feet to the bottom. DeCollado followed and Draper climbed back up and slid the manhole cover back into place.

The inside of the eight-foot box culvert that formed the drainage tunnels lay dark, damp and filled with a musty combination of decay and wet garbage. The first couple hundred yards led to a cross tunnel flowing ankle-deep in water. They waded through it and continued down a branch tunnel that they knew led to the outfall deep inside Nogales, Son.

"*Hijo de puta!* The words floated through the tunnel coming from further on and Draper and DeCollado stopped dead still and doused their lights. Both listened for several moments and heard nothing more. They moved forward slowly, listening, feeling their way along the tunnel wall until they could smell cigarette smoke. DeCollado touched Draper's arm, a signal to stop. They both peered into the dark looking for the faint glow. When the man sucked in on the cigarette they saw it not five feet away. Draper swung a fist at the lit cigarette, connecting. DeCollado's flashlight came on with the sound of the impact. Draper grabbed the man's head and with both arms shut off his carotid arteries. In seconds he collapsed, his body loose and Draper eased him to the concrete without a sound. Both men knew the stranger would be out for at least a couple of minutes and likely wouldn't remember anything about what happened. By that time they'd be long gone.

"Nice," DeCollado whispered.

"Let's go!" Draper said.

Chapter Eighteen

Sonora, Mexico

It took another hour of feeling their way along, using only one flashlight pointed at the tunnel floor. They passed two more cross tunnels, both with varying amounts of water in them, before they were sure the outfall lay nearby.

Draper couldn't remember the last time the moon looked as good as it did when they stepped onto the concrete apron preventing drainage water from eroding the first couple hundred feet of the outfall. Almost full, the giant globe would make their walk into town easier, yet, at the same time, more dangerous. They rested ten minutes before beginning the long climb up the brush covered hill into Nogales, Son. They both knew they were likely bright white figures on a Border Patrol camera somewhere, but as long as they didn't move closer to the fence, no one would care.

At the top of the hill a few makeshift houses, hand built and barely adequate to shield the occupants, lay surrounded by discarded household junk and garbage. Another image of the Middle East reminded Draper of the sharp contrast between the haves and have-nots. While Nogales, Arizona is a small town, Nogales, Son is a sprawling metropolis of nearly a half-million souls. Dressed so as not to draw attention, Draper and DeCollado walked in an unhurried pace, moving deeper into the city through a maze of shops, dentist offices and eye doctors designed to attract American tourists. Mixed in subtly were cantinas, dance halls and whorehouses. Draper followed DeCollado's lead, not exactly sure where they were to meet Diego Ferrez.

"Hope you know where you are going," Draper teased.

"Apache always knows, only white man get confused in cardboard box."

They followed Fenochio Street south until it became Abelardo L. Rodriguez and turned east toward Highway 15D. A block short of the highway Draper spotted the Peugeot sitting in front of one of the many cantinas populating the street. Draper and DeCollado jaywalked with the crowd across the street and stood a short distance from the car. The Peugeot fit perfectly into the surrounding mix of autos, all ancient, all with questionable body work and multi-colored paint. After a few minutes Carlo Escar stepped out of the Peugeot holding a rolled cigarette and said, *"Ha coinciden, señor?"*

"Sí," DeCollado said, digging in his pocket and retrieving a package of matches. He struck one and held it in a cupped hand.

"Gracias, señor. Podríamos dar a levantar en alguna parte?"

DeCollado turned to Draper and said, "These nice gentlemen are offering us a ride."

"That's good of them," Draper said, looking disinterested and going along with the play.

Draper and DeCollado squeezed into the back of the Peugeot. The limited room in the old French car guaranteed Draper a bloody nose or a black eye from his knees if Ferrez hit any sized chuckhole, a road feature common to Mexican byways.

Draper sat quiet as Ferrez circled the block to merge onto 15D where he sped up heading south toward Hermosillo. "Okay, what was that all about?" he said, his internal alarm sounding.

Escar turned around, his face serious, "There have been a number of innocents killed . It's almost as if the cartels suspect something and are randomly targeting citizens as some sort of intimidation tactic. It's a favorite of theirs. The local police are unable to stop it."

Draper sat silent his mind whirling. "They won't be able to as long as there is no reprisal," he said.

"What do you mean?" Ferrez said, twisting his head around.

"Just drive and listen," Draper said. "You hit a bump and you'll have to bury me."

Escar laughed. "Our American friend does not fit so well in your car, Diego."

"Not my fault he's so big," Diego countered. "I want to know what you're thinking."

"History is full of examples of corrupt societies suppressing the people," Draper said. "In every case either war resulted or the people rose up and forcibly ejected the criminals."

The car sped down Highway 15D with its occupants staring straight ahead for several miles. Draper's words lay unanswered as each man considered the consequences of what he'd said.

"So what does that mean?" Ferrez said, cranking the wheel to avoid a pothole. The highway skirted around the town of Magdalena before meandering on to Santa Ana where Highway 2 branched off to the Northwest.

"Isn't Alter just up that road a ways?" Draper said, trying to remember where everything lay during their flight north and ignoring Ferrez's question for the moment.

"Yes," Escar said, "why?"

"About ten miles north east of Alter there's one hell of a construction project going on. It looks big enough to be a tunnel portal."

"That's what all the materials in Hermosillo are for?" Escar said.

"My guess," Draper said.

"You didn't answer my question," Ferrez said.

"I'm not ignoring you, Diego; I'm trying to formulate an answer that doesn't make me look like some kind of nut case."

"I need to know," Diego said. "Many of us are risking our lives and our families. We hope it isn't for *nada*."

"I'm not going to lie to you, Diego. This is a war, and in war good men and women get horribly injured, maimed, and some lose their lives; that's a fact. Good leaders try to hold it to minimum, but there's no getting around the reality, people die."

Silence ensued again as everyone absorbed Draper's words. He waited to see what they'd say, wondering if he'd misjudged their resolve. He didn't doubt Escar. The man was a different cut; he'd experience the bad parts of the world and came away changed maybe, but far from naive. Diego and his friends were a good deal less sophisticated.

They arrived at the Diego Ferrez farm a little after dark. Maria greeted them with *pollo* fajitas' covered with onion, green and red peppers sizzling hot, topped with sour cream and guacamole, one of Draper's favorites. The mood light, the men, including Escar joked and added brandy to their after dinner coffee. Maria joined them though she declined the brandy.

"I think it would be a good thing for you to talk straight to the men tonight. They will be here after nine to again practice their skills. I think you will be pleased," Ferrez said.

"Diego is right, they have come far," Escar said. "Unfortunately, as in any war, the true test will come when the enemy is shooting back. I think it is time to take them on a real sortie."

The group now expanded to eight, they started to arrive a little after nine. Draper, DeCollado, Ferrez and Escar waited in the barn until the last one poked his head through the door. When they all were seated, Escar stood and addressed them.

"Welcome, *compañeros*, you have made yourselves proud with your efforts these last weeks, but now it's time to test your knowledge. *Señor* Draper has returned and tonight we plan to begin hitting the cartel where it hurts. We will begin slowly at first, like a sidewinder eating the big rat. They'll hardly notice the first bite, and by the time they do, we will have bitten off their head".

The men sat silent, definitely a different group, Draper thought. He could see a touch of fear coupled with common resolve in their eyes. Escar looked at him and said, "*Señor* Draper has a few words to share."

Draper stood, looking over the group, seeing not a collection of helpless farmers, but a tightly knit faction ready to do what was necessary to wrestle their country from the cartels. He was aware it was like swatting flies; for every one you smack, two more show up. To a man they stared back at him, somber, ready and unflinching. It seemed Diego had chosen his friends with care.

"As Carlos has already told you we are going to run a test tonight. The target will be a *casa de putas*. The location has been selected and here's how it will go down. Escar, DeCollado and I will make the initial assault. Once we clear the bodyguards and any resistance, the rest of you will help us clear everyone out. We will confiscate any money, drugs or anything of value. It should be fairly safe by then but if you are threatened, shoot to kill. After everyone is out we will burn it to the ground."

Draper stopped, waiting to see any reaction as Escar reiterated his speech in Spanish. For several moments there was none until finally one man said, "What happens to the money?" Escar repeated the question in English even though Draper caught the man's meaning.

"It all goes to your organization. Mr. DeCollado and I will take none of it. What you do with it is up to you, but I suggest you use it to buy better arms and more equipment."

Draper saw a hint of disbelief and the same man said, "You mean steal it, just to be clear."

"Call it whatever you like, but you should consider it taking back what the cartels have stolen from you and your families, not to mention your grandchildren as well as future generations." Following Escar's translation, Draper saw agreement in the others and the single dissenter appeared to consider his words.

"These men are here to help you take your country back. The cartel consists of criminals who are living large off the youth of this country and mine. They take in more than twenty billion dollars every year. How does that compare to your income? I know it's a lot more than mine," Escar said.

The barn went quiet. "Perhaps Mr. Draper and I ought to let you men discuss it a while." DeCollado said, standing up and walking toward the door. Draper followed without a word.

"What do you think?" DeCollado said when they were outside of earshot of the barn.

"I think they're smart, especially the one that was doing all the talking. I believe they're with us, but it really doesn't matter. If they aren't nothing changes; we just do it alone." Draper said.

After a few long minutes, Escar opened the door and waved them back. Draper entered first and when he stepped into the barn the dissenter stepped forward with his hand out, *"Mi nombre es Felipe Cruz, Le siguen Regreso del infierno, El matador de hombres malos.*

Draper looked at DeCollado who was grinning. "He says they will follow you to hell and back, Slayer of bad men."

Draper took the man's hand and said, *"Gracias, Señor Cruz."*

"They call you that, you know," Escar said.

"It shouldn't be me, it's them." Draper thought about it a moment. "Perhaps we need something like that to rally the people. What if we use it to give a face to their organization, like a symbol or icon; an image that will rally the people against the cartel?"

Escar made the suggestion to Cruz in Spanish. The man seemed to think about it a moment before he said, "I like it. My English not so good to speak, but I understand many words." Cruz said.

"Well, Felipe, we should get along great; your English is way better than my Spanish." Draper said. He turned to Escar and DeCollado and said, "Let's get this group outfitted; we've got work to do."

A few minutes before eleven o'clock, Draper and DeCollado stood across the street from a non-descript three-story building supporting a stucco exterior. The lower story windows were heavily draped on the inside allowing no light through. The second floor windows were bare except for sun weathered pull-down roller shades. Only faint light escaped. The front entrance sat unremarkable and lit by a single crimson bulb. A burley man leaned careless against the stucco next to the door smoking a cigarette.

Escar stood next to Draper and DeCollado in a darkened doorway across the street. "We believe this place is a center for cartel activities in this area of town. The headquarters are on the second floor and there is a fire escape in the back they use for an entrance and escape route."

"You and the rest of the group watch the front. Don't make a move unless you hear from Bill or me. We will secure the top floor and work our way down. If it goes bad, get these guys out of here," Draper said.

"What about you?" Escar asked.

"We'll take care of ourselves. Your job is to join us if we call you or get the hell out if necessary," Draper said.

Without letting Escar answer, Draper and DeCollado crossed the street between cars and entered an alley that led them deep into the mix of buildings. A single bulb at the third floor marked their goal and shed just enough light to see the steps. Draper climbed the steel fire escape first, slowly working his way to the top, stepping near the wall to avoid making sound. When he reached the top floor landing, DeCollado started up. Draper stood at the door looking through dirty glass at two men sitting at a desk drinking. While he waited for DeCollado he withdrew his Glock and screwed on a suppressor.

DeCollado reached the top and touched Draper's back. Draper mouthed, "Ready?" and DeCollado nodded his head to the affirmative. Draper twisted the doorknob, threw the door open and stepped in. The two men, startled by the opening door, looked at the intruders and reached for the guns lying on the desk. Draper shot them both; his Glock barking a sharp snapping sound four times in the room. The door to the lower floor stood closed, and Draper stepped next to it, listening while DeCollado gathered weapons and secured the room.

"So far, so good," Draper whispered. He took out his cell phone and took individual pictures of the two dead men. "Might be useful later."

The top floor consisted of three rooms, two of which appeared to be storage. Other than a quick look Draper and DeCollado ignored the other two and quickly searched the desk and a locked closet. The desk produced the usual pencils, pens, notebooks and two more pistols, both .357 revolvers, chrome plated, and loaded. Draper had to pick the closet door, a process that took less than a minute on a cheap hardware store unit. Inside they found a metal lock box. "Change of plans," Draper said.

"How so?" DeCollado said.

"Let's grab this lock box and go back out. I'd bet this contains the cash. We can take the bottom floor next, take whatever cash there is down there and leave. Prostitution pays the overhead; it's the drugs that make the profit. This will hurt them locally, but do little to stop the operation; simply a good practice run."

"Can't argue that, let's do it." DeCollado said.

They made their way back down the stairway into the alley and followed the building back to the street where the others waited. Drapers mind whirled since he was making this up as he went along, a practice totally foreign to his training and past practice. He had a small, inexperienced, force with minimal training and little going for them except determination. He could only hope that would be enough.

"What happened?" Escar said when they reach him.

"Two dead and a lockbox," Draper said.

"What's in the lockbox?"

"Maybe nothing, but hopefully cash. We've decided on a little change of plans. The top floor is secure, so we take the bottom floor and leave. Neat and clean, no friendly casualties and we get away with whatever we find."

"Let's do it," Escar said.

DeCollado sauntered across the street, hands in his pockets, showing a weaving step, as if he'd been in more than one cantina already. The large man outside the door threw away his cigarette and watched disinterested having already dealt with a crowd of drunks. Draper walked up the opposite side of the street and crossed over, slipping between parked cars and coming up from behind. DeCollado had the man's attention when Draper slipped his arms around his neck and put him to sleep.

"You are getting good at that," DeCollado said.

"Practice makes perfect and I've had a few opportunities of late." He waved at the men across the street while DeCollado applied zip ties. As planned, Escar and two others joined them.

"Follow our lead, be ready but shoot only if threatened. There are likely only one or two bodyguards inside and the proprietor. She's probably as dangerous as the men," Draper said.

When Draper entered the main lobby, he was greeted by a barren room with a few hardback chairs around the perimeter. One rode-hard wingback chair was occupied by a sleeping former bad-ass covered with gang tattoos. Guessing his weight at two-fifty or more and his age pushing sixty, Draper figured guarding a proletarian whorehouse listed as a cartel retirement job. Across the room, a hotel-like counter/desk with cubby-hole cubes for mail behind it provided support for a granite-faced woman with deep-lined cheeks and steely eyes. Her dark hair stripped with more gray than its original color hung straight controlled only by a single white ribbon. Without looking at Draper she said, *"Cien pesos por media hora,"* which he translated to less than ten dollars for a half-hour session. When Draper stuck his still suppressor-mounted Glock under her nose, she didn't flinch, only responding *"Por supuesto, para clientes especiales podemos renunciar al cargo."*

"She says, for you they can forget the charge," DeCollado said, amusement in his voice.

While Draper zip-tied the woman, DeCollado tapped the over-sized guardian's forehead with his pistol. The man's eyes flew open and he sat stock still. "Quiver and you're dead," DeCollado said, handing him a zip tie. "Bet you know what this is for. Put it on your legs." The man complied and DeCollado handed him a second. "Lie face down on the floor and put your hands behind your back; do it nicely and you might live to see tomorrow."

The area secure, DeCollado and Draper searched the office and found an old metal cash box full of Mexican pesos. They struck out on anything else of value and were about to leave when, from down the hall, they both heard a door slam. A gruff voice, with muffled words floated through air followed by a softer pleading one. Draper ducked behind the counter while DeCollado greeted a burly man with Mexican gang tats dragging a young girl by the hair. The man looked at DeCollado and said "¿Qué diablos?"

Even Draper's limited Spanish allowed him to understand "what the hell." He rose up to see the man clawing for a weapon and shot him with his silenced Glock. The Mexican looked surprised and dropped his grip on the girl. He died before he hit the floor. DeCollado went to the girl, now sobbing, while Draper checked the casualty. When he stood, DeCollado had his arm around her looking helpless at Draper.

"So, now what do we do with her?" Draper said.

"Beats the shit out of me," DeCollado said, "you're the expert on rescuing young girls."

"We can't rescue them all."

The girl, mid-teens, Draper guessed, stood straight-backed, dressed in a thread thin pullover nightgown that fell inches short of her knees. Her dark black hair looked wild and in better circumstances would she be considered pretty. "See if you can find her some clothes, we can't take her out like that."

DeCollado spoke to her in Spanish and she indicated down the hall. "I'll go with her and guard the door."

"Hurry it up, we need to get out," Draper said.

DeCollado was back in minutes with the girl dressed in a ragged pair of jeans, a coat over the nightdress and barefoot. "Says she doesn't have any shoes," DeCollado said pushing her out the door with Draper following behind.

When Draper exited behind DeCollado he noticed a poster board sign on the front door, with a picture of a tattooed Mexican outlaw covered by a red circle with a red slash through it. Underneath in script were the words: *El matador de hombres malos.* Draper smiled; Escar had been busy.

Chapter Nineteen

Hermosillo, Son, Mexico

T he trip back to the Ferrez farm required that the young girl ride in the back seat of Diego's Peugeot squeezed in between DeCollado and Escar, neither one of which were small. Draper sat shotgun and when he looked back the girl's eyes looked like a wild animal seeking an escape hole and finding none. It was the same look he'd seen in Gabriella's eyes the night he corralled her in the desert. While that outcome had turned out well, he had doubts about this one.

They pulled up to the Ferrez farm after two a.m. Draper walked back to the old pickup and shook each man's hand. He was between men when he heard DeCollado yell, "Stop!" and he looked to see the girl run barefoot across the Ferrez front yard into a prickly pear cactus. She screamed in pain and stumbled headlong into the sand. DeCollado was on her in seconds, gathering her up and carrying her toward the house with Diego running behind.

"Looks like there's a little complication," Escar said.

"It happens," Draper said, "Nothing we can't handle." He wished he felt as confident as he sounded. "Let's get everyone in the barn for a recap."

Once inside Draper ran through the evening's events. "Just so you know there were three enemy casualties tonight; two on the third

213

floor and one on the first floor." I want you to look at the pictures on my cell and see if you recognize any of them."

"Him I know, he is a Barajas cousin," one of the men said, pointing to the picture of the man who had dragged the girl up to the front desk. "A real asshole named Riis."

"He's probably a procurer," Draper said.

"And what is that?" one of the men asked.

"Someone who finds young girls for illicit purposes, usually around fourteen or fifteen, runaways, girls from broken homes, or other difficult circumstances. I suspect more than a few are from Guatemala, El Salvador, Honduras, or name any Central or South American country. They come looking to get to the U.S. and they're easy picking for a procurer.

"They can't force them to work in the houses, can they?" Draper could tell these men, dedicated as they were about taking back their country, had a level of naivety akin to a liberal socialite.

"They can and they do," Draper said, "Starvation, repeated rape and beating, multiple times a day coupled with forced drug use are usually enough after a week or so. Some don't live through it."

The men stared in stunned silence. "That's only one of the reasons you're here. There are lots more, including murder, kidnapping, combined with the two biggies, drug and human trafficking. Tonight was just a practice run. Every sortie from now on will get harder. We need to use the same weapons the cartel uses; fear and intimidation. To do that we'll have to be tougher, meaner and faster than they are and willing to do whatever it takes to stop them. That means we'll have to kill a few cartel members. The body count tonight was three. Sometimes it'll be more and sometimes less, but it's always an option. Go home and come back the night after next. We'll wait a couple of days before we go again."

Draper stood and watched them file out, somber, eyes at the floor, thinking. He wasn't sure how many would return, but he'd bet on most.

"Tough talk," DeCollado said when they were alone.

"It had to be said."

"No doubt,"

"How's the girl doing?" Draper said.

"Last I saw, she was biting down on a wet rag while Maria pulled out cactus spines out of her feet."

"Both her feet? Damn, that's gotta hurt!"

"I know, I couldn't watch, easier to listen to you talkin' about killing folks," DeCollado said.

***

When she looked out the bedroom window of her forty acre walled estate southwest of Hermosillo, Marisol Barajas could see the deep blue waters of the Sea of Cortiz or *Mar de Cortés* as she knew it and Baja California in the far distance. The scene was one of her few real pleasures and she gazed long and often since it gave her a sense of calm, something she needed more of late. She remembered the trips to the seaside as a young girl with her father. She would run up and down the sandy beach, wade in the warm sea water letting the silt slide between her toes. Those were the good days, before the Mexican army hanged her father. Whenever she closed her eyes she could still see him swinging from a tall Mesquite tree, his feet at last still after many minutes of struggle. The deaths of her cousin, who she didn't particularly like anyway, and a couple of low level no-accounts bothered her little. There was the insult, of course; that would need retribution, a simple matter since anyone would do. They'd just randomly pick an easy target and blame it on this *El matador de hombres malos* person.

Pablo Castillo stood across the room watching his boss. The news he'd brought would normally have resulted in a fit of rage, yet today she stood looking out the window uttering not a sound. For a moment he thought maybe this was the end, that somehow all the money, drugs and sex would disappear, like a dream that seems real when you first wake, but fades with passing time; gone as if it never happened. Castillo was nothing if not practical. He'd squirreled away enough money to live comfortable, quiet on a sunny beach somewhere with a covey of female assistance. That was his plan and had been from the start. All that he'd done, good and especially the bad, was simply his stairway to the dream.

"Pablo," she said to the window, "I want his head. I want him found, executed as slowly as possible and his head displayed in the middle of the marketplace in downtown Hermosillo."

"And it will be, as soon as we find out who he is. Javier says they will turn over every rock in Mexico until they find him."

"Make it quick. Last night's incident is nothing. One day's receipts and a few dead is nothing. It's the principle of it. We can't let them get away with it."

***

Maria came to the barn in early evening where Draper and DeCollado were waiting to see how many of their little army showed up. Draper wasn't entirely sure Diego's wife was pleased with the interruption of their quiet existence. They'd dropped in from a foreign country, uninvited and unexpected, bring along considerable danger. Draper wouldn't be surprised if she wasn't a bit angry, even though Diego has indicated otherwise. Instead, she said, "the girl is awake now, you should talk to her. She is from El Salvador and doesn't speak English so I'll have to interpret for you. She is also very frightened, which is no surprise."

The thought, "Now?" formed in Drapers' mind, but he didn't express it. Maria obviously had something on her mind since her words came across as a statement and not a question. Draper followed her to the house and into a spare room where their new boarder lay on a narrow cot with a colorful quilt pulled tight under her chin.

Maria arranged two chairs, hers next to the girl and Draper's closer to the foot of the bed. She sat, took the girl's hand to reassure her and spoke to her in Spanish. Her dark eyes stared at Draper as if she expected him to hit her. He noticed she had her hair combed and tied with a piece of ribbon; obviously Maria's work and it left him wondering if she'd ever be able to look at any man again without fear and hatred.

"Her name is Charise Frases," Maria said. She and her family were trying to get to the U.S. and they were waylaid by *bandidos.* Her father and mother were murdered and they sold her to the cartel for five hundred *pesos."*

"Fifty dollars for a human life," Draper said, more to himself then to the room.

"Life is cheap in this country, it is unfortunate," Maria said.

"Tell her we are here to help her and anything she can tell us about the cartel would be helpful."

"I told her you where here to help, but I don't think she believes it yet. It would be better if you weren't so big and scary,"

Maria said. She gave Draper a little smirk, which told him she was pulling his leg.

"Can't help what God gave me," Draper said. "Ask her if she heard any names or any other information about the cartel.

The two conversed in Spanish a few minutes while Draper watched the girl's face. In a better situation, with nice clothes and a little makeup and some life in her eyes, Draper realized she would be a quiet beauty he'd expect to draw a respectable crowd of young men. He hoped she'd be able to find it.

"She says they took her to an estate somewhere east of here where she was beaten and raped continuously over several days. She doesn't remember how long because they kept her in a dark room and she lost track of time." Maria's eyes filled with emotion and she hesitated a couple of times trying not to lose control. "There was a woman the men called *la Reina* which means the Queen. The woman's brother was the first to violate her. She called him *Javier*."

"I know those names. Does she know where this place was?" Draper asked.

"They kept her blindfolded when they travelled. She remembers the men said it was east of Hermosillo."

"You tell her we will make sure no one ever touches her again and we are going to punish the men who hurt her," Draper said.

"Already did." Maria looked at Draper with grim determination. "My Diego says you are a hard man, but a good one, Señor Charlie. I believe that. Do what you have to, but be safe. I will take care of this one."

"I know you will," Draper said.

He walked back to the barn with a burning anger in his gut. When he told DeCollado about the conversation with the girl the older man swore. "Those sons-of-bitches, how could they do that? You should tell the others. Let them know what we're doing this for."

"No need. They saw her last night. I think they already guessed," Draper said.

By midnight, Draper learned his confidence in the small army he'd gathered had not been wrong. Not only all eight returned; they brought with them two recruits. One of the two, as tall as Draper and out-weighing him by at least thirty pounds, stood toe to toe staring straight at Draper with challenge in his eyes.

"I'm told you're a tough son of a bitch," he said in broken English.

"I don't play games, friend, back away. It's the only warning you'll get."

"And if I don't?"

Draper hit him, carefully, yet hard enough so that the man dropped like a pole axed steer. He didn't move for several seconds before looking up at his aggressor and rubbing his neck. Offering his hand, Draper waited for the man to recover and decide whether or not to accept the hand. When he did, Draper helped him stand.

"Satisfied?" Draper said.

"*Sí, señor Draper,*" my name is Vicente Mendez."

"Welcome to our little group Vicente Mendez. Next time you challenge me, I won't be as gentle."

"That, *mi jefe*, I believe." Mendez said.

"My name's Charlie."

"*Sí, señor Charlie, eres como ellos dicen, un duro hijo de puta.*"

DeCollado laughed, "He says you are as they say, one tough son of a bitch."

They spent the evening with more training, preparation and coaching. Considering the short time frame they had Draper was pleased. They weren't hardened enough yet, but those that survived a couple of sorties would be, of that Draper had no doubt. Draper also knew casualties were a fact of war, and part of the price of eliminating the cartel's death grip on the nation. He hoped it would be enough for the people to begin demanding change.

Later that night, after the others had returned to their homes, Escar approached Draper. "I know Mendez" he said. "You won't catch him unaware a second time. He's as honest as the day is long and he's also every bit as tough as you."

"Believe me, Carlos, I've already figured that out."

The next night they split the group into two five man teams with Escar and Mendez as team leaders. They decided they had enough manpower to attack the fenced compound holding all the equipment which undoubtedly would end up in the tunnel. Draper didn't have any real proof, other than a gut instinct, but that told him it was an unequivocal truth. Most of the material was palletized, crated or in wooden containers, setting fire to the lot would damage most of it to a point where it would be useless. It wasn't a perfect plan, but since they didn't have explosives it was the best he could fabricate. Escar and his team would eliminate the guards and Mendez would pack in the flammables and start the fires. Draper decided they need to be in and out in less than twenty minutes. Even counting on a slow response from the local fire dispatch and an overconfident cartel, he dared not expect more. His biggest liability lay in his inexperienced army.

At midnight they left the barn, each man armed and ready. During the short drive into Hermosillo, Draper sensed a combination of excitement and fear. They were prepared, but only the night would tell if their training efforts stuck. The plan itself outlined simple; catch the guards when they were separated and furthest from help, disarm them, and secure them physically. Use deadly force only if necessary, but don't hesitate. How well that worked remained to be seen.

Once the guards were eliminated and electrified fence turned off, Mendez and his team would bring in the flammables and begin soaking everything they could find that would burn. They planned on the fifty-foot bare ground space around the inside of the fence to confine the fire to within its borders. Everything hinged on Draper and DeCollado finding and turning off the switches to the electrified fence.

At twelve-forty-five a.m., Draper slipped up behind a small ten by ten building sitting outside the compound. Peering through a dirt-covered window he could see a single guard seated at a desk. When he stepped through the door the guard whirled in surprise and Draper hit him, dropping him to the floor. After securing the man with zip ties he inspected the electrical panels.

"Okay?" DeCollado said from the door way."

"Yeah," Draper said, "typical Mexican electrical work." He looked at a rust-coated service panel, sans the original cover with heavy wires exposed to the world. The two-hundred-ampere Siemens disconnect looked circa 1950 tied to carelessly inserted two-aught aluminum feeders. Draper tripped the breaker off and to be certain unscrewed the line-side lugs so he could pull the wires out. With a cable cutter he cut them off as close to the edge of the box as possible.

A good electrician would be able to reconnect them, but he'd have to work at it.

"Are we good?" DeCollado said.

"Yes," Draper said. "If the guards are secured, let's do it."

By the time Mendez pulled up in his pickup loaded with cans of gasoline and five of the rebels, Draper and DeCollado had the gate open. The men moved through the compound with clockwork precision spreading gasoline on anything flammable. Draper and DeCollado started at the far end lighting the gas-dampened crates and working toward the entrance. In minutes the entire compound blaze lit the night sky. Carlos Escar nailed a freshly printed poster on the door of the gate shack in the last moments before he and his group left. With all the men accounted for, they drove back to the Ferrez farm slow so as to not attract attention. Draper felt confident that tunnel construction would be delayed for some time.

Over the next week, they kept a low profile. Trips into Hermosillo were only routine drives and as few as possible. Draper and DeCollado stayed close to the farm for the first couple of days on the assumption the cartel would be watching for strangers. On the third day after burning the storage facility lot, Escar and Mendez arrived after dark fell for what was supposed to be a short strategy session.

Draper went over the details of the girl from El Salvador's comment on where she'd been taken east of Hermosillo.

"There is a lot of open country out there with many large estates built by the upper class because of its view of the Gulf. Many still live out there. It would be hard to tell one from another without getting up close and personal which would be hard to do undetected," Ferrez said and Draper watched Escar and Mendez agree.

"It would take considerable time to check out each one and the risk would be great," Mendez added. "I don't suppose there's any way the girl could give us more information."

"I don't see how. She's pretty traumatized after all she when through. I guess I could try talking to her again and see if she remembers anything new, but I won't without Maria's permission. She's got a pretty good handle on how the girl is doing and I wouldn't want to risk causing a relapse," Draper said.

"I can tell you from experience that my Maria wouldn't let you within a mile of that young lady if she thought it would further traumatize her, but I will volunteer to broach the question and see what she says," Ferrez said.

"I know your Maria, also," Escar said, "and it's likely, my friends, he will come back with pussy-whip lashes all over him."

Everyone laughed at Ferrez, who only grinned saying, "You are jealous *mi amigos*, my Maria when she wants to makes the punishment worth it many times over."

"Okay, Diego," Draper said, suppressing his vision of Ferrez bearding his lovely spouse, "if you feel up to the risk, give it a try."

Diego was gone only a few minutes and when he returned his smile telegraphed the response. "My Maria says if you come, Charlie, she will let you listen while she talks to the girl, but not to expect much. And she says you are not to harass me or she'll quit cooking."

"None of us believe the last part," Escar said.

Draper went to the house and found Maria in the kitchen with her daughter, *Calliste,* who at no more than seventeen was not much older than the girl in the next room. A mirror image of her mother, she would soon be a heart-stopper. It reinforced Draper's desire to stop the cartel any way he could, because these people deserved better.

"Good evening, *señor* Draper," *Calliste* said, practicing her English.

"Good evening to you," Draper said. "Your English is much better, but you should call me Charlie."

"*Si*, Charlie," *Calliste* said, looking at her mother for approval.

"Charlie would like me to help him talk to our patient, so would you finish dinner for me?" Maria said.

"Of course, *Mamá*," the younger Ferrez replied.

When they were in the hallway, Maria said, teasing, "Ah, they grow up so quickly. Already she likes to admire handsome men," and she poked Draper in the back. "What is it you want to ask?"

"Anything she remembers about the trip to wherever they held her; a road marker, signpost, a house, landmark, anything that would help us find the place she was held."

Draper listened while Maria talked to the young girl. She looked much more aware than she had the last time he'd seen her. Her eyes, though still wary, brightened more, despite looking at Draper with distrust and a little terror. At first she shook her head, saying "*nada, nada*," but Maria kept at it, speaking softly, in a conversational tone, engaging the young woman without pressuring. Draper had to admire her technique; like an experienced inquisitor, she began drawing the girl into the conversation and probing for information. As Maria worked, the girl began to communicate.

After fifteen minutes of rapid Spanish, of which Draper understood less than a half dozen words, Maria's face brightened. "She says when they turned off the paved road there was a sign."

"Big sign, little sign, words, color, anything that could help us find it?" Draper asked.

"She's not sure. The blindfold slipped a little and she could see only than it was a small sign with the name of a place and 4.8 kilometers. She didn't know the place so she can't remember the name other than it contained *Bahía*. She probably means *Bahía de Kino,* a small town on the coast toward *Baja.*"

Draper felt a twinge of elation, not a large one but one nevertheless. At the very least they had a general direction to look, something that they didn't have before. Draper knew, because much of this part of Sonora lacked real definition, finding a single estate in the vast expanse of the desert would mirror sorting sand granules with an excavator. The young girl had given them a starting point, but little else. He walked back to the barn trying to decide what to do with this new bit of information other than wandering aimless.

Chapter Twenty

Sonora, Mexico

Marisol Barajas' anger bordered on livid when she aimed her nine millimeter automatic at Pablo and pulled the trigger. The bullet missed his head by a couple of feet, embedding itself into the ornate mahogany crown molding surrounding the room. Pablo knew, because he stood unharmed and still lived, she intentionally aimed high. It didn't calm his fear however, and his body shuddered. He knew better than to say anything since past experience told him it was best to hold his tongue. This knowledge did little to slow his pounding heart.

She walked toward him following the chrome plated Smith and Wesson automatic she favored, its barrel making small circles around his nose. "Pablo," she cooed, looking at him with deep eyes that mixed cruelty and sexiness in a weird way he found mesmerizing. That same look terrified him deep in his gut. He'd seen hints of it before once or twice, almost as intense but she'd never shot at him. When she pressed the cold barrel alongside his cheek, his bowels weakened and he thought for a moment he was about to meet *el diablo*. He saw the dream, his magic pot-of-gold fading, guarded by female fire-breathing dragon that could easily eat him.

"Pablo," she said again, dragging the first vowel to an aaaah; caressing one cheek with her hand and the other with the nine millimeter, "you will find the ones who did this for me, won't you, Pablo?"

"I will make sure Javier is on it," Pablo said, his voice hoarse.

"My brother is a fucking moron!" Marisol Barajas spat, slamming the automatic into the side of Pablo's face. He felt the front sight bounce off his back molars and blood running onto his chin. He bit his tongue to keep quiet. The cartel Queen walked away, pacing, yelling at him, "Javier couldn't find his ass with both hands if he had two sets! I want you to do it! Find those assholes, this *El matador de hombres malos"* who dares to interfere with our business. The Russians will be extremely unhappy that the tunnel will be delayed. They will demand their money back or our heads. We need to find the perpetrators and stop this now!"

Marisol Barajas stopped. Looking at Pablo she saw the line of blood oozing from his cheek, *"Oh, mi Pablo!* I'm so sorry, did Mamá hurt her baby?" She went to him and kissed him hard before licking the blood off his face. As she worked, she whispered, "You will do this for me, *mi Pablo, sí?* And come back to me when it's arranged and you will be rewarded."

Pablo Castillo left the bedroom/office of Marisol Barajas with trepidation eating at his chest. He'd long ago lost the fear of dying. It was a risk, but an acceptable one, tempered by his dream of riches and pleasure somewhere a long distance from Sonora. He drove into Hermosillo in his last year's BMW sedan. A loaded to the hilt machine, it cost more than the annual income of most Mexican citizens. This fact bothered him not the slightest, since his boss had added it to his regular stipend. He considered Marisol Barajas a silly bitch, spoiled rotten by excess, mean as hell, with the morals of an alley cat and the body of a Greek goddess. He knew that last fact because he'd explored every inch of it.

Castillo began a round of visits to his favorite haunts, the *las cantinas* and *prostíbulos* in particular, looking for information before attempting to locate Marisol's brother, Javier. Both places were the best information source if there was anything to learn. At the third *las cantinas* he chanced onto the guard from the main gate of the storage compound. The man, still dressed in his uniform, sitting three tequilas passed sobriety, had raised his captors to giants with weapons of mass destruction. Likely he'd been asleep and hadn't seen a thing, but Castillo decided it was worth a try. He flashed a red hundred peso note under the guard's nose. "Describe this giant man to me, *mi amigo*; do a good job and this note is yours."

Sí, señor, I saw him for only a short time before he hit me with a large club. My neck is still sore"

"What did you see?"

"He was an americano, very big. *Fui golpeado por un americano muy grande*"

"Was he alone?" Did you see anyone else?

"Maybe, it was very dark."

"Did you see anyone else or not?" Castillo began to lose patience.

"*Sí, tal vez un viejo mexicano?*"

"How much older was this Mexican?"

"Maybe sixty," the guard said, eying the hundred peso note.

Pablo Castillo wasn't sure it was worth it, but he gave the man the note. It was only a hundred pesos and there were plenty more where that one came from. He now knew he was looking for an *americano*, probably not giant-sized, but likely over six feet. In Hermosillo, such a man would stand out and cause talk. An hour later, minutes before the cantinas began to close, Castillo stopped at a popular place and was conversing with the owner, a heavy-set bearded man whom he knew well.

Castillo ordered a shot and dropped a five hundred peso note on the bar. "I'm looking for an *americano, muy grande,* what have you heard?"

"Just tonight, several *hombres,* they whisper between themselves but I heard one say the raid on the storage compound was led by a *norteamericano, gringo, hombre blanco.*"

"A white man?" Castillo said,

"*Sí, amigo mío, un hombre blanco.*"

Castillo pushed the note toward the owner who slid it off the bar top and into his pocket like an expert. "*Gracias, mi amigo, has sido de gran ayuda.* You have been a big help. Let me know if you hear anything else or see this white American. I would be very appreciative."

Pablo Castillo's next stop was a visit to the *jefe de plaza* or the local elected official who ran all things political for the cartel. Ramón Gómez González was born in a shack north of town and scratched his way into cartel favor at the tender age of fourteen by shooting his father who, in a drunken rage, beat his mother to death. Ramón emptied the revolver putting the last bullet in the man's head at close range for good measure. By sixteen he graduated to cartel shooter and never looked back. At thirty-one Ramón retired from active killing and took up politics since it left him more time to sample tequila and friendly *puta.* As Chief of Security and Enforcer or *jefe de plaza* in the town, Ramón, defying tradition, adopted his mother's last name instead of his father's for obvious reasons and went by Ramón González. Castillo knew González from childhood when they'd played in the streets together. At ten they were accomplished thieves developing a street-gang comradeship that lasted into adulthood. His official office sat on the top floor of a three-story cantina/*burdel* which Castillo considered akin to building a fox den above a chicken coop.

The third-floor office door locked, Castillo beat on the thick oak with his fist and hollered, "Ramón! Open the damned door; I need to talk to you!"

It took several minutes before González answered, pulling the door open a bare six inches. "What the hell..." followed by, "Ah, *mi amigo*, I am busy right now; go down and have a couple of tequila's on me and I will join you *en un momento*."

"Now, Ramón! Get rid of the *puta*, we have business to discuss and I don't want any listeners." Castillo pushed hard on the door, forcing his old friend to stagger back. "And put on your pants, for Christ sake!"

"Okay, okay, Pablo, you're so serious, *¿qué pasa?*

"Just do it quick. I don't have time to stand here all night."

González returned to the room shirtless but buttoning his pants while pushing a young girl wrapped in a bed sheet ahead of him. Castillo guessed she had nothing on underneath because as she passed him she starred at the floor, never raising her eyes. Lord, they get younger every year, he thought; or was he just getting older?

When the door slammed shut, González turned, his face dark, saying, "What the fuck was so damned important, that it couldn't wait an hour?

"There's an American in town causing trouble. The people are calling him *El matador de hombres malos,* they think he's some kind of savior," Castillo said.

"You mean the destruction of our equipment for the tunnel?"

"Yes, he's apparently recruited some locals to help. One man couldn't have pulled off that raid by himself."

"Where would he find such fools? We have them scared of their own shadows," González said.

"That's what I want you to find out." The Russians will not be happy with the delay."

"What's the big deal? We move tons of drugs across the U.S. border. The miniscule amount the Border Patrol catches is a cost of doing business, a percentage of the total hardly worth worrying about."

"That's not why the Russian's want a tunnel."

"If it's not for drug and human smuggling, then what is it for?" González said.

"There is no doubt the tunnel would allow us to substantially increase our flow, but it won't increase the market. The Russians have bigger ideas. I don't know all the details, but they have plans to destabilize U.S. economy with a variety of methods not the least of which might involve so-called 'dirty bombs'. The tunnel would be a clean way of transporting such a weapon into the U.S. undetected. Why do you think we flood the U.S. with immigrants from every country south of the border? It's to drag their economy down and create a larger market for drugs."

"So, what do you want me to do?" González said.

"Ramón, *mi viejo amigo*, you must help me find this *americano*." Talk to all your contacts and tell them I will pay *cinco mil pesos,* to the one who brings information about his name or whereabouts. That's nearly five hundred American dollars"

"Whoa, that's a bundle; I may try to collect that myself."

"You won't have to; that's over and above the five thousand American we will pay you," Castillo said.

"I will start immediately," González said, "I should have an answer within a week or less."

"Make it days, though I know it won't be tonight. The minute I leave you will be downstairs dragging that girl back up here."

"Ah, *mi amigo*, you know me well, but a man must have his pleasures."

***

The girl didn't go back downstairs as she was instructed. She knew she was risking a severe beating if caught, but stood instead outside the oak door with her ear against the wood. She had no trouble hearing and caught every word after 'there's an American in town causing trouble.' Alivia Lopez at fifteen had been looking for a way out for months. So far her efforts had resulted in savage beatings, and little else. Her face unmarked because the cartel didn't want to lower her earning ability, she hurt almost everywhere else. The last time she'd endured chest pain from obviously untreated broken ribs. Every breath sent sharp flashes of pain rumbling through her chest for nearly six weeks. The beatings did little to dampen her resolve. She was going to get out or die in the attempt. Her heart beat rose as she stood on the stairs clutching the dirty sheet around her and memorizing everything she heard. When it sounded as if the meeting was over, Alivia bounded down the stairs and dashed for her room. When the door to her room closed she leaned against it amazed that she hadn't been caught. After her breathing slowed she slipped into bed and tried to sleep, knowing she would soon be interrupted.

Draper and DeCollado agreed that a day or two of quiet would leave the cartel wondering what was next and a little off balance. The men came and practiced in the barn each night but other than increase the intensity of their training, they did nothing for two nights. Draper spent the time pacing, his mind roaring in many directions without coming to any conclusions. His sleep ranged from shallow to nonexistent, his mind analyzing recent events. He tried concocting a scenario where they could do some real damage to the cartel without endangering his simple army. He lay wide awake at four a.m. on the third morning when Diego Ferrez pushed the sliding barn door aside. Draper's hand immediate reaction was for his Glock, gripping it tight before he realized it was his host with one of the co-conspirators. Draper sat up and greeted the two, wondering if something was wrong.

"Sorry to wake you up, but Manuel has a problem which may have some bearing on our little war," Ferrez said.

Draper knew the man beside Ferrez to be a competent soldier and fast learner. Given time and considerable more experience, he would likely become a leader in any resistance force that developed out of their efforts. He was also a damn good shot, a talent learned from childhood necessity. His name was Manuel Hernandez and Draper liked him. "So what's so important you have to wake me up at four in the morning," Draper said.

"It shames me to tell you, but my seventeen-year-old son, Jesus, came to me this morning and confessed he had visited a *burdel* this night," Hernandez said.

"Not as if that should come as a surprise, my friend, given the availability in this country," Draper said.

"It was not his first time. Apparently, he has formed a relationship with one of the girls and wants to know how to get her out of there." Hernandez hung his head, obviously shamed by his son's actions. "I would not bother you with this matter except my son says she told him she overheard the *jefe de plaza* say there was an *Americano* causing problems and they were looking for him. I think that is you, *señor Draper*."

"What's a *jefe de plaza*," Draper asked.

"He is the political head of the area, kind of a Chief of Security or law enforcer and a very bad man. His name is Ramón González *señor*. He is one who will kill without hesitation, because he knows he can get away with it."

"Can you bring your son here?" Draper said.

"He is just outside, I will bring him."

Hernandez's son stood tall for a Hispanic male. He filled the air almost half a head more than his father and bulkier. Draper didn't have any doubt the kid was a favorite of the local girls. He cultivated a hint of facial hair and sported a laced tattoo on one arm. His eyes shone strong tempered by a sheepish smile that made Draper like him right away. Draper guessed that if he hit the kid, it wouldn't matter how hard, he'd fight back to his last breath. As he did with everyone he met, Draper tucked that little bit of information away for future use.

"So, you've been banging the *putas*, huh," Draper said, teasing to see what the kid would do. He got the reaction he expected.

Hernandez's son swung a roundhouse fist that took forever to reach its intended target. Draper stopped it midway and swung him into a hammer lock with his other arm underneath the kid's chin in a choke hold. "Don't struggle, Jesus," Draper said, "Just so you know I could kill you in an instant if it became necessary. I had to test you because if I'm going to help you, I have to trust you implicitly, with no doubts, *comprender?*

DeCollado repeated Draper's words in Spanish before the kid said, "*Sí.* Let me go *señor*, I speak a little English."

When Draper released him, he stepped back defensive, in case the kid wasn't done. Instead, Jesus turned and held out his hand. "My father said you were a good man and tough. He didn't lie, and I'm glad because I need your help."

"So, tell me about it, son," Draper said.

"It started a few months ago. Some friends and I were sharing a bit of tequila and on a dare we went to the *burdel*. I met this girl, she was very young, much younger than I expected. I was just going to talk to her."

Draper wasn't sure that last wasn't for his father's benefit, but said, "We don't need explicit details, Jesus, just facts."

"I touched her, because she looked so scared and she cried out. When I asked her what was wrong she said the *jefe de plaza* had beat her. She had huge bruises on her back and it hurt very bad when she took a breath." Jesus looked at Draper as if expecting a response.

"Go on, we need to know it all," Draper said.

"I went out and paid for the whole night so no one else would bother her. We talked until morning. You wouldn't believe what she told me."

"Yes, I would," Draper said. "I can almost tell you most of it."

"Can you help me get her out of there, soon?"

"We can try, but you must understand it could get her killed."

"I don't know that it matters. She risks death every day and she told me it would be preferable. I've been going back as often as I can and paying for the night, but I'm running out of money. That is why I decided to tell my father."

"Listen, Jesus, give me some time to come up with a plan. You say this guy is the boss man, right?"

"Yes, he has an office upstairs in the *burdel.*"

"Excellent! We might be able to work with that information." Draper's mind filled with possibilities yet one fact worried him. They were looking for an American. He wondered how they knew. The one thing it told him was they didn't have much time before Diego's family would be at risk.

By mid-morning Draper had formulated a plan. He and DeCollado went over it bit by bit, changing the scenario slightly here and there to minimize risk. They both knew it would also require a bushel of luck as well. Late in the afternoon they notified the troops to come prepared that evening. Ferrez called the Hernandez home and requested both he and his son come early. They arrived shortly after seven that evening.

"Manuel, I'm going to ask you if you are okay with letting your son participate in tonight's activities. I wouldn't normally consider it, but we don't know which girl and there is too much danger involved in one of us trying to search for her during any kind of firefight."

"What's your plan?" Manuel Hernandez asked.

"Jesus goes in first and buys time with the girl."

"Her name is Alivia Lopez, she's not just 'the girl'" Jesus Hernandez said, looking a Draper with defiant eyes.

"You're right, Jesus, my apologies. Jesus goes in first and secures Alivia Lopez. DeCollado and I follow and secure the front of the *burdel*. Then Jesus brings Alivia out and takes her back here to the barn where they wait until we return; questions?"

"I have no money," Jesus Hernandez said.

Draper nodded at DeCollado, "We can take care of that."

"Anything else?" When silence ensued, Draper looked directly at Jesus. "You, young man, understand this; you go in and bring Alivia out when we tell you to, you take her to your father's vehicle, drive straight out here and wait for us to return. No heroics, no questions, no nothing; understood?"

"Yes, sir, I thank you for doing this."

"Save your thanks for later when we have her safe. There are no guarantees here. And keep your fucking head down. I'll kick the shit out of you if you do something stupid."

"I need to go early, so I can pay for the night before she gets busy," Jesus said.

"No," his father said, "that is too risky."

Jesus put his hand on his father's shoulder, "I'll be fine, *mi padre, señor* Draper is right. Besides, I'll need time to convince her. She'll be terrified."

Jesus Hernandez left at seven-thirty, a half hour before the rest of Draper's little army began to drift in. He took his father's battered old Honda Civic, leaving the older man nervous as a cat pacing in a cage. Draper felt his pain, knowing it wasn't easy sending a son into harm's way untested and untrained. He wished there could have been another option, but both he and DeCollado agreed there weren't any that didn't expose everyone to more risk.

"You look worried, my friend," DeCollado said.

"I am. We're depending a lot on poorly trained troops with very little intel. I hope we don't find ourselves in a real firefight. I'm not convinced the outcome would be what we want. Am I wrong to send a snot-nosed kid into the lion's den?"

"No. I think the kid's up to it," DeCollado said.

"I guess we'll see."

Chapter Twenty-one

Sonora, Mexico

Gathered in the alley behind the *jefe de plaza* headquarters, Escar and Mendez had already briefed everyone on the detail of its layout. The building, larger in size by double than their first target, the building sat stuccoed, whitewashed, and blow-sand eroded at the end of a winding street terminated by a cul-de-sac filled with parked cars. The first floor housed a bustling cantina floating music onto the street with matching revelry sounds. Draper hoped the noise would cover any disturbance. The front entrance to the second floor *burdel* lay inside the cantina at a stairwell to an upstairs balcony. It was guarded by two cartel gorillas armed with illegal AK-47s.

Similar to their first target, the back supported a steel fire escape stairway used to transport their illegal wares in or out. These stairs, also guarded, led up the side of the building to service each of the upper two floors. The back of the cantina had a double door entrance and a small loading dock. There were no outside handles meaning it could only be opened from the inside.

Draper and DeCollado walked up to the two guards and asked for cigarettes. Draper held his suppressor-fitted Glock behind his right hip and when the men started searching for smokes, he shot them both.

Without hesitation Draper started up the stairs with DeCollado close behind. They knew the men behind them would stash the bodies. Draper's first concern was to get Jesus Hernandez and the girl out. At the second floor landing he tried the door and found it locked.

"Shit," he mouthed at DeCollado, "these assholes don't trust anyone."

"Shut up and pick the damn thing," DeCollado hissed.

The lock was an old and worn from years of use model that Draper had open in a few seconds. They stepped into a dimly lit hallway presenting a row of closed doors on both sides.

"The kid said to look for room number twelve," Draper whispered.

They found it in seconds and DeCollado tapped on the door while Draper stood lookout. The door opened a crack and Jesus Hernandez said, "Come in."

Inside the room with the door closed, Draper could see Alivia Lopez standing behind Jesus, her eyes a wide combination of excitement and sheer terror. Medium height, maybe five-five or six, emaciated and wasted, she looked to Draper like the prisoners he'd seen in Southeast Asia. Her facial features were sunken and fear painted her face like a mask. She wore a plain cotton dress hanging desperate from sunken shoulders. Draper suppressed an urge to go back and shoot the two guards in the alley again.

"Alivia, these are the men I was telling you about. They are here to get you out," Jesus said.

The young woman began a silent cry, tears rolling down her white cheeks in small rivers while she bit her thin lips. Jesus put his arm around her and said, "It will be over soon in just a little longer. These men will protect us."

Draper checked the hallway and finding it clear, waved the two kids out and pushed them toward the outside stairway. When they got to the bottom, the older Hernandez looked relieved when he greeted them both.

"Get them to hell out of here, Manuel, take them to the barn and wait for us." Draper said.

Draper turned to DeCollado and said, "Round two, *mi amigo*, let's go kick some ass!"

They climbed the stairway again, this time with Escar and Mendez following with two others of the gang. They left the rest in the alley to guarantee a secure escape route. Mendez and two others reentered the second floor prepared to empty the rooms and take out the two guards in the cantina. They checked cell phones to coordinate their attack. Draper, DeCollado, and Escar climbed to the third floor. The first task was to find and take out the *jefe de plaza*.

Again, the lock proved to be a simple pick job and Draper opened the door slow expecting noise. There was a slight squeak, almost indiscernible given the revelry below. He stepped in, scanned the room and saw a large ornate desk, filing cabinets, closets, piles of cardboard boxes in one corner and an open door into a second room. Draper slipped across the floor and followed his silenced Glock through the door.

The woman saw him first, naked, sitting astraddle of a man in mid-coitus. She screamed and dived toward the floor in a flurry of flesh and bedclothes. The man's reaction was different. He scooted up against the headboard and looked at Draper with hate-filled eyes. "*Usted nunca saldrá de este edificio vivo, idiota.*"

"He says you will never leave this building alive," DeCollado said behind Draper.

"I guess we'll see about that," Draper said, "keep your hands were I can see them or you will die before I do."

DeCollado translated and the man's hand reached under a pillow and when Draper double-tapped him the woman screamed again.

DeCollado stepped across the room, pressed his pistol against her head and growled, *"gritar de nuevo y vas a morir hoy."*

"Por favor, señor, déjeme ir," the woman pleaded.

"Vístete." DeCollado said.

"What?" Draper said.

"I told her if she screamed again I'd shoot her, then she pleaded for us to let her go and I told her to get dressed."

"You're such a suave son-of-a-bitch," Draper said.

"I try," DeCollado said.

"When she's finished dressing, tie her to the bed while we search the place. I'll go start."

Draper signaled Escar to join them, called the cell number and said, "Go!"

Draper began a systematic search of the upper floor, starting with the desk. While the desk itself, a beautifully constructed mahogany piece with intricate carved drawer fronts and trim that time had aged to a deep, darkened color that seemed to glow was intriguing, its contents were not. Draper moved on to a couple of closets finding little of interest. He discovered a stairway down to the second floor.

"Check that stairway out and make sure it's secure and see if Mendez is okay," Draper said. Escar nodded and started down.

Draper was about to continue searching when he heard a sharp crack of a small caliber pistol followed closely by DeCollado's voice, "You goddamn bitch!"

242

Draper had his Glock out before he made half the distance to the bedroom door. The woman, now half-dressed was on her knees scrambling for a small automatic in a corner. DeCollado was on the floor bleeding from an arm wound yelling in pain, "Watch her, she's got a gun!"

When Draper stepped into the room she had it in her hand and was coming around. He double tapped her and dropped her dead. Watching for movement, he stepped to her body and retrieved a tiny .25 caliber Colt automatic.

"You okay, Bill?" Draper said with his Glock still pointed at the woman.

"No, Goddamn it, the bitch shot me," DeCollado said.

"Let me see," Draper said, inspecting the wound. The bullet had passed through DeCollado's upper arm exiting out the back and embedding itself in the far wall. "I think you'll live but that arm's going to be sore as hell for a day or two."

"I must be getting old," DeCollado said, "I should have checked her clothes."

"Forget it; you'll have plenty of time to beat yourself up later. Right now we need to finish searching this place and get the hell out." Draper tore a strip from the bed sheet and wrapped the wound. "Not very sanitary, but it'll keep you from bleeding all over the place."

"Son-of-a-bitch hurts," DeCollado said.

"Don't doubt it," Draper said. You're lucky it wasn't something bigger."

"Goddamn, bitch!" DeCollado said, again.

After Draper bandaged the wound he made DeCollado sit at the desk while he finished the search. It puzzled him that there was nothing of interest anywhere he looked. He stood in the last room, studying it trying to figure out why it didn't look right.

"What's behind the picture?" DeCollado said behind him.

"I don't know, never looked."

"Seems a strange location for a picture that big, doesn't it?"

"Yeah, it does." Draper walked across the room and picked the picture off the wall and set it on the floor. Behind it was a four by four foot oak door with sturdy hinges and a combination lock on it. "Need a crowbar," Draper said.

"Why not just pull the hinge pins."

"There's that," Draper agreed. "There's tool kit in one of the closets in the other room."

DeCollado returned carrying a small hammer and a punch. "Couldn't bring the whole kit; you know I'm wounded right?"

"Forgot that," Draper said, while driving the pins out of the hinges. When he was done he used the claw part of the hammer to pry the door out of its jamb. The door fell away and hung on the lock hasp. Looking inside Draper said, "Holy shit!" to no one in particular.

"That is an understatement," DeCollado said.

The compartment, built into the space above the stairwell down to the second floor and about four feet deep stood stacked three-quarters of its height with American one hundred dollar bills.

"How much do you think there is?" DeCollado said.

"I don't know, but if it's all hundreds, it's got to be millions."

Escar entered the room and said, "Everyone's out, the second floor is secure and the boys are cleaning up on the first."

"Go down and bring back two or three if they can spare them, we are going to need some help here," Draper said.

Escar looked at the hole in the wall, seeing its contents for the first time. The stunned look on his face mirrored Draper's response when he first opened the door. "Is that what I think it is?"

"It is," Draper said, "there's enough here to finance a revolution and then some."

Escar returned with Mendez and two of the gang after sending the rest back to the barn. They all looked at the money stunned silence. Draper said, "Grab some of those cardboard boxes out there, dump out any contents and bring them it here and we'll start loading them up."

"What if we load one box with loose bills?" Escar suggested. "You know, cut the bands off."

Draper looked at him and voiced the obvious, "Why?"

"What if we take that box down and dump it on the crowd; like sharing the wealth? We'll shout *El matador de hombres malos* while they are scrambling for cash. We couldn't get any better advertizing."

Draper thought about it. His initial reaction was getting out as soon as possible since they'd been in the building much too long already.

"Idea has merit," DeCollado said. "We get the populace on our side; it'll make the cartel efforts to find us more difficult."

"Do it," Draper said, stuffing packets of bills into a box, "but do it to half the boxes. We'll dump a couple of boxes on the crowd and four or five more on the street of town."

"Why would we want to do that?" Escar said.

"The money is basically worthless. In large bills it's difficult to spend without arousing suspicion, unless..." Draper hesitated, his mind whirling.

"What?" Escar said.

"It's everywhere. Half the town has at least one bill found in the streets.

"Goddamn, you are a devious son-of-a bitch," Escar said, smiling. "I like it."

"Aw, shucks, I didn't know you cared," Draper said.

Escar threw a packet at Draper. "I don't, so don't get any ideas."

"All right, girls, tend to business," DeCollado said. My arm hurts and I'm pissed about it so let's move it."

It took forty minutes to pack up twelve boxes, more time than Draper wanted, yet he could see the benefits. Dumping two boxes into the drunken crowd below the balcony caused a scramble that he was sure would continue long after they left. They took a circuitous route through town throwing out fistfuls of hundred dollar bills until all the loose ones were gone. When they arrived back at the Ferrez barn, they had five remaining boxes which they took into the barn.

"How much do you think we have left?" Escar said.

"Just a wild guess, I'd say, maybe three or four million. I counted about one hundred fifty packets per box at five thousand dollars per packet that's seven hundred-fifty thousand per box, give or take a few thousand bucks," Draper said. "Don't even think about spending a nickel of it, or you'll have both the *policía,* the *militar* and the *carteles* all over us and we'll be lucky to see the light of day again in this century".

The men grumbled, but agreed.

"What happened to all the girls in the house," one of the men asked.

"Some disappeared into the night and some just stayed. Apparently they didn't have anywhere to go," Mendez said.

Draper remained silent. It was a sad fact that he couldn't rescue them all. He had to be content with few and hope that his efforts would change things. His gut told him though, that as long as there was a demand for drugs, the cartels would happily furnish the product.

"Where are Jesus and the girl?" Draper asked looking around the barn and realizing the two were absent.

"My guess," Diego Ferrez said, "is that my blushing bride has found another child to mother."

They piled the money boxes in the hay loft of the barn and covered them with loose hay and sent everyone home as the thin clouds above began to turn crimson with the dawn. When they were alone Ferrez said "Let's go to the house and see if there is anything for breakfast." They walked across the yard in the beginnings of daylight listening to a couple of great horned owls hoot from a nearby mesquite tree. The owls were hunting, searching for small prey for breakfast. Like humans, they had to eat also.

Maria Ferrez's kitchen assailed Draper's senses with aromas of cooking food raising immediate hunger. Alivia Lopez sat next to Jesus Hernandez and across the table from Charise Frases, the young girl from El Salvador. Neither girl spoke despite Jesus' encouragement. Draper couldn't help wondering if either one would recover completely without the kind of internal fire Gabriella had. He hoped so but wasn't going to place any bets on it.

Maria buzzed around DeCollado with soapy water, antiseptic, and gauze bandages. Draper watched thinking his partner might be considering taking a round for team was worth the attention.

***

Pablo Castillo looked down at the body of his friend, Ramón González, the *jefe de plaza* and the woman lying next to him. The *policía* were fumbling around asking questions that defied answers.

Castillo had looked into the empty hole over the stairwell knowing there should have been at least ten million in U.S. currency stashed there. There wasn't. The hole sat empty as the day it was constructed, the door hanging from the padlock hasp. He wondered if that was where the one hundred dollar bills he'd seen floating around the *cantinas* had come from. He thought it likely. It seemed obvious that it was the work of the mysterious American, whose identification now looked difficult. No evidence existed anywhere that his friend had started looking for this man. Castillo slammed his fist into the wall, angry because his friend had let *puta* get in the way of business and knowing he'd have to explain the loss to Marisol Barajas. He kicked himself mentally, angered because all he gained was bruised knuckles and a sore fist.

Castillo walked down the stairs to the *burdel* floor where doors were mostly open and the rooms unused. He had men out trying to round up the women since half of them had disappeared. That part didn't bother him since they could have replacements in place and the revenue stream restored quickly. It was the inconvenience that graveled him. Under his breath he cursed his friend for being an idiot. Standing at the top of the balcony overlooking the cantina floor, Castillo saw Javier Barajas sitting below and moved to the stairs to join him.

"It is not a good thing, Javier," Castillo said.

"Fucker's! Who the hell do they think they are?" Javier Barajas said, his voice a tequila-caused morning growl.

As usual, Castillo thought, Marisol's brother appeared hungover, unwashed, and sloppy-dressed supporting a five-day beard that instead of tough made him look like a juvenile punk. Castillo, confident that in a real fight the younger Barajas wouldn't last past the first punch, would have liked to put the kid out of his misery.

More trouble than he was worth, he lived only because of his sister. Castillo learned early on not to depend on the kid since he could be easily sidetracked by booze or women, and especially both in combination.

"Marisol wants you to find the American who is responsible for these problems and kill him," Castillo said.

"I will find him and kill his ass," Barajas said, "but I need a drink first to clear my head." He grinned at Castillo like they were drinking buddies, which they weren't. "Goddamn my head hurts. We need to start carrying a better quality of tequila."

"What you need is a pot of coffee and some guts," Castillo said, angry because he had to babysit this piece of shit.

"You watch your tongue, asshole; you're nothing but my sister's whore. One word from me and she'll hang you from a mesquite tree by your balls." Barajas said.

Castillo took a moment to control his flaring temper. Realizing it was pointless to antagonize the man, Castillo softened his tone saying, "Come on, Javier, let me help you, together we can find this American asshole and take care of him along with those who dare help him. I tell you what, you work your contacts, talk to everyone you know and find someone who knows who this American is and where he is. Someone has to know; promise them money, women, booze or whatever it takes, but find out whom and where he is. Find out who is helping him."

Castillo stared at this worthless brother of the woman he knew to be the driving force behind local cartel activities and saw the weak link. Realizing it was a dangerous one, he considered shooting the kid if only he could figure out a way to blame the American. There were too many witnesses here, but somewhere, somehow, he determined to find a way, one that would leave him blameless or better yet find a patsy to take the blame. He'd have to work on that.

Chapter Twenty-two

Sonora, Mexico

Draper slumbered until early afternoon trying to recover from the late night. He stared at DeCollado's empty bed, feeling as if he'd overslept. The air in the barn smelled of fresh hay. Outside the temperature had begun to climb into the nineties and in not too many hours would cross the hundred degree mark. Laying his head back, he let his mind trash through the last few days trying to see if they'd accomplished anything or were they just reacting to other events. Sadly, he decided it held a combination of both. He rose, dressed and sauntered toward the house continuing to analyze the previous evening.

Maria stood alone in the kitchen stirring the contents of a large bowl containing a mysterious mixture Draper couldn't identify. She looked both beautiful and domestic. He knew when whatever was in the bowl crossed his tongue his taste buds would jump into overdrive. She smiled at him and said, "Would you like some coffee?"

"Desperately," he said, pulling back a chair and sitting at the table.

Maria brought two cups, setting one in front of Draper and the other across from him. She filled the cups with steaming brew, placed a small pitcher of cream between them and sat across from him. She took a sip from her cup starring at him over the rim."

251

"What?" Draper said.

"I'm curious as to just who you are, Charlie Draper."

"Is that so?"

"Yes. Do you have a woman?"

"I do."

"Tell me about her." Maria said.

"She's a lovely lady who accepts who I am. She doesn't like it necessarily because she's in law enforcement and for some time it mattered, but now, I think she tries to ignore it."

"Kind of like the good outweighs the bad?"

"Something like that, although I'm not sure she believes the scales are balanced."

"More bad than good?"

"Probably, but its closer to even than it used to be. We have an adopted daughter who has made a difference. She's had a lot to do with making us whole."

"Yet you still kill people?"

"If need be. What else would you do with a rabid dog?"

Draper could feel the woman analyzing him, puzzled that it didn't bother him. He'd normally have become defensive, but instead he wanted her to know even if she didn't understand. "Our Gabriella came from the same environment as the two you have here. I didn't have any qualms about killing the one's that put her there, no more than I'd have shooting a rabid animal."

"You feel these ones you kill have no good in them?" Maria said, still looking at him with doe-eyes that seemed to peer into his soul. Draper wondered what she was seeing in there, mystified that he didn't mind her probing.

"No, those who prey on the helpless or indiscriminately destroy lives with drugs and forced prostitution ask for punishment.

252

Sometimes they deserve killing. If I see the need, I accommodate them."

"That's a dark outlook on life, isn't it?"

"Not really, most folks are basically good, hard working and do what they can to make the world better. There aren't too many really bad ones, it just seems like they move around a lot."

"Your woman, what is her name?"

"Molly Sorenson, she's the Sheriff of the county I live in."

"Would you kill for her?"

"If I had too; the cartel tried to kill her and almost succeeded. She's still recuperating. It's part of the reason we're here.

"I ask because I wonder how I'd feel if someone did to my *Calliste* as was done to the other two girls."

"I think, Maria, you already know that answer."

"I believe you are correct, *señor* Charlie."

"How are they doing?" Draper asked. "The other girls, I mean."

"I think about as well as can be expected. They've both been through unimaginable torture. I want to keep them here for as long as possible to give them some stability." Maria said.

"What about *Calliste?* How does she feel about sharing her mother with strangers?"

"You should ask her yourself, I think you would be surprised by the answer."

"No, knowing her mother, I don't think I would be. I would like to talk to both girls though, with your permission and include *Calliste* if you think it would help; sometime soon if possible. I'd like to see if we can get a line on where they were kept early on."

"Are you talking about me? I heard my name," *Calliste* said, stepping into the room.

"I was telling Charlie how you were taking care of our guests," Maria said.

"*Señor* Charlie should talk to them. I think I have them convinced he wants to help."

They were interrupted by the Peugeot pulling into the yard. "I was supposed to tell you that William and my Diego went to town to look around. They didn't want you along because there's no disguising a leopard in sheep pen," Maria said, smiling.

DeCollado and Ferrez walked in followed by Escar who they picked up on the way to town. "So what's going on?" Draper asked.

"Lots," DeCollado said. "We have a price on our head, the *policía* are searching for some mysterious bad guys, though not very actively, since they've collected a considerable amount of U.S. currency in hundred dollar bills. Trying to figure out what to do with it is taking up most of their time."

"It's good to be busy," Draper said.

"Word on the street is the cartel is offering a reward for information about the ones who murdered the *jefe de plaza,*' Ferrez said.

Draper looked at Maria, his mind wondering how much they should discuss their actions while Ferrez' young daughter stood in the room. It didn't take long to find out.

"*Calliste,* maybe you should fetch you friends. Perhaps they should hear this," Maria said as if she read his mind.

"I think so also, *mi madre,* I will bring them."

Draper watched the young Ferrez child, thinking somehow in the last week or so she'd matured in some way. He couldn't put his finger on it but something had changed. She reentered the room easing to the ex-captives into the room as if showing them off. Of the two, Alivia Lopez, bathed, powdered and some rested, still had a deer-in-the-headlights look as if, despite Maria and *Calliste's* best efforts, she expected a hammer to fall. She held onto *Calliste's* hand tight surveying the room fearful. Charise Frases, on the other hand, had begun to blossom. Draper, only exposed to the ingenuousness of young women, could nevertheless see the difference. Her features had developed a blush color and her mouth hinted a smile when she entered the room.

"Have the girls sit across from Mr. Draper next to me," Maria said, gathering her flock.

Draper directed his attention to Charise Frases, originally from El Salvador and the stronger of the two. "Ask her if she remembers anything new about the place she was first kept after the kidnapping," Draper asked.

Maria nodded at Calliste who asked in Spanish and translated the answer. "Charise and Alivia have talked and what they both remember is clouded by fear and blindfolds. Sorry."

"Nothing to be sorry about," Draper said. "Tell them we are protecting them and nothing bad will happen from now on."

Calliste repeated Draper's statement in Spanish. Alivia Lopez, holding tight to the hands of both Calliste and Charise, said *"¿Has matado a Jesús?"* Draper could see tears welling in deep green eyes mixed with hate. He felt it would take a gentle hand and considerable time to erase the memories in her head, if ever. His own anger boiled in his gut, knowing he'd make sure someone would pay. He looked to Calliste for interpretation even though he was sure he knew what she said.

Calliste spoke a few words to the girl before interpreting, "She asked if you had killed Jesus Hernandez. I told her no, that Jesus was safe and well. I think it would help if Jesus could come visit her." She looked at Draper with a furtive smirk and continued, "She would then know that you don't kill everyone."

Draper could see a young version of Maria, smart, judicious beyond her years, and nearly as devious as her mother. He considered it likely Diego had not a prayer of surprising these two.

Over the next week, the training continued and Manuel Hernandez began to bring his son, who always visited Alivia Lopez. Maria told Draper that the young women had begun to heal albeit slow. DeCollado, Escar and Mendez went every day to town separating to different cantinas and drinking with the populous in order to listen to the talk. There was plenty of that and the problem became separating fact from fiction. On the fifth day, DeCollado struck gold.

***

Javier Barajas sat alone in the *Oro Ram Cantina* at ten in the morning, nursing a classic hangover with a second tequila. His head ached just above his eyebrows as if someone had driven a railroad spike into his head. He barely remembered the previous night with only flashes of faces that included at least one unsuccessful session with a *puta*. Faint images told him he probably beat her for his own weakness, but he preferred to think of it as her fault. Barajas stood under five-seven even though he claimed to be five-eight. His pock-marked face, the result of adolescent acne and a lack of personal hygiene, gave him a distorted appearance in contrast to his sister who was two years older and beautiful. Javier hated her. Thinking in his mind that he should be boss, he hadn't yet gathered the courage to challenge her. He thought about it often, plotting her demise by sliding a knife between her breasts and watching surprised fear fall across her face. It irritated him that she stood two inches taller. Inheriting her height from her father rang as a constant reminder of his lower stature. His favorite knife, an eight inch beauty with a mother of pearl handle lay on the table in front of him as he daydreamed of killing his older sibling. At twenty-seven, he'd spent much of his life swilling tequila in the time since his parents died at the expense of any useful endeavor.

"Te invito a una copa, señor?" a voice said.

Barajas looked up at an older Hispanic whose hair hung long, more silver than black, standing six feet tall with hard eyes. The offer of a drink stifled his initial apprehension and company fit into his mood. He needed someone to bitch at, someone who would sit quiet and listen to his rant. He felt he had a lot to rant about.

"Mi nombre es Guillermo," the man said, using the Spanish form of Bill.

"Sit," Barajas said.

"You are Javier Barajas, am I not mistaken?" the stranger said. The man's accent sounded slightly northern, though not overly so, and Barajas overlooked the warning, his pride at being recognized smothering his caution.

"You are head of the Sonora Cartel?" the man asked.

"Yes," Barajas lied, "what is your interest?"

"I'm told you are in need of good shooters."

"And where did you hear that?"

"Word on the street."

"Are you any good?" Barajas took a long swallow of tequila to calm his excitement. Maybe, just maybe this stranger could be his salvation.

"None better."

Barajas felt the tequila burn his throat on the way down landing in his stomach like a ball of fire. The liquid laid gentle warming his insides and bolstering his courage. Javier tried to look mean and only partially succeeded. "I might have a job for you and if you're good enough there will be more work for all the money you can spend."

"I like money," the stranger said.

"Any problem with killing a woman?"

"No more so than a man."

"Well, I have this woman; actually she's my sister, but a big pain in my ass. She's dangerous, so don't underestimate her."

"How dangerous?" the stranger asked.

"She carries a Smith and Wesson nine with her at all times and she knows how to use it."

"I doubt the nine millimeter will help her much against a long distance sniper rifle. She steps one foot out of her house, she's dead. All I need to know is where she lives."

An hour later, Barajas' voice began to slur, and shortly thereafter he slid to the floor in an alcohol-induced coma.

His companion smiled, glanced at the bartender who looked purposefully in a different direction while DeCollado emptied the sleeping man's pockets. He found a U.S. one hundred dollar bill that he placed on the bar top before leaving. The prize was directions to the Barajas estate. On a sheet of plain white paper lay lines scribbled by a drunk bragging about his grand holdings, the information extracted by an accomplished infiltrator.

***

DeCollado walked into the barn in mid-afternoon to find a pacing Draper, frustrated by having to spend days depending on others to move their plan forward.

"Tell me something good," Draper said, grumpy and ornery from a lack of sleep.

"I think it'll make you happy, but I won't tell you unless you ask me nice."

"What?" Draper said, not in the mood for games. "It better be good or I'll shoot you in annoyance; how about that?"

DeCollado grinned at his friend. "How about if I tell you I have the location of the Barajas estate?'

"Then I'd probably be tempted to kiss you instead."

"God, I hope not, you're not my type. Too damn ugly."

"No shit, you've got it."

"I have *mi amigo!*"

"Let me see," Draper said.

DeCollado handed Draper the folded paper. "I found Javier Barajas hung over and trying to cure himself with more booze. The man's a lush. The rumor we'd heard that he was the weakest link is certainly true. The dumb-ass hired me to kill his sister."

"No shit!" Draper studied the paper and it didn't tell him much. "I hope you know where this is."

"I don't, but I'm sure either Carlos Escar or Vicente Mendez will be able to interpret these chicken scratches. That and what he told me should land us right on the Barajas doorstep."

"Did he give you a way to contact him?"

"Of course he did. I went to spy school. They taught a course on how to obtain information called *Fucking Over the Enemy 101.*

"Okay, smartass, I guess I deserved that," Draper said.

"As long as you apologized, I'm to meet him every Tuesday afternoon at 2:00 p.m. for tea."

"How much is he going to pay you for this job?" Draper said.

"He mentioned a hundred thousand peso's."

"That's under ten grand; when did you start working so cheap? You should have held out for more."

"Couldn't; I don't think the poor asshole has the cash. Sounds to me like the sister has her thumb firmly planted on his ass."

Escar and Mendez arrived after dark. They left Mendez to continue the training and Draper rode with Escar and DeCollado. They borrowed Ferrez' Peugeot for the trip. The mission objective included nailing down the location of Barajas estate and recon for a potential assault.

"Understand you are working with the enemy," Escar said to DeCollado.

"Only temporary, Draper doesn't pay for shit so I had to take a temp job." DeCollado said. "You should have seen that poor slob, he damn near begged me to kill his sister. Apparently there's no love lost there. Here, Carlos, take a look at this and see if you can make heads or tails out of it or its location."

Escar studied the drawing. "Not much detail here. It could be a test to see if you can pull off the kill without a lot of information."

"I'd agree normally, but frankly I don't think Javier Barajas has the brains God gave a morning dove let alone be that devious," DeCollado said.

"The area south and east of Hermosillo runs mostly to rolling desert with saguaros, palo verde, scrub creosote and an occasional mesquite. It's hard to see very far in most places and there are not many roads. The existing ones are bladed desert sand with paving only on the highway and an occasional high-end estate," Escar said.

They took the highway toward Baja, a narrow, winding thoroughfare, similar to riding a rollercoaster and minimally paved. Three roads bisected the highway heading south and none looked remotely similar to the scrawled map. After forty miles they turned around. Both sides of the highway were screened with desert flora masking whatever lay hidden beyond.

"There!" Escar exclaimed. "See the road sign? Didn't you say one of the captive girls said she saw a sign where they turned?"

"Yes, she did. It had 4.8 kilometers to someplace on it." Draper said.

Escar slid the Peugeot to a stop next to an upright steel fence post coated with rust and a narrow sign that read *Hermosillo 80 km.*

"That can't be, it's the wrong way and too many kilometers." DeCollado said."

"Wait a minute," Escar said, opening the Peugeot's door and stepped out. He knelt next to the post, brushing away sand to retrieve a second sign. It read *Bahia de kino 4.8 km.*

"Bingo!" Escar said, passing it into the car to Draper sitting in the back seat.

"Excellent, Carlos, we just might buy you a drink as soon as we get done here," Draper said.

The road heading south looked well-traveled, filled with vehicle tracks, some of which were fresh and others, sand-filled.

"What do you think," Escar said, looking back at Draper.

"Let's go see what we find."

The landscape south varied little from along the highway. More saguaros, scattered palo verde, mesquite and creosote mixed with thorny low-growing cactus capable of inflicting serious hurt. Escar drove slow, scanning both sides of the road for signs of a turnoff.

"Barajas said I couldn't miss it. There is a tall column with a masonry B in it," DeCollado said.

They drove until the coastline of the Sea of Cortez became obvious between dips in the rolling desert on their right. Draper estimated it was about five miles as the crow files. Draper mused later that the entrance to the Barajas estate would have been impossible to miss. On both sides of a smooth driveway a ten-foot masonry wall extended fifty feet on either side into the desert. The three foot thick walls supported an enormous arch connecting the two walls over the driveway. At its peak the construction rose tall enough to allow even the highest vehicle to pass. On the center of the arch, reaching up to scrap the sky was a granite obelisk with a large B carved in relief. They would have had to been blind to miss it. In front of the arch and alongside the road, a masonry covered guard house stood manned by two dangerous-looking thugs with AK-47s.

"Wow," Escar said.

"Stop," DeCollado said, "I know it's hard, but try to look inconspicuous back there." His reference was to Draper, his long body wrapped in obvious discomfort in the Peugeot's back seat, with an incognito sombrero tipped forward. They all hoped the dusk would hide his pale face.

One of the guards stepped forward pointing his AK-47 in DeCollado's general direction while the second guard covered the car occupants. Draper couldn't help thinking they'd had some training. That made them dangerous.

"Unless you have business here get back in the car and keep moving." the first guard said.

"What is this place; is there a cantina here?" DeCollado said, slurring his speech a little for effect.

"Nothing for you, *abuelo,* you've got five seconds to get back in the car and move on." The guard made it clear their bodies would forever rest in Sonoran sand if they didn't *vamoose.*

Back in the car, as Escar pulled away, DeCollado groused, "The asshole called me grandpa for Christ sake. I should go back and shoot his ass."

"You may get your chance later," Draper said.

On the way back to Hermosillo, they discussed various ways to breach the estate's probable defenses that would minimize casualties. It was Draper's opinion that it wasn't going to be easy. "I think we should look for someone that at one time had the Barajas' ear but for whatever reason now hates them," he said musing in the back seat.

"Good luck with that," DeCollado said, "those people are usually called dead."

Chapter Twenty-three

Sonora, Mexico

D raper hated the intel gathering part of any operation especially when his level of patience stretched close to the breaking point. When he was younger it was especially difficult and almost got him killed, twice. Those incidents sat fresh in his mind twenty-odd-years later. On both occasions DeCollado had saved him from a dim-witted youthful error. DeCollado didn't have to say anything when Draper bitched about their apparent lack of progress. He simply looked at Draper with that same *you are going to fuck it up* look he used in the past and Draper immediately wised up. They were in the barn, sitting on straw bales, by themselves and working the plan.

"I think the guards are the key. It's likely there is some deadman code they have to trigger regularly so that the house knows automatically if something is wrong at the front.

"Agreed," DeCollado said.

"So someone needs to know the code, switch, button or whatever, that can continue to send it while we move inside."

"Again, I agree. I need to get it from Javier Barajas before we make a move."

"So why are you sitting there harassing me, go get it," Draper said.

"Can't, have to wait until Tuesday."

"How about we try sooner?" Draper said.

"Barajas may be a lush, but he's wily in a coyote sort of way. When there's food around he'll go for it, but not before circling it a while."

"And your point is...?"

"I do it the Apache way, go to the cantina, hang around, have some fun, and let him come to me," DeCollado said.

"What about backup?"

"I'll take Carlos; your ass is too white for serious undercover work."

Draper watched them leave. It didn't improve his mood, yet he knew DeCollado to be right. He spent the next hour disassembling his Glock and cleaning it. It occupied his mind and made the gun ready. After he was done he felt better knowing the weapon shined and smelled of fresh gun oil. Armed, his Glock resting under his left arm, Draper walked to the house to beg for coffee.

Maria was in the kitchen with Calliste and the other two girls, cooking as she always did meals in advance for her newly expanded family.

"Sit," Maria said, pouring a cup of coffee Draper hadn't yet asked for. She handed it to Calliste who added some cream and passed it him.

"Thank you," Draper said.

"You are welcome," Calliste said, forming each word deliberately, almost without accent.

"Very good," Draper said.

"She's been practicing," Maria said.

"Where's Diego?" Draper asked.

"He's working the fields south of the house. You could probably find him if you want him."

"No, I won't bother him. I'm waiting for Bill and Carlos to return. We are trying to find out something about the setup at the Barajas estate."

"Do you want me to ask the girls?" Calliste asked.

"Sure, go ahead. We need information about the guard house." Draper didn't expect information and only agreed to pass the time. Both young women were recovering, but Maria Ferrez and her daughter, try as they might, would not be able to erase all the dark memories. Softening them with kindness and support was all they could do. Likely both captives would live the rest of their lives shouldering a heavy dose of shame and heartbreak.

Calliste turned to both young women and began questioning them in Spanish. At first there was little response until Charise Frases spoke and a long conversation ensued most of which Draper missed because of their rapid chatter. Calliste turned to Draper and said, "There's a button in the guard shack they must push every fifteen minutes. Otherwise an alarm alerts the house. She knows this because she overheard them talking once when a guard went to sleep. She heard a loud bell, like a fire alarm."

Draper couldn't help a twinge of excitement. If DeCollado came back with the same information they'd not only know about the alarm, they'd have conformation. "Tell her I thank her very much and she likely saved our lives."

The moon rose above the horizon and left saguaro shadows crisscrossing the Sonoran hills before DeCollado finally returned. Draper's pacing wore a path in the straw-covered barn floor inches deep by the time the old Apache stepped in and muttered, "I'd rather try to hold a conversation with a fence post than a drunken Javier Barajas. I'd probably get more information, too. It took hours to drag anything useful out of him and I don't know how accurate it is."

"What'd he tell you?" Draper asked.

"Well, apparently there is a button in the guard shack that someone has to push every once in a while or else some kind of alarm goes off in the house. That's about all I got. If we take out the guards, they'll be ready for us inside."

"It's a bell, like a fire alarm and they have to push a button every fifteen minutes," Draper said.

"And you know this how?"

Draper tried not to look smug when he said, "Expert detection."

DeCollado didn't answer at first. "One of the girls told you. You might have tried that before I spent half the evening messing around with Javier."

"I didn't think they'd know. Besides, now we have confirmation."

"There's that," DeCollado conceded.

"What do you think, full force assault tomorrow night or the next?"

"I think we can be ready by tomorrow. If we have a full-staffed planning session tonight and then hit them tomorrow night, we'll have a little less moon light but enough to see without night-vision equipment."

"Sounds, good," Draper said

The training session, followed by a two-hour briefing, lasted until minutes short of two a.m. They worked with each man separate from the others, outlining their role and exactly what needed to be done followed by a session on what not to do. With their raw recruits, there were more not's than do's. Their list of do's included neutralizing the guard shack, pressing the dead man button every fifteen minutes without fail and, of course, staying alive. Escar and Mendez, each with a four man team would deal with any other guards and possible resistance.

"DeCollado and I will go in first. We will neutralize as many as we can without causing an alarm. Once an alarm is triggered we hit them hard and show no mercy. Everyone in the building is the enemy. Do not..." Draper stopped a moment staring at each man, "hesitate to kill. Wounding is not allowed. A wounded enemy is an enemy that can kill you."

Draper continued to sweep the room with cold eyes, looking for the one who might have second thoughts. The one whose split-second hesitation would get him or worse yet his buddy, killed. There was only one, a short, slightly over-weight individual on Escar's team who during training had struggled to keep up but had always been enthusiastic. Only when live ammo danced around his head would his psyche know for sure. When Draper mentioned it to Escar, the man said, "I've known Juan for many years. He's one of those that to look at him you wouldn't expect much, but when it matters, he'll be right in the middle of the fray."

At two a.m. they sent everyone home except Escar and Mendez. Draper and DeCollado spent another hour with them before both felt they'd covered everything possible.

"Possibilities for success?" Draper asked.

"The only thing we don't know as I see it is the total size of the opposing force. How many are in the house are capable of resistance? Will kitchen and wait staff resist? Is there anything else dangerous that we don't know about?" Escar said.

"All good questions, Carlos," Draper said, "the simple answer is be prepared for any contingency, clear rooms one by one, until the whole floor is clear. Then start on the next floor. You know how this works. We all have ear buds and cell phones so we can be in constant contact. If you get into trouble I can't guarantee instant help, but we'll get there as soon as we can."

"Like all operations, there are risks, we'll minimize those we can and deal with the rest as it happens," DeCollado said.

"Last thing we do on the way out is collect all the weapons we can find. We'll try to pick up a few AR-15s or M4's on the way in, and if we do, so much the better. Grab any ammo you see also," Draper added.

"I haven't kicked any ass for a while, I think this will be fun," Escar said.

Draper rose early the next morning and went for a walk in the shallow darkness. He climbed a hill covered with creosote and prickly pear cactus watching his step as he moved. The thin clouds to the east began to turn first a pale crimson then turning deep red as the sun rose. The low angle lightshow lasted less than fifteen minutes and Draper watched the entire performance. Finally the misty clouds turned back to white their colors evaporated by the golden ball peaking over distant mountains. Not a follower of organized religion, Draper's belief in some sort of higher power centered on other mysteries. The universe around him excited as well as puzzled him. Facts as wondrous as the similarities between things alive and the rocks under his feet caused him to think. There was a complicated organization there too, along with questions that rose to roll around in his head until his brain hurt.

DeCollado sat on a bale of straw tying his boots when Draper returned to the barn. It promised to be a long day and an even longer night.

"You are up early," DeCollado said.

"We'll need two vehicles," Draper said.

"Already done," DeCollado said. "Mendez is bringing a nine passenger van. The forward group, that's you, me and Escar will neutralize the guard shack folks and Mendez will bring in the van on our signal."

"Breakfast is on the table", Ferrez yelled from the door.

Draper and DeCollado followed Ferrez to the house. Draper, in his already overloaded mind, walked wondering if they weren't endangering the quiet serenity of Ferrez' family. When dark fell they would attempt to severely damage the cartel's ability operate in Hermosillo. Draper had no illusions that the effect would be permanent. The goal remained to weaken them long enough that the local authorities could finish the job. Diego and his wife had to be the catalyst that would demand change. There was a lot of strength there, and the little mini-army they'd trained would have to rise to the occasion in ways they didn't know about yet. This evening's outcome would make or break the future.

Escar and Mendez arrived shortly after dark. The rest of their crew, only slightly larger than a platoon, arrived around nine. They loaded the troop into Mendez' old Ford Econoline with Draper, DeCollado and Escar riding in a beat up Honda Civic with Ferrez driving. Escar sat shotgun with Draper and DeCollado in back. Their plan hinged on a different car and a different driver than the previous visit in case the guards hadn't been rotated. Mendez would stay back until the entrance to the Barajas estate had been secured.

Escar stopped the Civic in the middle of the road a couple hundred yards short of the entrance to the estate. Draper and DeCollado exited. They were dressed all in black with hoods over their faces with narrow eye slits. Maria designed and made their outfits, with help from Calliste and the two captives. Claiming the work would be therapy for the young women, Maria secured a bolt of black cotton and set to sewing. Draper like the idea, calling them uniforms. His one request was to make his and DeCollado's tops like a light jacket, open in front, so they could access their shoulder rigs easily. Without a word Maria modified them all.

There wouldn't be much of a moon that night so they'd timed their initial rush on the guard shack to the period before moonrise. The advance on the main estate building would have just enough light to operate without night-vision equipment.

The first hitch in their plan rose immediately. Both guards were inside the small enclosure. Not knowing exactly where the button was located meant they had to wait or somehow draw the two out. Draper elected the latter. He coughed, not loud, more like a throat-clearing noise, followed by lip sounds. He'd heard a deer make that sound once and tried to imitate it. He doubted it would matter since it wasn't likely the guards were familiar with deer noises. It would sound like a strange noise, not alarming but needing investigation.

Draper heard their surprise, followed by discussion in Spanish and movement. One of the guards peered out the door, waited for his eyes to adjust to the dark, saw nothing and followed his AK-47 around the building where Draper put him to sleep and DeCollado grabbed the gun to keep it from hitting the ground. Silence ensued. A moment later the second guard looked out. *"Héctor?"* The second guard made the mistake of stepping into the dark from a lighted room. For several seconds a person is blind. He didn't see Draper standing beside him in the dark.

While DeCollado zip-tied their two captives Draper searched for the alarm button, found it and pushed to reset it. Now they had fifteen minutes before it had to be pushed again.

"Bring the boys up, Vincente, we are secure," Draper said into his cell.

The van arrived. Mendez unloaded the men, turned the vehicle around for a quick getaway and parked it off the road. The two selected to man the guard house and push the alarm reset, were armed with handguns and a twelve gauge shotgun each. Shotguns were useful in close quarters but useless otherwise. Circumstances required them to do with what the men had. Because handguns and most other weapons were illegal in Mexico only the army, local *policía* and, of course the cartels, had any real firepower.

Escar and Mendez spent the next twenty minutes organizing the assault, with Draper and DeCollado making a recon trip up the driveway toward the main estate since they were clueless as to how everything laid out.

The main estate grounds were also walled with the main house sticking above the walls by a full story. An armed guard paced back and forth along the top of the outside wall. They could see him only when he moved but there wasn't any doubt what he was there for. The driveway ended at a set of massive double doors the full height of the walls which Draper estimated at least ten feet. To the right of the big doors was a smaller walk-in door.

"Christ!" Draper whispered, "That's not an estate it's a goddamn fortress!"

"Feeling a little undermanned?" DeCollado returned.

"Just a little; since we have time I suggest we make a circle around it and assess what we're up against." Draper decided this unexpected problem deserved investigation.

"Good idea," DeCollado said.

They walked around the walls staying far enough into the desert to avoid detection. It burned almost an hour, both of them moving carefully to avoid proliferating thorny flora common to the Sonoran Desert. The local flora was capable of painful, long-lasting wounds. Returning to the driveway told them the only entrance lay right in front. Both men could see above and to the right of the big doors, situated over the walk-in door, an open, stuccoed, guard station sat staffed by two men with AK-47's.

"Looks like they have to come down and open the big doors for visitors. The small door is in case they want to check a vehicle before letting them in.

"Got any ideas?" Draper said.

"Maybe we can get them to come to us?"

"How so?"

"Build Indian fire. High up they should be able to see it."

"All right, I'll bite, what kind of fire is that?"

"White man builds big fire, has to stand far away; Indian build small fire, stand close and make white man curious. White man comes to investigate and Indian hit with tomahawk."

"I'm a little fuzzy on the analogy, but I don't have a better idea. It might work."

Firewood lay scarce in the desert and it took a bit to find enough creosote wood and dead saguaro frames to build a fire. They constructed their ruse in the middle of the driveway feeding fuel slowly to keep it small. It took seventeen minutes on Draper's watch for the first guard to come and investigate. He walked up to Draper sitting in the road next to the fire and said, *"¿Qué demonios estás haciendo?"*

"Trying to get you to come out here so I could shoot you," Draper said, while DeCollado stepped out of the shadows and flattened him. He dropped as if pole-axed and DeCollado dragged the man's limp body into the dark and secured him with a zip-tie. They hoped any sound wouldn't carry to the other guard. In the man's pocket they found a small white plastic card with a magnetic stripe on the back. It looked like a credit card with no markings.

Draper had voted originally for death to any resistance they encountered, his mind changed by DeCollado supporting the idea that stealth and mercy might add to the mystique of *El matador de hombres malos*. To cope they'd brought a bundle of zip-ties. After reflection, Draper warmed to the idea, conceding that an air of mystery might work in their favor.

Chapter Twenty-four

Sonora, Mexico

P ablo Castillo drove toward the estate with worry plaguing his mind. He had Marisol Barajas' Jaguar XKR-S Convertible, gunning the 550 hp engine to ninety-six miles an hour, much too fast for the likes of the Mexican highway, but the sheer g-force against his body was almost sexual, pressing him into the seat like Marisol did during their love-making, fierce, demanding, and powerful. When he felt the car lighten going over the small rises, he eased up on the accelerator and let the car slow to a more reasonable speed. He'd watched Javier in the cantina, appearing to negotiate with a stranger, an older Mexican. His trust of the younger Barajas sibling never complete, Castillo watched long enough to know that there was something afoot Marisol wouldn't like. His first thought, given Javier's loose morals, was some sort of *puta* party, especially when a packet of cash changed hands. He gave his favorite bargirl a hundred peso's to listen in and her response scared him. "He wants the older man to kill someone," the girl had said. "It sounded like a woman." When Castillo had pressed her, she confirmed, "*I heard, I want you to kill her.*" Castillo knew instantly he meant Marisol.

Decision made, Castillo turned the Jag around at the highway junction and raced back to town. Again parked outside the cantina he looked in the lift-back trunk area and found a chrome S&W 9mm automatic, Marisol's weapon of choice. He checked the magazine and found it full, racked the slide to load the chamber and dropped the safety in place. He had weighed all the options and found no other. Javier's death would cause no loss. He knew Marisol would feign sorrow, breathe a sigh of relief and forget she had a brother inside of an hour. The rebels who attacked the cantina and stolen their money caused a temporary setback, but not an insurmountable one. The cantina was back in operation in hours, the *burdel* in less than a day and the money a minor amount when compared to their monthly take. Castillo felt confident that his next move was a necessary task that no person, not even Marisol, would question. He glanced around the cantina and Javier was gone. The bargirl pointed up the stairway. Upstairs, the *burdel* hostess gave him the room number and a master key. He felt the hard steel of the automatic in his pocket as he pulled it out and thumbed the safety. Without a sound he unlocked the door and shoved it open.

Javier Barajas stood in the middle of the room and died as he'd been born, naked and clueless with the added weight of two nine millimeter slugs in his chest. The woman sat on the bed, terror in her eyes, grasping the sheet under her chin in a death grip.

Castillo turned and walked back to the stairs. As he passed the *burdel* hostess he said in careless humor, *"Usted tendrá que limpiar la habitación,"* telling her she had a room to clean.

Castillo drove back to the estate, this time with a sense of relief. Marisol's brother had been a long-term pain in the ass and he spent the hour drive perfecting his story to Marisol He had proof the man was plotting to kill her, had paid an assassin, an act that could be confirm by the bargirl. Castillo doubted he'd need the girl's testimony, and expected his boss to rant a bit, shed a couple crocodile tears, and forget she had a brother in minutes.

As he passed the guard house he waved at the sentinels, his mind filled with the evening's events and he missed the fact he didn't recognize either man. A tiny flash of warning came, but he ignored it, his mind filled with the vision of Javier standing stupid and bare-ass naked ten feet in front of the nine. Then the admonition was gone as he accelerated the Jaguar down the driveway with a satisfying spin of tires in loose sand.

***

Draper and DeCollado moved to the wall of the estate searching for more guards. If their count was right there should be two more, probably in the tower cubicle at the top of the wall. DeCollado climbed the steps and shot two guards, finding them reading magazines and not paying attention. He looked back toward the main road and saw car headlights dancing off the desert flora coming toward the estate.

"Vehicle coming!" DeCollado hissed down at Draper.

The long, black car slid to a stop in front of the doors to the estate. Draper didn't recognize the make, thought it probably foreign, expensive and an ostentatious example of cartel greed. When he walked up to the driver's side window, the man looked at him surprised and said, "*¿Quién diablos es usted?*"

Draper didn't answer, not understanding question but guessing it to be something about his ancestry with a curse word or two included. He didn't know who this clown was, but nevertheless it was likely he wasn't one of the good guys so Draper shot him, the Glock jumping twice, its noise muffled by the suppressor. The man slumped over bleeding on expensive upholstery.

"Who is he?" DeCollado said.

"Beat's the shit out of me, but I couldn't let him raise an alarm."

"What are we going to do with him?"

"I'd vote for nothing. He and the car will block the entrance to the estate in case we have to make a quick getaway."

"Works for me," DeCollado said.

"Let's call in the troops and see if we can get inside. I can't wait to see what the inside of this place looks like."

Minutes later the Ford Econoline parked behind the Jaguar after he'd turned around to quick getaway position. They added two more AK-47's to their arsenal, making a total of four, giving two to each team.

Draper and DeCollado held counsel. "The small door gets us inside. We don't know who all is inside but don't trust anyone. Try to round them up alive, but if you encounter any resistance shoot to kill. Do it just like we trained you, one room, and one floor at a time, starting on the ground floor; any questions?" There were none. The men stood nervous, their weapons checked, loaded and deadly.

Draper found the card swipe and used the plain white card they'd found on the first guard. The lock clicked to unlock. Draper went through the small door first, following his Glock, checking the area cautious, making sure no one was aware of their presence. His first scan showed a wide area of gardens, carefully manicured. The landscape contained an artfully selected array of desert flora planted around small areas of Bermuda grass. Carefully tended and illuminated to emphasize its beauty, the gardens surrounded the house on all sides. Draper could see a wide variety of desert plantings broken only by flagstone pathways winding throughout the garden. Someone had spent considerable time and effort not only creating the area, but maintaining it. Mid-center on Draper's side of the house sat a giant, two-hundred year-old multi-armed saguaro cactus standing like a guardian over the design. Draper took a moment to appreciate its beauty before searching for baddies. The first floor of the house had many windows that looked as if they went all the way around allowing Draper to see the garden on the other side. Inside, people moved around doing routine tasks in lighted rooms looking very domestic, like kitchen and dining areas. There were no signs of alarm.

Draper and DeCollado made a sweep of the garden finding nothing before signaling the troops in. They surrounded the house, covering the four exits into the garden. Draper stood at one door and counted bodies, five inside, all appearing to be domestics. Two women stood washing dishes; two were cleaning furniture while the single man swept highly polished colorful tile flooring. Every part of the decor smelled of money. The ceilings were high, lined with frieze boards and cove molding cut from exotic hardwoods. Draper couldn't identify them but suspected cherry or some other expensive species.

Draper stepped inside followed close by DeCollado. Draper held a finger to his lips suggesting silence. They all saw the Glock, staring as one at the man wielding it.

DeCollado said, "*¿A alguien más aquí?*"

The man pointed at the ceiling while the women looked terrified.

"*No estamos aquí para hacerte daño. Las malas personas arriba?* DeCollado asked.

The man said, "*Sí, la mujer, ella es muy malo.*"

"I told them we are not here to hurt them and when I asked if there was anyone else in the house that's when the guy pointed at the ceiling. Then I asked if there were any bad guys and he said yes, a woman and that she was very bad," DeCollado said.

"Okay, call Escar and have him bring a couple of guys to watch this bunch while you and I search the rest of the house," Draper said. "Let's leave the rest outside so we don't get surprised from behind."

DeCollado called and Escar and his two men came in.

"Watch these people, we think they're innocents but I don't want to take a chance. This has been way too easy, which makes me fearful we've missed something.

"Could be cartel arrogance, we're deep in Mexico and they think they own it."

"Maybe but let's not take any chances. Stay alert."

Draper and DeCollado moved through the door on the interior side of the kitchen and stepped into a large entrance hallway where the ceiling reached all the way to the roof and housed a supersized chandler decorated with hanging glass prisms. In the center a massive curved stairway swept down from the second floor landing with oversized banisters, decorative moldings and a glossy finish. In his mind's eye Draper could imagine a beautiful woman descending in a long white gown to her awaiting paramour; he remembered the same scene in a movie somewhere. It was that kind of staircase. With DeCollado covering him, Draper ascended slowly, watchful, following the Glock ready to beard man, beast, or woman. They found nothing. The upstairs consisted of five oversized bedrooms, each with a walk-in closet, private bathrooms in sparkling white tile, extensive decor and huge beds with expensive looking furnishings and fancy spreads.

Draper and DeCollado met at the top of the stairs, both puzzled. None of the bedrooms looked lived in. All were spotless, everything in its place and could have been boudoir ads in a fashion magazine.

They returned to the kitchen and DeCollado again questioned the domestics. They all stood silent and Draper could tell they were puzzled that the woman couldn't be found.

"I didn't see a back stair way or a butler's stairway. Most big places like this have one," Draper suggested.

DeCollado asked and received blank stares and shoulder shrugs.

"Ask them which bedroom upstairs they usually see her in.

DeCollado asked and turned to Draper. "They say the one in back on the right.

"I'm going back upstairs for a look see," Draper said.

"Be careful," DeCollado said.

On the way up the staircase Draper noticed something he hadn't observed the first time. The second floor wasn't balanced and floor space appeared missing. First, there were three bedrooms on the right side and two on the left. The two on the left Draper remembered, were quite a bit smaller. He stood at the top of the stairs and studied the hallway. The layout of the doors tended to fool an observer since they matched up across from one another. One would assume the rooms were the same size. But they weren't. He was sure of it.

The women in the kitchen said they always saw her in the right rear bedroom so that's where Draper elected to look closer. He entered the room and stood for a minute but nothing caught his eye. Simply out of curiosity, Draper began opening doors. There were several closets, two with shelves and two with rods, all stuffed with women's clothing. A fifth closet had neither shelves nor rods. Empty except for a few boxes, Draper studied it several minutes before he saw it. A craftsman of considerable talent had installed a door in the back of the closet. A casual glance would miss it. Looking close revealed the faint outline fitting so well as to be almost invisible. There was no hardware so Draper pushed, hard. Nothing moved.

Draper rested his back against the closet doorjamb, and raising his right foot, he kicked at the hidden door at lock height. I gave in a little, then held firm. He kicked a second time and felt the shock of the impact run though his leg. Grimacing, he felt certain more than a couple more kicks would leave him unable to walk. Draper went back to the closest closet and dumped all the clothes on the floor, removed the inch and a quarter oak closet-rod and returned to the hidden door. His foot had left a hole large enough for him to insert the rod. He began to pry, his mechanical advantage increased by the rod and the door began to move ever so slightly until suddenly it popped open with a sharp crack. Draper dropped the rod and drew the Glock pointing it down a narrow hallway. He could see the other end twenty feet or so, its outline formed by an unseen light source. A short walk told him it was obvious he was in the sixth bedroom, similar to the others but larger and grander. The ceiling rose at least twelve feet, accented by a gaudy gold chandelier and heavy drapery on the walls. The floor covered with bleached white, long shag carpeting, it looked like a rake would be needed to comb it.

Marisol Barajas lay in a monster four-poster bed with a lacy canopy the color of 'Hot Lady' roses. The carved intricacy in the wood frame made it look heavy; solid walnut, Draper guessed, king-sized and fitted with gold-colored silk sheets. The woman was indeed stunning; obviously naked with deep auburn hair highlighting her sun-darken skin. She looked at him with smoky black eyes.

"Charlie Draper, I presume; I've been expecting you," fell out of sensuous lips she used to distract an opponent.

"You are going to jail, lady, or hell if you prefer," Draper said, leveling his Glock .40.

"You are the *El matador de hombres malos* who comes to rid Mexico of graft and corruption?" She made it a statement more than a question, letting a hit of loathing leak through.

"Think what you want, it ends here." Draper didn't believe for a second she would give up without a fight.

"Come now, surely we can negotiate. Why don't you join me and we can discuss terms." The queen of the Sonoran Cartel used her left hand to pull the pink top sheet down to her waist. Cupping her right breast with her other hand she continued cooing in a melodic tenor that Draper bet had seduced more than one enemy. "I think you and I could have a lot of fun together. Come on, Charlie, what have you got to lose?" she whispered in a soft, husky, inviting tone, not unlike a hungry black widow, Draper supposed.

"Keep your hands where I can see them," Draper said, seeing her left hand begin to sneak under the gold sheet. The hand stopped when he spoke but didn't retract.

"I can make you richer than you ever imagined. How does ten million dollars sound and with it you get me any time you want. Isn't that better that some scrawny lady sheriff?" Draper ignored her right hand caressing an erect nipple, looking instead straight into her black eyes and seeing death starring back. She knows about Molly, Draper thought, watching that left hand. When he didn't respond the hand moved again and he squeezed the trigger of the Glock and shot her twice between those magnificent *los pechos*.

"That's for the lady sheriff, *perra*, and she isn't scrawny," Draper said, though no one heard him. He walked over to the bed and pulled the sheet back; not that he cared, but sure enough, nestled in her crotch, with her trigger finger on the trigger guard, laid a fancy tooled, chrome-plated Smith and Wesson automatic with the safety off. Draper grabbed his cell phone and took a picture, a not very flattering one to be sure, but including the automatic; after which he selected an email address and pushed send.

Draper and DeCollado stayed in Mexico another week. They left the three guards zip-tied in the center of the plaza in Hermosillo. At first they simply disappeared, but days later were found hanging off a third-floor balcony. Almost poetic justice, their throats were cut and bodies mutilated. Draper didn't know how it happened and didn't want to, but talk in town believed it to be the work of the mysterious *El matador de hombres malos*. It told him that it was likely they'd started at least a small revolution where perhaps the people would seize the opportunity to take their country back. How long it would last remained to be seen.

In the barn at the Ferrez farm Draper and DeCollado prepared to return home. They were half done when Escar and Mendez entered.

"I'm going to run for *jefe de plaza*. If I win we will clean up the town and make it a place where families can be proud to live."

"I know you will," Draper said. He didn't add 'try' since he didn't want to dampen the man's enthusiasm. Reality told him crime and corruption was like a cancer, once it took hold, it was hard to dislodge. Strong medicine and sometimes years were required and often it raised its ugly head again. Something told him the war wasn't over; it was more likely only a lull in the battle.

Draper was asleep when he felt a gentle hand shaking his arm. When he opened his eyes he saw Maria kneeling beside him. "Charlie," she said, whispering, "Would you go for a walk with me?"

"Sure," Draper said his mind cloudy and sleep deprived. He rose and followed Diego's wife out of the barn and into a moonlit night only after grabbing his shoulder rig and the Glock. He looked at his watch and saw four-thirty a.m. clueless as to Maria's reasons. Outside the barn, while he was struggling into the rig, Maria looked him smiling, "You won't need that. I'm mostly harmless."

They walked without talking down the driveway until they were out of site of the house. Boulders lined the roadway and Maria selected one. She pointed at another and said, "Sit."

Draper sat. Still puzzled, he felt wary, though not sure why. He knew her to be a complicated woman, domestic in the usual ways, but fiercely protective of her family and probably willing to do whatever it took to ensure their safety. She said nothing for a couple of long minutes as if deciding on the right words.

Finally Draper, now fully awake, started the conversation with, "Okay, Maria, what's on your mind."

"My Diego, he is a good man, he works hard, but he'll always be a farmer. He loves the land, growing crops, harvesting, nursing the animals and all that, and he provides for us the best he can."

Maria stopped; she stared at the moon, as if planning what to say next. Draper waited for her to continue, mystified as to where she was headed.

"I love Diego, very much, he has treated me well and we've had a good life together. I also know that what we have now is all we'll ever have. When I was young I dreamed of going to the United States and attending school. I wanted to be a teacher."

"You'd have been a good one," Draper said.

"Maybe; but instead I married my Diego. He is not like you."

Sonoran Justice by Dave Folsom

"That's a good thing. I don't think you'd like the real me. I'm not a nice man. I've spent my life killing people. Most of them deserved it though."

"I know that, but it doesn't matter. I think deep down you are basically good. Can I ask you something?"

Draper wasn't sure he wanted to know the question, but said, "Go ahead, ask."

"Is there any way you could get my Calliste into the U.S. legally? Diego and I have saved a little money, but we will save more and send it to you for her education."

Draper noticed Maria had put her hand on his and squeezed a little. Draper looked into her dark eyes and saw a woman wanting her daughter to have better than herself and would consider any length to achieve it.

"I'll tell you what I can do. I'm fairly certain I can pull some strings and get her a student visa. Then I'll help her find a school. I have some extra money so, in payment for your help the last few weeks, I will pay her tuition. We can work out the details later. When does she finish school here?"

"This next fall she finishes what you would call high school."

"Okay, then it's settled. There are lots of good schools in Arizona so she won't be too far away."

"I have one more request."

"And what is that?" Draper said. He swore later to himself that her eyes sparkled like momentarily the devil had taken over.

She moved forward and kissed him. It was gentle, sweet at first and moved into passionate, leaving Draper stunned when she held it until he returned it. And then she pulled away smiling and stood. "By the way," she said, "Diego knows I am here with you and why. He'll never know about the kiss though. That's from me. I just wanted to know what it would be like."

Then she was gone, running up the road and disappearing into the dark.

"I'll be dipped in shit!" Draper said to the empty rock.

Draper sat a while on his rock before returning to the barn, his mind whirling with the events of the last few weeks, thankful that it had worked out. He watched the moon and Orion's belt move across the sky in their nightly travel thinking about the eons they'd made that journey and wondering if anything would really change. He'd spent a lifetime fighting assholes and every year there were more. He wondered if someday he'd cross paths with his own goddess Artemis; the one asshole stronger, faster and more cunning than he was. He tamped that thought down, deciding he just missed Molly and Gabriella, and Maria had reminded him. Draper walked back up the road to the barn, saddened a bit and wondering if he'd really made the world any better. He hoped so, at least a little.

Diego Ferrez entered the barn when Draper and DeCollado were getting up. The sun had heated the barn already and Draper felt as if he'd overslept. Ferrez came up to Draper and touched his arm.

"Thank you, *mi amigo*", Diego said. "You are a good man." With that he turned and left the barn.

DeCollado looked at Draper and said, "What was that about?"

"Nothing," Draper said.

"Bull shit," DeCollado said, "have you been pretending to be a good guy again?"

"Can't help it, it's just my nature."

"Yeah, and I'm the fairy godmother. What'd you do?"

"I'm going to help Calliste go to school in the states." Draper said.

"Have anything to do with Maria dragging you out of bed for a little tryst last night?"

"So you heard us?"

"Of course, I'm half Apache. Apache know almost everything and can guess the rest."

"Don't worry, it was innocent and Diego knows about it. We were discussing Calliste."

"Are you sure about that?" DeCollado said.

"Pretty sure," Draper said.

Chapter Twenty-five

Sonora, Mexico - Southern Arizona

Two days later, Diego Ferrez drove Draper and DeCollado to Nogales. Draper doubted the Peugeot had one more trip in it, but it ran up the road with ease. The trip went mostly silent with DeCollado and Ferrez sharing the driving duties. Draper tried to catch up on his sleep but spent a good deal of the long drive rehashing their trip. He concluded little would change in Hermosillo until the government in Mexico City relinquished its iron-fist control of things fiscal and political. Mexico's presidents in recent years, some good and some not so good, did little to change things as political assassinations and poverty reined king everywhere.

Diego dropped them off on Fenochio Street in Nogales, Son. They were a short distance from the International Border and close to the flood drainage outfall. The sun had dropped below the western mountains bring on the night. Outside the ancient Peugeot and standing in the street, Ferrez shook their hands. To Draper he said, "We will bring Calliste up this fall whenever you say."

"Good enough. I'll let you know when I find a few school options," Draper said.

Draper and DeCollado walked a crowded street filled with many American tourist shoppers, collecting Mexican trinkets to take back home, getting teeth fixed or opting for an eye appointment. Draper knew many families in Mexico depended on these transactions for their livelihood. In recent years the numbers fell due to cartel violence, though many still came. Few, however, ventured any distance into the city beyond a few blocks.

Reaching the outfall, Draper and DeCollado watched a coyote lead a group twelve men and two women into the mouth, hopefuls they guessed, looking for a better life in the U.S. They waited a half-hour to give the group time to get ahead before entering themselves. Once inside they saw no one and reached the iron steps in the manhole without incident.

The black Lincoln sat where they'd left it and Draper felt good to be back. He reached for his keys and was about to unlock the doors when a voice behind them said. "Border Patrol Agents! Put your hands on the car, please, where I can see them, do it now!"

Draper and DeCollado both knew the drill. They placed their hands on the roof of the Lincoln and stood still and silent.

"Any weapons, knives or guns I should know about?"

"Yes," Draper said, "we are both legally armed, in shoulder rigs."

The voice reached around and expertly removed the Glock and did a pat down. Subtle sounds told Draper the voice did the same to DeCollado. Draper waited patiently, knowing any resistance or comment would only extend the delay.

"This is your vehicle, Sir?"

"Yes," Draper said.

"Are you an American citizen?"

"Yes."

"How about you?" he said to DeCollado.

DeCollado said, "Yes."

"Your car hasn't moved for three weeks. Why is that, Sir?" The voice was back to Draper. He looked down at the tires and saw chalk marks, kicking himself mentally that he hadn't thought of that.

"Took a trip up north, with a friend, we used his car. He just dropped us off so we could retrieve this one." His story sounded weak, but he counted on the chance they couldn't or wouldn't bother to test it.

"Give me you right hand behind you back. For my safety, I'm going to handcuff you both and then we'll talk some more at the station."

Draper did as he was told and heard the click of the restraints falling into place. When he turned around he faced two no nonsense Border Patrol agents.

"Save us both a lot of time if you'd call Detective-Lieutenant John Pérez Tucson Police Department, he'll vouch for us," Draper said.

"Have any identification that proves citizenship?" The BP agent appeared to ignore Draper's suggestion.

"Driver's license," Draper said.

"Not good enough," was the answer.

They spent two hours in a holding cell at the BP station before an agent finally released them, returning their weapons and personal affects with a comment, "Lot of firepower for a couple of innocent citizens."

They didn't get a courtesy ride back to the Lincoln. Halfway to the Lincoln, DeCollado said, "Probably should have parked the car in a private storage facility."

"Would have helped had you suggested that earlier," Draper mumbled.

The long drive to Henry and Sheila Aguila's secure fortress now out of the question, they drove to Green Valley and rented a motel room for the night.

At six a.m. when Draper woke, DeCollado was up and dressed. They grabbed a quick breakfast and coffee to go and hit the road by seven. They'd settled in for the drive when DeCollado said, "I was lying awake last night and I remembered something Javier Barajas said that night in the cantina in Hermosillo. It was kind of a bragging comment and he was beyond drunk so I didn't give it much credence, but during the night I began to wonder. Someone in Tucson ordered the hits on the undercover officer and his CI in Tucson. Remember the guy in the warehouse mentioned a Ricardo Ortiz, who was a big shot in the cartel activities in southern Arizona?

"Yeah, I remember. You think it was Ortiz that did it?"

"Positive. When I was trying to drag information out of him in the Cantina that night he bragged that after I took care of his sister there was a cousin in Tucson that was next. He wanted me to dispose of a high-level cartel asshole named, drum roll here, Ricardo Ortiz. Want to take a bet that this Ortiz is the one. Ortiz either did it himself or had it done."

"So you think we should take a run at him," Draper said.

"I do."

"We are going to have to drag his ass outside the city limits or Pérez will be pissed if we leave a dead body lying around in his town."

"May not be able to help it, and I think he'll get over it quick considering what Ortiz did to that undercover cop and his CI," DeCollado said.

"He'll still grump about it. I take it you think we should make a stop in Tucson?"

"Don't you?"

"Never doubted it," Draper said. "We know there was a couple of Russians hovering around Marisol and Javier Barajas. It's likely they'd search out the heir apparent. Want to guess who that'd be?"

"Don't have to guess, it would be our mutual friend, Mr. Ortiz."

***

Richardo Ortiz built an expansive Spanish-style home on the upper north side of Tucson's Foothills area. It sat in the shadow of *Mesa de la Osa* Mountain and two or three times a year the yard would receive a skiff of snow, a rarity for southern Arizona. In the basement he had a shooting range and a single lane bowling alley with a fully equipped bar. His cartel drugs and human trafficking income rising to a lofty level left little that Ortiz wanted that he couldn't buy, so he spoiled himself. Frequently, he bought two or three of an item. In his four-stall garage there were three new BMW M6 Convertibles identical except for different primary colors and a new black Ford F250 four-wheel-drive pickup with a six-inch lift-kit. He didn't drive the truck often, but felt it added class to his driveway. The top floor of the home had dual master suites each with private baths and walk-in closets. One side of the dual master suite Ricardo reserved for himself and the other side housed his *hija de puta* of the month. In order to maintain his lavish lifestyle with the least amount of interference, Ortiz faithfully smuggled the bulk of his receipts south into Mexico but the remaining still required hiring a gaggle of accountants to ensure he faithfully paid his million or so dollars in taxes to the IRS and local officials each year. He'd become a shrewd politician as he aged, fending off the occasional law enforcement inquiry while controlling the gang leaders with a sizable economic club. It didn't hurt that he was also a cold-blooded killer. , he more often ordered it rather than participating in person, but in either case lost not a minute of sleep over it. The news of the death of Marisol Barajas, her brother Javier and the complete breakup of the southern arm of the cartel however, shook him to the core. He saw it first as a catastrophe and the possible demise of his lifestyle now that his supplier of the cash crop was out of business. As he rolled it around in his mind another option opened. If he moved swiftly before the news spread too far, he might, in fact be able to seize control of the cartel himself. To do that, he would have to contact the grandfather of cartel leaders, a task not to be taken lightly.

Ortiz's second in command, a former gangbanger legitimized by wealth, wore sleeveless pullover shirts to show off his extensive body art. At six-foot-six in height and a shade under three hundred in weight, he considered himself bulletproof.

"Who did this?" Ortiz demanded of his second, the product of a Hispanic mother and a Black father who saddled him with the name Alejandro Jones.

"There's not much, only a bunch of rumors of a mysterious asshole they're calling *El matador de hombres malos,*" Jones said, his manner cool and unaffected by the news.

"Killer of bad men? What the hell does that mean?" Ortiz said.

"Don't know, Boss, what you want me to do?'

"Do what you do best. Get out on the street and find out who this asshole is. Somebody has to know."

"Rumor has it he's American." Jones said, using a wooden toothpick to work on a bit of stuck breakfast. It amused him that an

American white-boy could cause so much disconcertion among some real bad-asses. His thoughts wandered casually to just how this mystical vigilante gathered the cojones to take on the cartel.

"American? How could an American go after the cartel in Mexico?" Ortiz said.

"Must-a pissed him off somehow," Jones said.

"Find out what you can and be back here this afternoon. The Russians will be here and they are not happy. That American son-of-a-bitch destroyed all our tunnel equipment as well," Ortiz said.

"Don't like those Russians," Jones said. "They never smile; makes it hard to tell what they're thinking."

***

Draper made two phone calls as soon as they reached Tucson. The first was to an unlisted number back east. He briefed them on what was in the works.

"We received the picture," the voice on the phone said. "Nice detail, we were able to positively identify her, so the amount we agreed to is forthcoming. Is the matter you are calling about related to the picture?"

"Yes," Draper said. "There were a couple of Russians snooping around the cartel in Mexico. We'd like to know if it's possible they are in the U.S. If they are we'd like to lean on them a bit."

"We know about the Russians. They are currently in the U.S., in Tucson, Arizona as a matter of fact. You may lean on them, as you put it, but it's preferable that you don't eliminate them. However,

State will not object if it becomes necessary, and you can proceed without prejudice."

"I don't think it will be necessary, but it will be nice to use it as leverage to get them out of the country pronto," Draper said.

"Do it." the voice said.

Draper hung up and looked at DeCollado. "We have the green light, covered as usual with a coating of political bullshit."

"Okay," DeCollado said.

The second call was to Detective-Lieutenant John Pérez of the Tucson Police Department. Pérez answered with, "I hope to hell you aren't in Tucson, I have all the bodies I can deal with already."

"You keep this up and I'll begin to think you don't like me," Draper said.

"What was your first clue? What do you want?" Tucson's head detective, always up to his eyebrows in violent crime ranging from muggings to murder, perpetrated by a sizeable population of genuine assholes, was never friendly, although the two generally got along within limits.

"We're interested in a couple of Russians, probably traveling with State department visas on some kind of bullshit mission that has nothing to do with what they are really here for," Draper said.

"We have a pair and they have an interpreter with them. We've got a tail on them for security reasons. Please, for God's sake don't kill them. The paperwork would take until next Christmas to complete."

"Don't plan on killing them, just want to talk. Where are they?"

"Let me look," was followed by a full minute of silence. "Right now they are on their way to brunch at a restaurant called The

Garden Inn on East Broadway Blvd. What do you want to talk to them about?"

"Best you don't know. And we didn't have this conversation."

"Damn you, Draper!"

"Settle down, John, I promise I'll call you first if we have to kill anybody."

It took twenty minutes to reach East Broadway Blvd through moderate mid-morning traffic and Draper found a parking spot empty near the front door. Entering the restaurant, the Russians were already seated in a back corner, a dumb move Draper thought since they were easily trapped. He approached them while the hostess seated DeCollado where they requested, a short distance away.

"There are some friends," Draper said for the hostesses benefit and walked directly at the Russians.

"Gentlemen, please keep your hands on the table and no one will get hurt." Draper had the Glock in hand, partially exposed so they could see it. Their reaction was predictable and the interpreter said, "You can't arrest us, we have diplomatic immunity."

"Sadly, that has been revoked. But, if you are good and we have a nice quiet conversation and if there is no trouble, we can discuss reinstating it; up to you."

Draper waited while the interpreter translated to his two companions. Both mumbled in Russian in a way Draper assumed meant they were unhappy.

The one on Draper's left growled something unintelligible which Draper's limited Russian interpreted to mean "asshole."

"Tell the boys to be nice, now," Draper said, looking hard at the interpreter.

"What do you want?"

"You see the mean looking guy across the aisle? Listen carefully and there will be no trouble. Cause a problem; all three of you will end up dead, simple as that."

"You can't do this, the United States government has granted us diplomatic immunity," the man repeated.

"And like I said before, the government has rescinded that and given us, that meaning the one over there and myself, permission to shoot your asses if you don't cooperate. Personally, we'd rather just shoot you but it would kind of mess up the restaurant."

"All right, speak your piece," the interpreter said.

"We know all about your deal with the Mexican cartels, we know about the tunnel and the U.S. government is pissed about it," Draper lied, improvising. "You will get up and walk out of the restaurant with us, where we will get into your car and drive directly to the airport. My friend will follow us in his car. There you will board your plane and fly directly to mother Russia stopping only for fuel. Is that clear?"

Draper was guessing a lot in his story but the expressions of the two men as they listened to the interpreter told him was on the mark or close to it. They slid out of the booth and DeCollado moved in behind on the way out.

"It seems they decided to cooperate," DeCollado said.

"At least for now," Draper said, "but chances are they'll return; too much at stake."

Draper rode to the airport in a stretched Cadillac limousine. The two Russian dignitaries sat in the good seats staring at Draper with hate eyes. Draper sat in one jump seat facing the Russian pair with the Glock in his lap. The interpreter sat in the other, his status apparently not high enough for soft leather. At Tucson International,

Draper and DeCollado watched the three men load into a plush Boeing 777 with a big red star on the tail. They watched until the plane disappeared into the azure sky.

"Good riddance," DeCollado said.

"Wish I could believe they are gone forever. Whatever they are up to is pretty big. What I can't understand is why they'd be messing around with the Mexican cartels. What could they possibly gain from it?"

"Your guess is as good as mine," DeCollado said.

Draper called Pérez a short time later while they were cruising down E. Grant Road with DeCollado driving. Since it was near noon, they were both hungry. The phone rang three times before it was answered.

"What?" Pérez said, sounding pressured.

"You should calm down, John, your blood pressure is probably in the stratosphere by now," Draper said.

"What I really need is for you to leave town."

"How about I buy you lunch, a nice quiet meal somewhere, while you control your apoplectic tendencies."

"You out of town would do that. However, I could be pacified by you buying lunch." Pérez named a restaurant nearby and said he'd meet them there. DeCollado pulled into the parking lot two red lights later and found a spot. They entered the place, a chain-type purveyor of fairly good food in weight-gain quantities. Good or bad, it was the type where no matter where in the world you find one the menu is exactly the same. Cops tend to frequent them because they can usually choke down the food in the short times between calls of criminal activity.

Draper and DeCollado selected a booth and sat only an instant before a harried waitress started wiping the table and multi-tasking by placing menus and gathering drink orders. Draper ordered coffee and DeCollado agreed.

"We are waiting for a third," Draper said, to a teenaged young woman, tall, pretty and thin as a rail who added another menu to the pile. The waitress checked back twice before Pérez showed.

"Had to take a report on a couple of Russian diplomats who had a sudden desire to leave our town escorted to the airport by a big ugly guy and his Hispanic friend. I suppose you two don't have a clue?" Pérez said, sliding into the both next to DeCollado.

"No big deal," Draper said. "They wanted to go to the airport; so being good neighbors, we showed them where it was located."

"Fancy that," Pérez said, "and you even rode in the car with them, which was a nice touch; friendly and all. I'm certainly glad I don't have any cops like you two on my squad. I'd be writing reports twenty-eight hours a day."

The tall waitress brought their order, dropped the bill on the table and left them alone. They ate in silence for a couple of minutes before Pérez said, "So, what is it you want?"

"What makes you think we want something?" Draper said.

"Please, you offer to buy lunch, what am I supposed to think?"

"I'm crushed," Draper said. "But as long as you brought it up, we could use some info on Ricardo Ortiz."

"Got reams of information on that guy, it would take a couple of semi's to bring it all over. Be specific, what's on your mind? We have cartel connections, first-born children, income sources, local contacts, whatever, we've got it. Rooms full of bad behavior and haven't been able to convict him of jay-walking." Pérez took a bite out of his sandwich, and chewed without sound, staring at Draper. "Are you two going to litter my town with bodies? If you are I want to pay for my own lunch so I won't feel bad when I have to arrest your asses."

"Not if we can help it. Besides, you don't have any probable cause," Draper said.

"Sadly, not yet anyway," Pérez said. "Are you Feds?"

"No."

"Spies?"

"Not anymore," Draper said.

"But you were?"

"Not really."

"Okay, I give up. What do you want to know?"

"An address where to find him would be nice. Or you could arrest him and tie him to a tree somewhere and phone us the location," Draper said.

"Yeah, right, and you'd just come and talk to him." Pérez starred into his coffee a minute or so as if making a decision. "Address is easy. Everyone in town knows it. You could look it up on the internet or in the phone book. What is it you really want?"

"Deep background; we would like something that will help us take him down."

Draper could see the man was conflicted. Pérez' past experience with Draper and DeCollado warned caution, yet that same knowledge somehow told him they were the good guys.

"It would help if you two would be honest with me. I'd sleep better at night."

"Fair enough," DeCollado said, "Charlie and I are ex-Feds, part of an arm of the CIA that no one talks about. We sometimes do contract work."

"That's kind of what I thought. Who do I call to confirm that?"

"You don't," DeCollado said.

"What would happen if I arrested you for murder or some other heinous crime?"

"An attorney would show up with a release order and any seized evidence would never see the light of day," DeCollado said.

"I've heard rumors, just didn't believe it. How many of you are there?"

"Not many."

Pérez gave them the address. "Call me before you go in so I can field the hard questions from my boss."

"Deal," Draper said.

Chapter Twenty-six

Southern Arizona

D raper and DeCollado sat in the Lincoln a half block from the Ricardo Ortiz estate while the mid-afternoon sun drove the outside temperature into the nineties. Draper thought of it as an estate in contrast to a regular home since it had a short wall around it. Maybe six-feet in height, he guessed, the three-foot thick enclosure lay covered with decorative stucco in a desert gold color. Between the wall and any buildings, desert landscaping requiring a full-time gardener screened the main house. The three-storied living quarters fell short of a mansion, but only in size, indeed not in opulence. A concrete-surfaced driveway weaved through the gardens to a four stall garage.

"What do you think?" Draper said.

"Wouldn't mind owning it except too many other folks around," DeCollado said.

"I mean, how do we approach it?"

"I know what you meant, just had to comment on the way rich people live. Looks like direct is the only approach," DeCollado said. "I'd bet on motion sensors, security camera's and at least two or three really big, tough security people."

"Only three? What are you going to do while I'm taking care of them?"

"Supervising," DeCollado said. "A wise warrior feigns right and goes left."

"Think we ought to wait until dark?"

"Always easier to catch enemy sleeping that way." DeCollado said.

"You okay? How's the arm?" Draper said.

"A little sore, but shouldn't hinder me any." DeCollado said.

They waited two hours until the sun dropped behind mountains, dark crashed around them and the temperature slid a meager two degrees. "Good night for stealth," DeCollado said, "pansy-ass white man sit close to noisy air conditioning. Can't hear shit."

There were two outside guards. Their jobs so boring that neither appeared alert, the first sat on at decorative boulder designed to accent the flora but proved a convenient resting spot. The glow from his cigarette shone orange in the dark. Draper could smell the smoke long before he located the man's outline. One step at a time until he was able to grab the man's neck, Draper put his lights out. The man slumped limp against Draper who lowered him gentle to the ground. Zip-tied and gagged, he wasn't going anywhere for a while.

DeCollado appeared and said, "We good?" in a low voice. He looked down at the sleeping guard. "I just hit mine with a sap, little more bloody, but just as effective."

Draper and DeCollado circled the house, looking in windows for signs of activity or alarm and saw none. "I can't believe there aren't any alarms yet," DeCollado whispered. In one first floor window at a desk in an office-like room a black man worked at a set of ledgers.

"He looks big enough to take us both on without breathing hard," DeCollado said.

"Might be necessary to shoot that one," Draper said. "I'll take the back door; it looks closer to the big dude."

"You don't think I could handle him?" DeCollado said.

"No doubt in my mind, but at your age you'd have to shoot him in both knees first."

"You better be nice to me or I'll shoot you."

"Take the front, but be ready to help me. He's a big asshole."

Draper knew the two rules of combat by heart. *Never* underestimate the enemy and *never* give him a break. The back door was locked and DeCollado's voice in his earpiece told him the same was true in front.

"Hold a second, I'll be right there," Draper said, picking the deadbolt. The locks, in spite of the house opulence, were contractor grade, a step up in pretty but not in quality. He had the door unlocked in under a minute. He moved off the porch, walked around front and unlocked the street-side door.

"Give me a thirty count to get around back," Draper whispered.

Draper turned the back door handle slow avoiding the click sounds and eased it open. Faint squeaks rose to his ears that he hoped didn't travel. He could see the outline of the hallway and moved toward the door he suspected led into the office occupied by the black man. When he reached it he turned the knob until it stopped, threw the door open and stepped into the room following his cocked and ready Glock.

The large back man jumped and rolled his chair back with his hands raised. "Easy cowboy, I'm not a threat."

"Hands behind your neck; face forward and remain seated." One wrong move and I blow your fucking brains all over that far wall."

The man complied and Draper handed him a zip-tie. "Since I suspect you know what this is for, make a loop and put your hands in it behind your back. Do it now before I get nervous and trigger-happy.

His hands through the loop and behind his back, Draper pressed the Glock against the back of his neck and jerked the zip-tie tight. He used a second tie to bind the first to the chair. Satisfied, he stepped in front of his captive and stared at him with the Glock pointed between the man's eyes. He saw a well-built black man, probably intimate with different types of weight-lifting. Big, solid, and confident, Draper mused that in a fair fight with the man he'd probably get hurt. There was also the likelihood he'd lose unless he cheated. Cheating was rule number three if rules one and two failed.

DeCollado entered the room and said, "First floor is clear. I see you have our friend here secured."

"You ready to do the other floors?" Draper said.

"Might I inject a word," their captive said.

"Free country," Draper said.

"Draper and DeCollado, right?"

"Maybe," Draper said slow, wondering how this guy knew.

"Name's Alejando Jones; DEA undercover. I can give you a code word and a phone number to check. Kind-a-been expecting you guys."

"Okay, enlighten me," Draper said, pulling out his cell.

"You two are somewhat infamous in DEA circles." Jones gave him a number to call and a code word.

Draper dialed and listened. When asked he mouthed the code word. Without any further speech he hung up and looked at DeCollado.

"Seems to check out; we have a choice, believe it or just shoot him."

"I vote for shooting him," DeCollado said. "We can't take chances."

"How about we compromise? We don't shoot him but we leave him tied while we finish our work. I'd hate it if he tried to arrest us before we were done."

"I can live with that," DeCollado said.

"Okay, I'm impressed with the intimidating bullshit but I hope you'll hurry since these zip-ties aren't exactly comfortable," Jones said.

"Don't you go anywhere, we'll be right back," Draper said.

"You should know the second floor is clean but Ortiz is in one of the third floor suites with a woman. She's a good kid so try not to hurt her. All the support staff has left for the day. I'd guess from the fact you two are inside unscathed, the boys in the yard· are incapacitated. Am I right?"

"Good guess," Draper said, noncommittal. "Thanks for telling us about the girl. We'll be careful with her."

Draper and DeCollado treated the second floor as their training required. They cleared each room, one at a time before moving on to the next. As Jones had said the rooms were a combination of bedrooms and baths, all empty.

The stairway leading to the third floor continued alongside an elevator system that serviced all three floors. Each of the steps machined from quarter-sawn, close-grained red oak, they were finished with hard acrylic and polished to a high gloss. Draper felt a twinge of guilt stepping on them without cleaning his shoes. The stairs led to the third-floor landing with more oak and polish ahead of an open hallway. Each side supported a large set of double mahogany doors. The hallway was lined with large oil paintings in gold-leaf frames.

"Talk about living large," DeCollado said, under his breath.

"Pick one," Draper said.

"Doesn't matter, whichever one we pick will be wrong."

"Right," Draper said, and moved toward the right door. He tried the gold lever handle and it moved. When it bottomed out he pushed gentle hoping for well-lubricated hinges. The door moved without sound and in seconds they were in the first suite.

The bed occupied most of the first room. It looked large enough for most any sport, covered by a spread that appeared to be silk with a lace fringed border and embroidered with a delicate design. Next to the main room sat a walk-in closet lined with women's clothes over numerous drawers of varying sizes and a bathroom with a soaking tub and a walk-in shower large enough for a crowd. The rooms were empty.

"That leaves the other side," DeCollado said.

Back in the hallway, Draper tried the left-hand door. This time it was locked. The tools came out and Draper raked the pins as gentle as he could hoping the activities within would cover the noise. Finished, Draper pressed the lever down and pushed on the door. The layout of this room mirrored the other and they entered another large room nearly filled by a bed. Occupied by a young woman whose eyes enlarged wide when she saw the two men, Draper pointed the Glock at her and put a finger to his lips. She nodded her head and pulled a silk sheet up to cover herself.

"Where is he?" Draper hissed.

"Shower," she answered. "He has a gun."

"Take care of her, I'll check the bathroom," Draper said to DeCollado.

The bathroom door was closed with water noise obvious. Draper tried the door and it opened. He followed the Glock inside remembering the layout of the other suite. Ricardo Ortiz stood facing into the water letting it pound into his face.

"Freeze asshole," Draper said, shouting over the shower sounds.

Ortiz turned, startled for a moment before he went for the gun hanging just above the water. The small automatic was in his hand as he dove toward the floor. He must have practiced that move, Draper thought in the instant before a slug flew by his head and the Glock barked twice slamming Ortiz against the cold tile flooring, dead. DeCollado was standing behind him when Draper stepped forward and picked up Ortiz' automatic.

"You okay?" DeCollado said.

"Yeah, the son-of-a-bitch was fast or I'm getting slower."

"Guys like him practice a lot. There are too many young bloods coming up with take-over on their minds."

"Girl secure?"

"Yes, she's getting dressed, shaking like a leaf."

"I don't doubt it. I'm a little shook myself."

They took the young woman downstairs with them and returned to the room where they'd left Jones. They gathered another chair and tied the woman to it.

"Alright," Draper said when DeCollado finished, "now we are going to have a little confab, just us chickens, no foxes around. You claim to be DEA and the number I called seemed to verify it. But then Bill and I weren't exactly born yesterday. How do I know who was on the other end?" Draper said.

"It was DEA headquarters in Phoenix," Jones said.

"I know, that's what you say, but put yourself in our shoes. I let you loose and then how do I know you won't shoot me or my friend Bill, first chance. I think we are going to let the Tucson cops make that decision. You and your girl friend will have some time for conversation before they get here. If I were you, I'd spend it getting your stories straight."

"He's not my boy friend, he works for the cartel," the woman said.

"See," Draper said, "there you go. You can see the predicament Bill and I are in. It seems prudent to us to let the boys in blue sort it out."

"You put it that way; I can see your point," Jones said.

"I'm glad you agree. It shouldn't be too long."

Draper reached for his cell phone and dialed Perez' direct line at the Tucson Police Department.

"What do you want now, Draper?"

"You have caller ID. Are the poor citizens of Tucson paying for such frivolous options?"

Of course they are, dumbass, don't waste my time with nonsense," Pérez said.

"Remember the address you gave me earlier?"

"Yeah, what about it?"

"Probably better get over there. We've got two gun-totters, a woman and a big dude who claims to be undercover DEA tied up here; oh, and one dead guy."

"Only one dead guy; you're slipping, Draper. Don't you dare move or I'll arrest you ass for jay-walking or something."

"Okay, if you insist. We'll stick around, but you buy dinner."

"He hung up on me," Draper said to DeCollado grinning.

"You should think about being nicer to him, more bees with honey sort of thing."

"I know, but he's so much fun to irritate," Draper said.

They heard sirens minutes later and the first arrivals surrounded the house and waited. In five minutes, the brass arrived. Draper and DeCollado watched from the living room while the Tucson police ran their hostage situation playbook. Pérez used a bullhorn to say, "Step out on the porch, Draper. Keep your hands where we can see them."

Draper and DeCollado complied.

Pérez walked up with a uniformed officer sporting sergeant stripes. "Which one of you did the dead guy?"

"That would be me," Draper said.

"Clear your piece and hand it to the Sergeant. We'll need it for ballistics," Pérez said.

Draper did as he was told.

"Got a backup?"

"You know I do, John," Draper said.

"Okay, you can keep it for now. Sergeant Garcia, take these two clowns to a restaurant somewhere close by, make them buy you coffee and take a statement, detailed. I want a minute by minute account," Pérez said.

"Yes, Sir," the Sergeant said. "You two, follow me."

They sat in a restaurant, drinking coffee while Garcia grilled them on the evening's activities. Garcia used an iPad4 to take notes and his fingers flew over the digital keyboard. Hispanic in his late twenties, Garcia bonded immediately with DeCollado. They chatted in Spanish while Draper admired the waitress. Slim, leggy, and pushing forty, she wore a wedding band set with a small diamond that she was too proud of to take off while she worked. Draper liked that and imagined she and her husband worked long and hard for the money to purchase it. She scurried off working the late night crowd by herself.

Pérez showed up an hour and a half later, with Alejando Jones in tow. "Thought you two ought to meet Jones, without the need for zip-ties," Pérez said.

Standing next to the booth, Jones looked even bigger. He folded into the booth leaving his long legs sticking into the common area.

"No hard feelings, I hope," Draper said.

"None," Jones said. "I probably wouldn't have been as nice. I am interested in your recent activities down south. I understand you two almost single-handedly wiped out the upper management of the Sonoran cartel."

"Not true," Draper said.

"And what is the truth?"

"Some of the people got together, formed a little army and did it themselves. We only offered technical advice and a little training," Draper said.

"You're not the *El matador de hombres malos* I've heard about?" Jones pronounced it perfectly with a mid-Sonora accent.

"Definitely not; it was their idea, right Bill?"

"Absolutely," DeCollado said. "It's the name they selected for their little army."

Jones looked back and forth between Draper and DeCollado with question eyes. "I will say this; you two are almost as good at bull-shit as you are at some other things."

By the time Draper and DeCollado sat alone the clock read 10:45 p.m., too late to drive north so they settled for a motel. Alejando Jones recommended one close by and they found it easily.

Chapter Twenty-seven

Tucson, Arizona

Draper's dream included a fist pounding on the motel room door. The noise had an impatient tone to it. Each beat a little harder and closer together. Someone calling his name penetrated sleep fog deep enough to drag him unwilling into semi-consciousness. His name again, demanding, with more pounding and finally he opened his eyes. "What?" he yelled. More pounding so he planted his feet on a cold tile floor and started for the door. Halfway, he stopped and turned back to the bedside table and his Glock. No way in hell he was going to open that door in the middle of the night without his friend Glock. The gun firmly in hand, standing beside the door with his back to the wall, he unlocked it. "Come in!" he yelled and slipped the Glocks safety off.

The door opened. "Draper, you up?" a familiar voice said.

"Pérez?" Draper couldn't figure what the Detective Lieutenant was doing at his door in the middle of the night. Only it wasn't the middle of the night he realized because sunshine poured through the open door. "What the hell time is it?" he said.

Pérez pushed his way into the room and looked at Draper. "Except for the gun, you aren't very scary standing in the middle of the floor in your jockey shorts."

"Don't you have crime to solve or did we clean it all up for you last night." Draper said walking to the closet and pulling on his pants. He selected his last clean shirt and pulled it on.

"I came to buy you breakfast only now it's closer to lunch," Pérez said.

"What time is it?" Draper said.

"Ten-thirty."

"Just because you are buying, I'll tag along. Did you get Bill up?" Draper said.

"He's been in the car waiting for twenty-minutes."

Pérez drove them in his neutral-colored police-issue sedan with hidden lights and siren. The restaurant was a quiet, upscale place noted for its fine cuisine and drop-dead breakfasts. The hostess seated them and said their waitress would be by shortly.

Draper looked at Pérez and said, "Okay, while I'm hungry and appreciate a free meal anytime, what gives?" You win the lottery or something"

"No, you did."

"How so?" Draper said.

"Feds had a fifty-thousand dollar reward for information leading to the arrest of high level persons involved in drug distribution. Guess that would be you."

"Take it and send it to your favorite charity," Draper said. "Bill and I have already been paid."

"Shit," Pérez said, "Now I'm going to have to consider liking you, Draper. Hate that idea, but not enough to refuse."

"Why did you think I did it? It was worth making you uncomfortable." Draper said.

"Got some other news I think you'll like," Pérez said.

"What's that?"

You know the guy, Damian Sanchez, they were holding in Florence for trial on shooting your Sheriff?" Pérez said.

"Yeah, please don't tell me he escaped."

"In a way, he did. Somebody shanked him in the shower early this morning, deader than hell."

"Can't say I'm going to shed any tears," Draper said.

Henry and Gabriella stood at the gate waiting, an indication to Draper that Henry's auto-detection system was alive and well. The old Apache had his arm around the shorter young woman in an affectionate way that sparked a twinge of jealousy in Draper. It was dumb he knew and he would never admit to it, but there it was, bigger than hell, as if she was his natural progeny.

Henry opened the gate while Draper drove through and stopped. When he stepped out of the Lincoln, Gabriella dove into his arms and buried her face in his chest. "I'm glad you're back, Pops," she said, her voice muffled by Draper's shirt. She held him long moments before looking up into his face.

"Believe me, darling daughter; we are glad to be back. How's your mom?"

"She's grumpy, but doing well. She's up and walking around almost all day now, though she still gets tired toward the end. I know she's doing better because she keeps saying she needs to go back to work."

"I know," Draper said, "Damn woman thinks the Sheriff's Department will fall apart if she's not there."

"Maybe it's because she's worried it won't," Gabriella said, wise far beyond her years.

"There's that possibility," Draper said.

DeCollado drove the Lincoln over to Henry's machine shed with Henry riding shotgun. Draper and Gabriella walked to the house with Gabriella's arms around Draper's right arm and her head against his shoulder. She looked childlike from a distance, her height barely reaching the top of his shoulder.

"I have something to tell you, Dad."

"What?"

"I've already told Mom and she said I needed to tell you."

"Okay," Draper said, clueless as to where this was going."

"Brad Gutierrez has called me almost every day since you've been gone."

Draper felt another twinge of jealousy, puzzled because he'd never thought it possible. "What have you told him?"

"I told him all he needed to know the first time he called. He surprised me by calling back the next day. We've talked a lot on the phone," Gabriella said. "He wants to drive up this weekend. I told him he had to have your permission."

"He doesn't need my permission. You're legally an adult."

"I know, but we both want it, even if we don't need it," Gabriella said.

"What if I said no?" Draper said, looking at her with a smile creeping into his mouth.

"I told Brad you wouldn't say no because I could wheedle a yes out you with my feminine ways. Molly and I decided you wouldn't have a chance between the two of us."

"More truth than fiction there," Draper said. "So tell him to come. I can always shoot him if he doesn't behave."

"He's already on the way," Gabriella said.

"Somehow I knew that," Draper said.

Later that night Molly lay next to him in the Aguila's spare bedroom. When she asked, Draper told her about the weeks spent in Mexico and Marisol Barajas.

"You shot her without knowing if the gun was there?" Molly said.

"Yes, it didn't matter if the gun was or wasn't there, she knew about you, which put you in danger. Besides, she wasn't a very nice woman. She either murdered or caused the deaths of hundreds of people, likely even thousands, so it wasn't an option to let her live. She also ordered the hit on you."

"But the gun was there, right?"

"It was."

"Was she beautiful?"

Draper considered the question a moment before he said. "No, physically I suppose some would say so, but inside there wasn't any question. She held an ugliness that ruined any physically pleasing attributes. Another moment and she would have shot me without shedding tear."

"I'm very glad you shot first," Molly said.

Two weeks later Draper sat on his front porch in the semi-dark of dawn waiting for sunrise with a half slice of bread resting on the porch rail for George. He'd driven Molly into Ajo the night before after dinner, dropping her off at her own place. They'd argued over it because she planned on returning to work in the morning. Draper had tried to talk her out of it to no avail.

Draper drank an entire pot of coffee alone at home with only Dog to keep him company. Midway through the pot the desert became alive in a new day. The dog was now his semi-permanent companion even though Alice Quinn still retained ownership and visiting rights. She claimed it was part payment for his help, but Draper knew it was only temporary for as long as she continued to teach in Phoenix. On the positive side Alice was spending weekends at Bauer's place.

He spent most of the day puttering in the hanger, not doing anything constructive, but at least it passed the time. He spent most of it gazing out the hanger door and thinking about Molly. After lunch he washed the 182 and swept blow sand off the concrete run-up pad. After supper, at a loss for further tasks, he poured a glass of wine and retired to the front porch to watch the sunset. He drank the wine, watched the sun fall behind the mountains, and went sound asleep with his feet on the porch rail serenaded by Dog snoring beside his chair.

Dog woke him with a deep growl. Draper opened his eyes to complete dark and instant awareness. He couldn't hear or see anything out of the ordinary. He listened hard, intent on discovery and heard nothing. That was it, he decided, there wasn't any sound. He reached down and touched the dog, petting him soft and slow, letting him know they were a team. After a moment he rose, stepped into the dark house and found his Glock and holster rig. Without turning on a light he felt in the front room closet for one of the M4s. Slow and easy he racked the slide to load the chamber and slipped the safety on. He felt confident they'd eliminated everyone who knew his name or where he lived. It puzzled him that there'd be danger out there, but his dog and his instincts didn't lie; especially the dog.

Next he felt for night-vision goggles and strapped them on. Then he could see, the greenish-yellow contrast colors outlining everything in the room. He stepped to the front door and did a careful scan of the desert in front of the house. There was no movement with everything in its place. Draper stepped onto the front porch one foot at a time, scanning always, and seeing nothing. He made a complete circuit around the house slow, cautious and watchful. Dog followed emitting a low rumbling sound every five or six feet. When they returned to the front the dog growled again, low. Draper began to think paranoia had slipped into his brain.

"What's the matter, Dog," Draper said, reaching to pet the dog's head. Again, he could hear a low rumble from the dog.

Draper mounted the porch and the dog followed. When he sat in his chair the dog stood beside him.

"There's something out there, is that what you are telling me? Well, we'll watch a while and see what happens."

They waited a half hour before Draper saw them. He could see a car, large like a Lincoln or Cadillac, dark color, moving very slow, creeping up the driveway and parking a couple hundred yards out. No lights; barely any sound from the motor. Draper slipped down behind the railing and fed the M4 between the stiles. They sat in the car another fifteen minutes, cautious, making sure, planning their move. Through the rifle's scope Draper could see faint movement in the windshield, two men at least, maybe more in the back. He debated taking out the front passenger first just in case and decided against it. Better to wait until they were all out of the car where he could pick them off one by one. The front passenger opened his door and stepped out. A low squeak reached Drapers ears and he move the barrel of the M4 enough to place the scope's crosshairs in mid-chest. The man laid a long tube-like weapon on the top of the open door when Draper's first 5.66 mm soft-point blew a hole through his middle just under his first coat button. His second shot went through the windshield on the driver's side. Draper waited. He couldn't see the driver and no one exited from the back. He was sure about the first shooter but not about the second. He waited ten minutes. When there was no movement, he circled the car trying to get a view of the driver's side.

A slow track to the right using the sparse vegetation for cover whenever he could, Draper moved car until he could see in the driver's door. There was no movement. He moved a little more to the right until he had a clear view of the driver's door before he moved closer. Dog matched his movements close behind. Slow and careful, the M4 on three-round automatic and pointed at the car's left-side door, Draper eased up on the car.

The driver, missing a large portion of the back of his head slumped against the steering wheel lifeless. Draper walked around the car and looked at the passenger. His body crumpled on the ground, it covered the business end of a hand-held, recoilless, Russian RPG-7 anti-tank grenade launcher. Loaded and ready with a PG-7VL HEAT grenade, the weapon would have blown Draper's home to smithereens and incinerating the contents. He and the dog included. Draper stood stunned. He hadn't seen that type of heavy weaponry in years and his thought process had trouble moving from drug dealers to all-out warfare. He rolled the man over to clear the weapon and received a second surprise. The man would never be mistaken for Hispanic. Draper guessed Eastern Europe, most likely Russian. The driver, even with all the damage to his head, Draper knew he was also Eastern European. Draper walked to the hanger to find a pair of nitrile disposable gloves taking the RPG-7 with him along with the grenades. He figured he'd earned them. An untraceable weapon like that might come in handy one day. The hanger was locked and he had to fumble for keys. He hid the weapon in the hanger and dialed the memorized number that wasn't in his address book. Even though it was the middle of the night, he knew someone would answer.

"Got a problem," he said into the phone.

"Go ahead," the voice said.

"Two dead guys, likely Russians, bent on destroying my home with an anti-tank grenade."

"ID's?"

"Haven't checked yet, but I doubt it," Draper said.

"Check and call back for instructions."

Draper hung up. Grabbed a pair of gloves and walked back to the car he now knew was a Caddy, nearly new, with rental plates. He emptied both men's pockets and found nothing of interest except round-trip airline tickets from London's Heathrow airport to Phoenix, Arizona, car rental papers and phony identification Good quality though, almost impossible to detect. The men were low-level muscle, Draper thought, and expendable.

He called the number again. "Nothing on them except phony papers" he said.

"Can you dispose of them?"

"Yes," Draper said.

"Permanently; no chance of discovery?"

"Yes," Draper said, again. "What about the car."

"Can you get it to a major highway where we can pick it up?"

Draper answered to the affirmative.

"Good. Call with the GPS coordinates when you get it in place."

The cover-up was on. Draper knew the government didn't want to deal with two dead Russian nationals in the Sonoran Desert or any place else for that matter. The car would be taken somewhere and crushed. A shame, he thought, nice car, a little messy though.

Draper's first task was the bodies. As he'd done before, he cranked up the Farmall M tractor, loaded the two men into the bucket and set out across the desert toward Thumb Mountain. The tractor's lights played mysterious on tall Saguaro's and scattered Palo Verde as Draper guided the old workhorse around patches of prickly pear cactus. The lonely howls of desert coyotes reached Draper's ears, their hunting songs searching for carrion or the occasional Gambel's Quail.

Draper's destination, in the shadow of Thumb Mountain was the wash that traversed the desert near his property boundary. Secluded, dry, and known mostly to desert creatures of all sizes, it was a perfect dumping place for inconvenient dead bodies. The coyotes would take care of disposal in a matter of days, leaving no trace other than soon to be bleached bones scattered on the wind. It took two hours before Draper was back to the car.

Draper looked in at the driver's side of the Cadillac. The seat, covered with considerable blood and other indescribable matter, wouldn't be pleasant to sit on. He walked to the hanger to get a plastic paint drop cloth. While there, he checked his nitrile gloves to ensure they were still intact. Satisfied, he walked back to the car, opened a back seat door and Dog jumped in. He closed the door and slid into the driver's seat and started the engine. Draper had time during the drive to speculate about the unsuccessful hit. It had to tie to the Mexican cartels and the now delayed tunnel, but Draper couldn't understand the why of it. The Russian element puzzled him and added a new factor. Try as he might, he failed to see a reason for their interest in a low-class, albeit lucrative drug and human smuggling operation. Finally, he gave up, deciding if there was a reason, he'd find out soon enough. For now he wanted to rest.

Draper knew it was less than four miles to the Interstate highway. He had a place in mind, at exit forty-six, where the highway crossed over a county farm road and the exit approaches dipped down deep because of the bridge. At the bottom next to the stop sign for the county road, a wide spot, used by truckers either tired or out of hours and needing to let their log book to catch up; that would do. It sat empty when Draper pulled in and stepped out. He left the keys in the ignition and called in the GPS location.

"Everything okay?" the voice said.

"Yes," Draper said.

"We don't want to hear from you for a long time," the voice said. "Make it as lengthy as you can."

"Works for me," Draper said.

The moon, almost full, shone bright on a soon-to-be-destroyed Cadillac sitting in the shadow of a highway bridge, alone on a dark, quiet Arizona Interstate exit. A retrieval unit would arrive before long and make the car disappear. Clean-up they called it. Draper started the hour long, lonesome walk home with Dog following behind. He didn't look back.

###

Books by Dave Folsom

Finding Jennifer

Scaling Tall Timber

The Dynameos Conspiracy

The Zeitgeist Project

Running With Moose

Available at:

Amazon.com - http://ow.ly/9JUGh

Barnes and Noble.com - http://ow.ly/areTc

Smashwords.com - http://ow.ly/dc1Vt

Also many other online bookstores

www.ingramcontent.com/pod-product-compliance
Lightning Source LLC
Chambersburg PA
CBHW070806180626
46818CB00001B/121